M000218868

THE MAGI
OF MIRIAM

"In her novel *The Magi of Miriam*, M.K. Sweeney conjures up a magical realm in the tradition of C.S. Lewis' Narnia and J.K. Rowling's Hogwarts Castle. Her spirited prose brings to life a fantastic cast of characters—royals and lords, good and evil, dragons, Magi, and one bewildered boy—in the memorable Land of Miriam, where the universal battle of Darkness and Light is re-enacted with engaging originality, imagination, and verve. The pages turn themselves."

Charles Scribner III

"M.K. Sweeney's delightful, fanciful *The Magi of Miriam* is reminiscent of fiction by other authors who use initials, including J.K. Rowling, C.S. Lewis, J.R.R. Tolkien and J.M. Barrie, to name a few. This absorbing work also echoes biblical and philosophical writings about goodness and evil, the nature of faith, and dilemmas in choosing the light or darkness. Moving magically in a seeming time warp from the present day to a kingdom of flying dragons and other oddities and back, this is a novel that readers of all ages will relish."

Richard H. Amberg Jr.

"I love everything about this book."

Vivian Woodrum
5th grader, Atlanta, GA

M.K. SWEENEY

THE MAGI
OF MIRIAM

The boy who saved the kingdom...

AMBASSADOR INTERNATIONAL
GREENVILLE, SOUTH CAROLINA & BELFAST, NORTHERN IRELAND

www.ambassador-international.com

The Magi of Miriam

© 2023 by M.K. Sweeney
All rights reserved

ISBN: 978-1-64960-130-8
eISBN: 978-1-64960-180-3

No part of this publication may be reproduced, distributed, or transmitted in any form or by any means, including photocopying, recording, or other electronic or mechanical methods, without the prior written permission of the publisher, except in the case of brief quotations embodied in critical reviews and certain other noncommercial uses permitted by copyright law. For permission requests, contact the publisher using the information below.

This is a work of fiction. Names, characters, and incidents are all products of the author's imagination or are used for fictional purposes. Any resemblance to actual events or persons, living or dead, is entirely coincidental. Any mentioned brand names, places, and trademarks remain the property of their respective owners, bear no association with the author or the publisher, and are used for fictional purposes only.

Cover Design by Hannah Linder Designs
Interior Illustrations by Christopher Jackson
Interior Typesetting by Dentelle Design
Edited by Katie Cruice Smith and Susanna Maurer

AMBASSADOR INTERNATIONAL	AMBASSADOR BOOKS
Emerald House	The Mount
411 University Ridge, Suite B14	2 Woodstock Link
Greenville, SC 29601	Belfast, BT6 8DD
United States	Northern Ireland, United Kingdom
www.ambassador-international.com	www.ambassadormedia.co.uk

The colophon is a trademark of Ambassador, a Christian publishing company.

T. G. K. M., all my love.

To my parents, for your guidance.

Through frightful nights they fly,

Prying, with a watchful eye,

Seeking the weak—those filled with pride

Boring holes into our minds.

Blessed are angels who come in life,

Saving our souls from devilish strife,

Protecting us with a nurturing arm,

Soothing hearts that beat, alarmed.

Screaming, demons block my path.

She wedges herself between me and Hell's wrath.

Crawling for cover, I watch her—

An angel disguised as a mother.

CHAPTER 1
JESSE WALKER

Jesse wriggles in his desk. He scoots his rear from one side of the seat to the other to get comfortable, struggling to focus on Mr. Armstead speaking at the front of the classroom. As he does so, the letter in his pocket pokes him, piercing through the lining of his jeans, scraping him like a fairy-sized knife blade, as though alerting him. As if Jesse could forget about the letter!

For three days, he's been carrying it around. For three days, he's been opening it and smoothing out its creases, reading it over and over in spare moments, trying to make sense of the note's meaning, revalidating its existence with each rereading.

"But it does exist," Jesse mutters under his breath.

How, though? He's often wondered this since he found the letter tucked in his backpack three mornings ago. *And who put it there? It wasn't Mama.*

How could a letter from Mama end up in my backpack two years after her passing?

Jesse had recognized his mom's handwriting on the outside of the envelope the moment he first saw it. But he knows it wasn't his mother who put it in his backpack for him to find. That would be impossible.

The reminder of his mom's passing makes Jesse jerk. He bumps the bottom of his desk with his knee, shaking the desk; and his textbook, *Pre-Algebra: A Starting Place,* slips off the desk's edge before he has time to catch it. *SMACK.* The book hits the floor of the classroom. Mr. Armstead stops talking mid-sentence. A gloomy sense of foreboding fills the air.

The teacher tilts his head, his eyes narrowing to two slits. *"Ahem,"* he hisses, glancing at Jesse's book spread out on the floor, splayed open for all to see. "Do you have something you wish to share with the class, Jesse?"

Jesse flushes with embarrassment. Mr. Armstead is Jesse's least favorite teacher; it seems to Jesse that he has always had it out for him. Jesse stares at his empty desk. Without raising his eyes, he slowly shakes his head no in response to Mr. Armstead's request for an answer.

"Then sit still and pay attention," Mr. Armstead snaps at him.

Raising a pointer, Mr. Armstead darts his laser around the room, pointing it from student to student. "I suggest that all of you use this weekend to revisit your schooling. *Focus. Think.* Before you know it, you will be moving up from the seventh grade, kids. Summer, a time of frivolity and decay, is lurking before us. Next school year, there will be no spoon-feeding. There will be no coddling."

Mr. Armstead sighs a long sigh, building momentum. "I have tried to *prepare* you children. It hasn't been easy working with a group like yourselves. Nonetheless, I have educated you on the Puritan work ethic. I've tried to mold your minds to teach you how to think! But alas, I am afraid I have failed. I don't know that you're capable of meeting the demands of eighth grade, Class. Can you rise to the occasion? Or will you continue with your small-minded shenanigans? Will you throw away your time and your brains?"

RIIIIING! RIIIIING! RIIIIING! The bell rings loud and clear.

Students jump from their seats and rush for the door like minnows swimming, knocking against each other and high-fiving. *School's out. It's the end. It's the weekend.*

Smiling, Jesse pushes through the door in a throng of his classmates. Together, they walk out of the room for the last time for the week.

In the hall, the air is thick. Kids are everywhere, jumbling together like gummy bears stuck in a bag, clinging together from one sticky appendage to another. It seems impossible to break through the mass of kids swarming the building. Jesse takes a deep breath and wedges himself in. Making a beeline for his locker, he inhales the cheers rising up around him.

It's Friday. He puffs out his chest.

Reaching his locker, he jiggles it open. Books, crumpled paper, and pens spring out at him. He hurriedly shoves in his belongings and closes his locker with a *BANG*.

I don't care how heavy it is. Jesse grits his teeth, pressing up against the weight of his overstuffed backpack. He scrunches his face, determined. *I'd carry ten times as much if it means I can get out of here.* He thinks of his pack, bulging in every direction like a dead body is stuffed into it. *For two days, I can eat popsicles and sleep in. For two days, I don't have to do homework, or tuck my shirt in, or sit in a desk and be quiet. At least for the weekend, I can fish and explore all afternoon.*

Ankle-to-ankle, chest-against-chest, Jesse struggles through the crowd with his unwieldy backpack toward the school's exit. Bursting through the school's doors, leaving the incessant air conditioning, he greets the hot Alabama sun.

"Ahhh." He sighs, soaking in the warmth of the outside air on his still-clammy skin.

Stepping out of the fray, he finds a space away from the flow of students to wait for his best friend, Irvin. Jesse watches the kids flow out of the school like water bursting through a dam, and he reaches into his pocket, feeling for the familiar contours of the letter. Grabbing hold of it, careful not to crumple the paper, he takes out the folded letter. Gently, he unfolds it, smooths its ridges, and rereads the words he's already come to know by heart.

> *My dearest Jesse,*
>
> *If this note has found its way to you, words can't describe how sorry I am. I never wanted to leave you or Maddie or your dad. Please understand how much I love you. Nothing can change that.*

Never feel alone. I am with you. You are my everything—my energy, my soul, the core of my being—AND YOU ARE STRONG. I write this as I imagine you have questions, and I want to dispel any self-doubt or fear you may have as you learn about us—who you are, who I am, who I was.

My love, if you've been given this note, something bad has happened in the Land of Miriam. The kingdom, no doubt, has come for you. As much as it pains me to write this, you must go with them, Jesse. The Land of Miriam needs you. It is who we are. Perhaps I shouldn't have shielded you as I have, but I wanted you to have a true childhood, where you could discover things on your own time and in your own way. If you get this note, though, it is time. You must go.

If you are reading this, I am with God now, smiling down. Never fear, never doubt, never feel you are not good enough. You are everything you need to be.

I love you.

Mom

CHAPTER 2
EONIA

The Kingdom of Miriam

"Garumph!" Princess Eonia hears Ben kär, one of the Gors, grunt.

Eonia's come to know her captors' voices. The princess was sleeping when the Gors came for her in the night, but it's been hours since they first kidnapped the princess from the kingdom. Princess Eonia's shock has long since waned; and her wits, sharp for any girl her age, have returned. Low and panting, the two Gors named Schlom and Ben kär sound as much like animals to the princess as they do like men, but she notes the distinction between the two of them.

"Dis princess id heavy," Ben kär comments of Eonia, whom he is carrying, bound up in a sack, swaying hither and thither with each giant step the Gor takes. "I don't see why we 'ave ta always be da ones doin' da dirty work. Can't King Angus do anyting fer hisself?" Ben kär spits at the name of King Angus, the Gors' ruler.

"Mind yer tongue," the other Gor, Schlom, groans back at him, grabbing the bag with the princess.

"Don't dell me whadda do!" Ben kär bristles. "King Angus da Fangus shudda drug hisself over 'ere, riskin' his own sweet, li'l life. Instead, he walks around wid dat stupid crown on 'is head, barkin' orders ad us like we're some kinda idiots."

Schlom stops in his tracks and glares, the sack with the princess swinging mildly from the abrupt change of propulsion. "Unless ye want ta end up dead, Ben kär, ye better stop yer jabberin'. Ye've seen what King Angus can do. Mind yer business and shut yer mouth," Schlom growls.

Unable to interject her protestations and frustration, bagged and bound as she is, Eonia blinks away a pang of nausea from the sway of the sack and tries to focus on what the Gors are discussing. But as long as she's been stuck here in this sack, listening to them, they haven't said anything of interest. They've talked about food. They've griped about King Angus, their infamous king, the king of the Gors. They've discussed their bodily functions (at length). Listening to their drivel, grunting like animals, has been painful in its own right. They've no meaningful thought, no useful observations to give. As much as Eonia's focused on their words, though, and tried to understand what they're saying, they haven't so much as hinted at how they escaped from the kingdom with her. They haven't said a word about what they plan on doing with her.

Tasting a mixture of tears, blood, and spit, Eonia forces herself to swallow. She thinks of how her father trusted Lord Letch all these years, and her heart races. Eonia's known for a long time that Lord Letch is smarmy. For five years, he's been at her family gatherings, lurking around corners, peering around doors. She saw him put on airs and listened to what he said versus what he did, and she developed a dislike for him years ago. Yet she never suspected him of this! Even in her wildest dreams, she never thought Lord Letch would be so needy for attention, so desperate for power, that he'd pledge himself to Darkness.

But alas, she is here! It was Lord Letch who threw her to these prattling Gors; he's the reason she's here. It was Lord Letch who sat quietly by in her bedroom, watching the Gors kidnap her. He's the one who had her kidnapped! He directed them. She's being held captive to him, caught up in his sinister plan to take over the Land of Miriam.

But how did it come to this? Eonia wonders, squinting at her bound wrists in the dim light of the sack, pondering her situation.

Curled up, bound, swinging in distorted positions, she contemplates how Lord Letch, seemingly a spineless servant so incapable of his own thoughts and actions, made the leap to orchestrating her kidnapping from the kingdom.

For sure, Darkness has been whittling away at Lord Letch for years. But I'd bet anything he fell to the Dark when he found out Aunt Lillian was ill. She scrunches her face.

The king, Eonia's father, had been distraught when he found out his sister, Lillian, was sick. More than once when Eonia's aunt was still alive but dying, Eonia went looking for her father, only to find him alone in his chambers with the curtains drawn, wringing his hands, draining them of what little blood was left in them. The king loved Lillian. He didn't know what to do.

During that time, with Lillian inching closer and closer to death, King Mor had met with his advisors to discuss the next steps. Lord Letch, of course, is on the king's advisory board and is privy to information concerning the inner workings of the kingdom. The king told his advisors about the *Book of Good and Evil*. He told them about Lillian's role with regard to it. He even told them about Princess Eonia.

Oh, no, no. I bet he wants to kill father! Eonia clasps her hands, pulling the binding around her wrists taut. *Lord Letch understands the power he might grab. He wouldn't want my parents left in his way, reminding everyone in the Land of Miriam of what has been—and could be again. Sooner or later, he'll want them all dead!*

And heaven help me, he has unhindered access to them! How hard would it be for Lord Letch to kill the king and the queen and to stage it as an accident? Yes, he'll want to kill them. They'll be in his way! Eonia reels. *They're a threat to him! There's no question Lord Letch will sacrifice anything in his way to get what he's after.* She jerks, picturing the disturbing look of determination Lord Letch so often wears on his face, and the sudden movement from the sack forces Schlom to reposition his grasp. *He has relentless ambition. He always has.* Eonia shivers.

But first, he'll need to be sure he can use me! That's why Dark agents are kidnapping me—so they can stow me away until Lord Letch finds the book, and I can unlock it for them. She straightens her body, making Schlom curse. *That's his plan; it has to be. But then, there is a snag in his plan,* she resolves.

Lord Letch doesn't know where the book is—no one does. She bites down on the cloth in her mouth. *No one but for the four of us, that is—mother, father, me, and Barrington—know where the book is, unless I am mistaken.*

CHAPTER 3
JESSE WALKER

Jesse hasn't heard the words "Land of Miriam" since his mom died. He shivers, recalling the white slab walls of his mom's hospital room, where he'd last heard the words spoken. He had stared at those hospital walls a lot, even more when his mom was at her sickest, hallucinating, telling him about the Land of Miriam, which she claimed was her home. He'd stared so hard at those bare walls that he could've bored holes into them, wondering where his mama had gone, listening to her talk nonsense, babbling on about magic and battles of good and evil and her brother, the king.

She's gone crazy, he had thought at the time. *She's sick. They've put too many drugs into her.*

Was I wrong to think that? Jesse wonders now, palming his mom's letter outside of the school's doors. *Is it possible what Mama said was true? And if it is, who else knows? If it's Dad, why would he put Mom's letter in my backpack?* Jesse shakes his head. *It can't be Dad. Somebody else put the letter there. Somebody else wanted me to find it.*

Jesse hears his friend Irvin's laughter break through the drum of voices seeping out of the school like a cackling hyena. Irvin has a distinct laugh, the kind of laugh that makes others laugh, too. Jesse scans the crowd, and Irvin's face emerges from the sea of students. He levels his gaze on Irvin's. Their eyes meet, and Irvin's eyes flash. Jesse fumbles the letter back into his pocket and braces for impact seconds before Irvin tackles him head-on. Jesse knows Irvin has a habit of tackling in lieu of saying hello.

"Irvin, for somebody who looks like a twig, ya sure are heavy." Jesse coughs, rolling to get his friend off him.

Irvin's lips curl into a smile. "It's gonna be an awesome weekend," he says. Then unzipping his backpack, Irvin pulls out a brown peel. "Wanna play some ball?"

For at least two months, Irvin has taken to sneaking a football into his backpack to quarterback an impromptu game of football each day after school. Graciously, the school's administration has thus far turned a blind eye on the boys' game in the field at the front of the school. Children, parents, and teachers pass by, exiting the school grounds for the day as the boys run plays and wrestle each other to the ground.

"Sure." Jesse shrugs, answering Irvin. "I can play."

Together, the boys walk toward the field. Already a group of boys is gathering in the grass, waiting for the game to begin. Jesse sees Trey, a lanky sixth grader with a live arm; Barrett, a surprisingly fast, pudgy kid; Isaac; Jackson; Malik. And, oh brother, there's Bobby. Off to the side, standing away from the group of boys gathering, is a scrawny eighth grader with a mop of blond hair. Bobby grins at Jesse.

"Go long," Irvin shouts to Jesse, cocking his arm, preparing to launch the football up and into the air.

Jesse runs. The boys break into roughly equal sides. The game begins.

Up and down the field, the boys zig-zag. After the hard rain the night before, the field is squishy. Jesse tastes dirt. His shirt and pants, freshly laundered this morning, are smeared with mud. His knees, rubbed raw from grass burns, sting as he runs; and his right pointer finger, swollen from a jam, throbs. His squad is down twenty-one to fourteen.

"Run the flea flicker," Irvin whispers to the five boys, pressed together in a huddle.

The boys get into position. Isaac snaps the ball to Irvin who then passes the ball to Barrett. Barrett passes the ball back to Irvin. Jesse, who's been running as fast as he can since the snap, nears the end zone. Turning, he looks to make the catch from Irvin. The ball floats toward him. Perfectly positioned, Jesse moves his body toward the ball to make the catch. *BAM*. Bobby, who read the play from the get-go, slams his full weight into Jesse before Jesse can reach for the football. Jesse crumples to the ground.

Kids up and down the field scream, "Interference!"

Jesse, curled in a ball and groaning, remains on the ground. His head pulsates with mind-numbing pain. When he opens his eyes, he sees his mom's letter, which must have fallen out of his pocket during the play, several feet away from him, ground down into the mud. Jesse grits his teeth and rocks onto his hands and knees, crawling toward it. Before he can make it to the letter, though, Bobby swoops down and picks it up.

"*Nooooooo!*" Jesse gurgles. "Don't touch that!"

But Bobby is already reading the words Jesse knows by memory. Bobby's eyes lock in on Jesse like two daggers, his face creasing.

"What's this?" Bobby asks, taunting. "A letter from your mommy?" Bobby smirks. "I thought your mama was dead!"

Before Jesse can answer, Irvin, seemingly out of nowhere, hurdles through the air like a cat upon a piece of frayed string.

Jesse's never seen anyone else like Irvin. His skin is jet black and shiny. His eyes, light compared to the color of his skin, have an orange hue, like tiger eyes. Against his skin, the whites of Irvin's eyes and the white of his teeth glisten.

"You idiot!" Irvin glares at Bobby.

Bobby struggles to regain his footing and squares off with Irvin.

"You don't ask someone about their ma like that!" Irvin spits at him. "Don't you have any brains t'all? Give me that," he orders to Bobby, motioning to the letter.

Grasping the letter, Bobby tilts his head mockingly and takes a step back.

Irvin steps in. Arching his back, he cocks his arm and hits Bobby so hard that Bobby goes flying backward like a piece of ragweed caught up in a storm, somersaulting through the air and onto his behind. Irvin crouches down. He rips the letter out of

Bobby's clasped fist. "Don't you never ask Jesse about his ma like that again. You hear me?" Irvin squints.

"Come on, Jesse. Let's get out of here," Irvin says, turning to his friend. Irvin hands the dirty and crumpled letter back to Jesse.

When they're far enough away that they're out of earshot, Irvin says, "I'm sorry about your ma's letter. Did you figure out what it means?"

"Nah," Jesse, half-limping, mutters at the ground. "Thanks for getting it back from Bobby, though."

"It's cool. Bobby's a bully."

"Yeah," Jesse agrees. "Hey, wanna come over? We can get something to eat at my house."

"Sounds good to me." Irvin nods. "If we go ta my house, Ma's gonna try to make us eat some of them butter beans." Irvin sticks out his tongue and makes a retching sound. "She had three tins of those puke green mushed beans set out on the counter when I left home this mornin'. Yech—no, thank you. I do not need me any of them *butter beans*!"

Together, the boys walk toward the bike rack as Irvin continues to mutter, eyes wide, about the butter beans. Side by side, they ride down the sidewalk, past the flagpole, and away from school grounds. Pumping their legs, they cruise by the lines of gardenia bushes, flooded with their fragrant, white buds. Mr. Armstead's seventh grade pre-algebra class and Bobby's grin are already distant memories.

Turning onto West Barbour Street, the boys balance their packs on their shoulders like snails balancing beneath their shells. They wind down side streets and cross from the asphalt of the road to the bumpy gravel of Jesse's driveway. Their bikes rattle over the gray pebbles, and Jesse grips his handlebars tighter. The boys stop at a beat-up sedan parked in front of his house at the end of the driveway. Dents riddle the car's metal, and its paint is peeling.

"I guess my dad's not home yet," Jesse says to Irvin. "He's been working longer hours since he got promoted."

"So, that's Sophia's car?" Irvin asks, unable to hide his panic from creeping into his voice. "She's not gonna try to make us eat her cookin', is she?"

Irvin's as familiar with Sophia's cooking as Jesse is. Sophia's run the gamut in Eufaula as a housekeeper. She's worked for most every family in town, cycling through them faster than you can say, "I'm sorry to let you go." Jesse's dad can't bring himself to fire her. "She's a nice lady," his father tells him. And he's right—Sophia *is* a nice lady; but she's a terrible cleaner, and words can't describe how awful her cooking is.

Jesse turns the doorknob, opening his front door. Like a punch to the gut, the smell hits him. The scent of socks, chicken bones, and soap mixes together, curdling, wafting through the house like a mist shrouded with the scent of death.

"Ugh." Irvin groans. "It's like roadkill she's tried to rub soap onto. Sophia *is* cookin'! That smell's bad enough to gag a maggot! You didn't tell me she'd be here," Irvin whispers, his eyes big as saucers.

"I didn't know." Jesse shrugs apologetically. "She's usually not here on Wednesdays. Dad must've asked her to work an extra day."

Hearing the boys whispering as they scramble to figure out what to do, Sophia calls out to them, "Hurry on in. Sit down. I pour ya some stew."

Jesse and Irvin make their way through the house like prisoners to the gallows, following Sophia's voice into the kitchen. They find her hovering over a pot, stirring. Sweat beads on her brow. Her hair, dark and coarse, is pulled back behind a handkerchief. Wisps, escaped from the cloth, stick to her skin, damp with steam from the boiling cauldron. Sophia smiles. Gingerly, she grabs two bowls out of a cabinet.

The boys grimace as they watch Sophia ladle soup into the bowls for them.

What did Sophia put in this? Jesse looks down at the soup in front of him. Like tadpoles surfacing and gasping for breath, carrots, peas, and celery bob up and down, peering out of the gelatinous broth. And then, there's chicken and ground shrimp—at least, that's Jesse's best guess for the pink stuff. *But why is the broth bright green?* Jesse wonders, longing for a cheeseburger with fries, fighting the urge to plug his nose.

Irvin takes the first bite. Jesse watches his friend swish the soup around his mouth as his face turns pale. Irvin sucks in his cheeks, trying not to swallow or throw up—Jesse can't tell which.

"Irvin, you don't have to eat it," Jesse says quietly, putting his spoon down.

Sophia, who's mopping the floor, looks up at Irvin. "What? You don't like it?" she asks, the lines on her forehead deepening.

"*Gurg.* Ids delicious, Mizz Sofia," Irvin mumbles through his mouthful. "I'm jus' not dat hungry."

Motioning for Irvin to make a run for it, Jesse mouths the words, *Meet me in my bedroom,* so only Irvin can see him. Understanding, Irvin scoots his chair back and, still holding the soup in his mouth, races from the kitchen.

CHAPTER 4
EONIA

Isle of Mires, Land of Miriam

Eonia's nostrils flare. Pressed up against the burlap, she sways in the sack, straining to hear. Then the swaying stops; there's solid ground under her. There's a tug as her captors work to untie the sack in which she's bound.

Light floods in, chasing out the dank darkness. Eonia feels fresh air on her skin for the first time in days. Oversized hands pull off the cloth in her mouth. Her cheeks aching, Eonia rolls her tongue around, relieved at least to have the freedom to move her mouth, and sighs, expelling the staleness of the sack in which she's been wrapped. But as the air travels up Eonia's throat, making its way out her lungs and to the outside world, her throat tightens.

"Gaaaaaaaah!" she gurgles; and she begins to scream. Eonia is face to face with her captors.

The magic Lord Letch had used to disguise them has worn off; and in the morning light, there's no hiding the fact that they're Gors. Bending, Schlom pries Eonia out from the sack as she squirms. He picks her up off the ground, his eyes bulging as he lifts her. Pressed up against Schlom's chest, Eonia shudders, and waves of nausea ripple through her. His eyes are black as night. There's no whites. There's no iris. There's no glimmer of light shining from a soul that should reside within.

BANG—he tosses Eonia to the base of a boat pulled up along the shoreline. Then climbing aboard behind her, Schlom barks at Ben kär, "Don't jus' stand there, ye dum dum. Push us off of the shore."

"A'right, a'right, ya don't have ta yell aboud it." Ben kär grunts back, shoving the boat off the bank and jumping aboard himself.

As the Gors paddle, they steer the boat deeper into the water. Checking to ensure Eonia's still there, they train their colorless eyes on her with each stroke of the oar. Eonia understands that she's an object over which the Gors have taken charge to deliver. But deliver to whom and why?

"Why am I here? What do you want with me?" she asks them over and over, but the Gors remain silent, watching. "The Light will come for me," she tells them. "They'll find me. It's not too late to save yourself," she presses. "We can go back. You can take me back to the kingdom. We can set things right again."

The Gors ignore her pleas.

Giving up, Eonia curls into a ball. Cradling her legs into her chest, she rocks back and forth along the length of her spine, avoiding the Gors' eyes. She stares into the waves, wishing her arms and legs weren't tied. *If I wasn't tied up, I could jump in. I could try to swim.* Even if she drowns trying to get back to the kingdom, it's better than the fate that awaits her at the hands of these Gors. *Wouldn't death be better than the misery of living with these creatures?*

But she can't get away from them. She can't jump in. Not only are her hands and feet tied, but she's also exhausted; and she doesn't know where she is.

Eonia spends a while like this. Dejected, she gazes out over the chop of the sea. For a girl who's always felt a conviction of right and wrong pulsing through her as real and strong as her own blood, her sense of empty helplessness is alarming. "*Argh*, get me out of here!" she yells with frustration.

Then in the distance, rising up out of the tepid water, an island emerges. A canopy of green covers the island, making it difficult for Eonia to see beyond the brush and the trees. Two shapes launch, rising. Flying toward her, they grab at the air with their wings. As they come closer, Eonia sees how large they are. And in only a moment's time, they're hovering above. Eonia feels the wind from their wings.

"Dragons." She quivers, craning her neck, feeling as though the boat's being pulled out from beneath her. And these aren't just any dragons. From the striping on their underbellies, Eonia recognizes that these dragons are Kelptars.

The Gors start to yell. "Ye iddy-biddy brained idiots, go back! King Angus'll have yer heads fer dis. We've got da princess of Miriam 'ere on dis boat. Take yer oversized gud-fer-nuthin, fire-breathin' *freaky* back ta dat island an' wait fer us der."

"Th-th-this is it," Eonia sobs quietly, bobbing up and down on the boat like a lure in the sea. Closing her eyes, she waits for the Kelptars' fire to engulf her. But it doesn't come. She opens her eyes. *They're flying away.* Eonia smarts. "They're flying back to the island? Why? Why didn't they kill me?" She shakes her head with wonder, watching them leave. "Have two Dark forces, the Gors and the Kelptars, joined together?" Eonia cries out at the Gors, searching for an answer. "Is Darkness uniting as one?" Eonia reels.

The Gors train their eyes on the princess. A hint of a smile flutters across Schlom's swollen, lopsided lips, and Eonia quivers; her worst fear has come true, it seems.

Dear Lord, if the Gors and Kelptars have joined together, it can mean only one thing—they know about the book! Eonia shrinks, not daring to speak. *And if they know about the* Book of Good and Evil, *do they know about me?*

The Gors run the boat ashore. Docking near one of the Kelptars, Ben kär jumps off the boat and pulls it up onto the island's marshy banks. Preening itself, the dragon doesn't even glance up as Schlom grabs Eonia and throws her over the side of the boat and onto the shore. Landing, Eonia sinks into the soft earth of the marshland, collapsing. The mud makes a sucking sound as though swallowing her. "I would go with it!" The princess sobs. *If I could dive in and sink through to the center of the world, I would go if it meant I wouldn't have to live out this nightmare.*

Schlom jumps down beside her. He unties Eonia's arms and legs. Steeling herself, she looks Schlom in the face. She knows she's an affront to him—a Magi princess, an agent of the Light. She stands for everything he hates. Still, she pleads with him.

"Even here on this island in the middle of the sea, the Light will come for me," she tells him. "I am begging you—we can go back! Take me home, and I can help you! I can have my father pardon you. You won't get in trouble. Please, please, we can set things right."

Schlom snickers. He looks at her with his vacant eyes, seemingly devoid of all feeling, and jerks her to her feet. Grabbing her wrist, he pulls the princess behind him. He doesn't have to speak for her to understand that he wants her to follow him.

"The Kelptars"—Eonia breathes—"why didn't they kill us?"

For the first time since it all started—since Eonia woke in the night to the whispers in her bedroom, since they dragged her and gagged her and stuffed her in the sack—she gets an answer.

"They're with us," the Gor says.

And it's clear now he's smiling. The most sinister smile imaginable is spreading across his face. Drool slips from his swollen mouth, wetting his neck.

Eonia remains silent, but inside, she's whirling. Spinning dizzily, she passes out.

When Eonia wakes, she's being carried. Sweat drips from her face. She feels it in her armpits, pooling. "Ugh," she gurgles, banging against Schlom's broad back with each step he takes.

"Aye, yer awake now," Schlom mumbles, tossing her off his shoulder and onto the ground. "Hurry up. We don't have all day ta wait fer ye, Princess." He walks away, motioning for her to follow.

Eonia struggles through the marshland behind Schlom and Ben kär. She can't keep up with them. *Why am I even trying?* she wonders from time to time.

Growing impatient, Schlom backtracks for her and grabs her. "I told ye to come on."

"Let go of me!" Eonia fights to break free. Feeling a ripping sensation, she winces and falls, losing her balance.

The Gors laugh. "She don' look much like a princess, now does she?" Ben kär cackles to Schlom.

Slipping in the mud each time she tries to stand, Eonia wallows in it. The cool, slippery wet of the sludge is almost soothing to her, albeit smelly.

"Get ye up!" Schlom shouts, yanking again and again. He drags her behind him, pulling her through the marshland. She flails, and her legs buckle beneath her, refusing to cooperate on the shifting ground.

For miles, the trio mush like this. The Gors bark and laugh at Eonia, pulling her through the sodden earth like they're dragging a wet noodle. Finally, they break out of the marshland and onto a dirt path. Entering the Gor village, smoke mingles with the stench of feces and unclean bodies, accosting Eonia's senses. Gors run hither and thither. Stopping to stare, they glare at Eonia with an icy hatred.

The village is strewn with soiled blankets hung from poles as makeshift roofs. Bonfires burn and smolder. Gor children, dirty and bloody, run about in packs like wild animals. Stepping over raw sewage, Eonia cringes. "There's no infrastructure; there's no order; there's no civility here. God's left this place," she mutters, gaping at the mayhem that's before her. *No good could live here.*

Trembling, heartbroken and overwhelmed, Eonia cries out. And from the corner of her eye, Eonia catches Schlom's glee at watching her misery. Soaking up her sorrow like a weed soaking up a summer's rain, his black eyes glint with enjoyment. She bites down on her lip. *I will never let them see me cry again*, she vows solemnly in her head.

Eonia knows about Gors, after all. She knows they long for misery. They feed off pain like a parasite.

Magi and Gors, more formally known as Belephegors, were once the same. At the beginning, there were no Gors. There were only Magi like Eonia and all the other Magi in the kingdom. Over time, Darkness coaxed Magi to it. The Dark plucked Magi from the Light one by one.

Darkness didn't have immediate success. But over centuries, it built a coalition of fallen Magi. And as time passed, those fallen Magi came to be known as the Gors. Naturally, as one might expect, fallen Magi were as intelligent and capable as the Magi themselves. That said, the Dark approached an impoverished set of Magi. Identifying flaws like pride and jealousy in its targets, Darkness sought out those Magi who were prone to weakness to recruit.

That was the situation until around twelve hundred years ago when the *Book of Good and Evil* was penned. Twelve hundred years ago, the Dark succeeded in recruiting one of the Magi greats to its ranks, Count Vandermere. Count Vandermere was one of the most powerful Magi of all time. He was revered. The Dark, however, sensing Count Vandermere's pride, focused all its efforts on his recruitment. At long last, Count Vandermere fell into the Darkness.

Count Vandermere's course took an unprecedented turn, however. During the time that Count Vandermere was in the Dark's camp, he conquered the darkness within him; and he crossed back into the Light! Before Count Vandermere, no one even knew it was possible for an agent to cross from the Light to the Dark and then back to the Light again. The Dark was furious.

Dark agents hemmed and hawed. They howled and growled. They threatened and coerced, and they pounded their fists. But none of it had any effect on Count Vandermere. Undeterred, he held steadfast to the Light. All the Light rejoiced at his return. Singing, laughter, and love rang out through the Land of Miriam in celebration of Count Vandermere's triumph.

And as it turned out, Dark agents had done a very foolish thing. So enamored were they by the success of Count Vandermere's recruitment that they had displayed their secrets to him. At an opening banquet in Count Vandermere's honor, Dark agents strutted about like peacocks showing off their spells and their powers. So, when Count Vandermere crossed back from the Dark to the Light again, Count Vandermere wrote the *Book of Good and Evil* himself. Having witnessed firsthand the secrets of both the Light and the Dark, he chronicled the powers of each of them. He engraved the book with his initials and gave it to the Light to be used forever to keep Darkness at bay.

Agents of Light have lorded over the armies of the Dark ever since. For over a millennium, the Light has triumphed over Darkness without fail. Since the book was penned, recruitment from the Magi to the Gors dwindled. A Magus defaults to the Dark every now and then, but it's extremely rare. The Gors, meanwhile, have bred with themselves. Today, Gors and Magi are unrecognizable as having been derived from the same species. Their bodies, riddled with sin, are mangled and deformed. Their black hearts seethe with hatred. And their villages, separate from Magi cities, are marred with bloodshed.

Schlom comes to an abrupt halt. He plunks Eonia on the ground. She looks up from the ground to a hut in front of her; a beast of a Gor emerges. There's no mistaking him for who he is. King Angus, king of the Gors, stands before her.

CHAPTER 5

JESSE WALKER

Eufaula, Alabama

"What do ya think was in the soup?" Jesse asks Irvin, closing the door to his bedroom behind him and locking it.

Irvin looks like he's trying hard to understand what he's just eaten. "Snails," Irvin snarks. "And maybe tires an' dung."

Jesse pulls a box of granola bars out from under his shirt and hands a bar to Irvin. "Did you swallow it?"

Irvin looks down at his hands but doesn't answer. He unwraps the granola bar. Closing his eyes, he chews.

Wow, that soup must've really been bad. Jesse blinks, interpreting the silence to be an unmistakable yes to his question. "Come on. I've got somethin' to show you," he says, not wanting to make his friend feel any sicker. He dives into his closet. Batting back shirts and pants, Jesse feels for the cold, hard steel beneath his hand. Landing on it, he pulls his drone out from beneath a pile of clothes. He hands the drone to Irvin; and Irvin tilts the machine back and forth, studying it from different angles.

"Huh. So, this is the drone your dad got you for getting good grades?" Irvin asks.

Jesse nods.

"Man, my ma didn't get me anything for my grades but more chores to do; and I got an A in science, social studies, and pre-algebra last quarter," Irvin grumbles, holding the drone out in front of him as though it might explode. "How fast does it go?"

"Not that fast," Jesse tells him. "But it does go pretty high. Wanna go to Fairview Cemetery? We can fly it there."

"Yeah, I wanna fly it." Irvin's eyes flash.

They crack open Jesse's bedroom and slither through the doorway and down the hall toward the entrance like a platoon sneaking past enemy trenches; the last thing the boys want is to be called back into the kitchen to try more of Sophia's concoctions. Reaching the front door, Jesse and Irvin burst from the house like water from a spigot, and they run.

From Jesse's house, the boys ride up Kendall Drive. Turning onto Cherry Lane, they sail past Ms. Frazer's house, whose dog used to bark at Jesse like he was a well-seasoned rib eye—that is, before he died. Then off Cherry Lane, they wind their way up North Eufaula Avenue to Shorter Mansion.

Reaching Shorter Mansion, Irvin stops. Jesse looks up at the old house and shivers. From the top of the hill, the mansion scowls.

"This place gives me the heebie-jeebies," Jesse mumbles. "Always has."

He remembers first seeing Shorter Mansion when driving by in Noni's car, peeking out the window. Even then, the house's empty, shutterless windows and chipped paint, colored from age, made his skin crawl. *It's like an old woman bitter that she's no longer pretty.* Jesse wriggles his nose.

"You know the story about the house, right?" Irvin nods toward Shorter Mansion.

"Yeah, I know. Dad told me about the Shorters."

Jesse had learned that Eli Shorter, a cotton planter and a congressman's son, built the mansion. He learned, too, that when the house burned down, Eli and his wife (heiress to the S.S.S. Tonic Company) rebuilt the house in even grander style than they'd built it in the first place. Masons raised Corinthian columns imprinted with the letter "S" for Shorter; carpenters cut wood from faraway places for the floors, and artists slathered six-layer molding and mounted doors set with lead-plated glass. Eli and his wife spent a fortune on that house.

Jesse also came to know that Eli's daddy, Congressman Shorter, Sr., was part of the Eufaula Regency, a group of men made famous for seeking Alabama's secession from the Union in the 1850s. Concerned about the North's threat to slavery, Congressmen Shorter urged the Confederacy to rise.

Is it surprising then, Jesse thinks, standing before the house now, *that Eli, son to the leader of the Eufaula Regency, built a house like this? Shorter Mansion's purpose is the same as his family's. The house is designed to browbeat others into submission in the face of its prominence. This mansion wants people to cower.*

"Snap out of it!" Jesse shouts, waving to his friend. "Let's get outta here."

Irvin breaks his gaze, and the boys start to ride. From Shorter Mansion, they cut down East Browder Avenue to Fairview Cemetery, the same cemetery where Congressman Shorter happens to be buried. With the turn onto East Browder Avenue, the asphalt turns to gravel. Pushing against the weight of the pedals, the boys cross onto the dirt path leading into the heart of the cemetery.

"Why is Congressman Shorter buried here in the first place?" Jesse calls out to Irvin, as he pedals past the lines of graves, flanking the gravel road through Fairview Cemetery. He huffs, "Shouldn't the Shorters all be buried together in Shorter Cemetery?"

The Congressman's brother, John Shorter, who was Alabama's governor during the Civil War, isn't buried in Fairview Cemetery. Rather, the former governor is buried across town in Shorter Cemetery with the family's other relatives.

"When the Congressman croaked," Jesse muses, "was Shorter Cemetery filled to the brim? Did Shorter Cemetery, chock-full with dead Shorters from the war, spit back out the guy's bones? Or did Congressman Shorter feel the family cemetery wasn't worthy of his dead body?"

"Beats me." Irvin shrugs in reply. "I don't specialize in dead Shorters."

Passing a final line of graves and coming to a field, Jesse hops off his bike. *Although not the cheeriest of places, Fairview Cemetery is pretty.* Jesse scans the field and drops his bike on the soft grass. Magnolias spread out their branches like arms cloaked in glossy leaves. Great oaks twist and twirl among the graves like old men dancing. And best of all, the cemetery's caretaker keeps a wide field cleared and trimmed at all times. *It's the perfect place to fly a drone.* Jesse smiles, inhaling the scent of the freshly cut grass. He sets the drone down in the middle of the field.

"Back up a little," Jesse tells Irvin, switching the drone to the *on* position.

"Goodness gracious, that thing is awesome," Irvin yelps with delight as the drone rises higher and higher. "Have ya crashed it?"

"Oh yeah. I've crashed it loads of times," Jesse tells him. He loops the drone five or six times before landing it. "Wanna try it?"

Irvin raises his eyebrows. His eyes gleam like two flaming darts. "Of course, I wanna try it."

Jesse hands the control to Irvin. Irvin pushes the throttle forward and then hesitates. The drone dives toward the ground. Crashing, it disappears into a cloud of dust.

Crossing the field toward the drone, Jesse hears Irvin's thoughts. *Please don't be broke. I don't have any money, and Ma can't afford to fix it. The mower's not working. I can't even mow jobs to pay for a drone.*

It's hard to explain. Jesse doesn't know why it happens. It's just that sometimes, like phones crossing mid-conversation, Jesse hears what others are thinking. Almost as though spoken, he hears Irvin's thoughts as his friend thinks them.

"Uh, don't worry about it, Irvin," Jesse says. "I crashed the drone tons of times the first day I was learnin'. It's not gonna be broke. And even if it was, my dad would probably be able to fix it. Don't sweat it. I'd never expect anyone else to pay for it."

Irvin relaxes a little. "How'd you know what I was thinking?" he asks. Irvin narrows his eyes. "It's not cool when you pull that hooey, Jesse."

Instead of answering, Jesse shrugs. "Wanna try it again?"

Before long, Irvin's banking the drone and flying it like he's been flying a drone forever. Finally, though, with the battery dying and the engine sputtering, Irvin brings the drone to land on the other end of the field. The boys cross the empty field. As they walk, the grass, dry from the summer's heat, crunches under their feet. The hairs on Jesse's arms rise. A tickling sensation runs up the back of his legs and his neck.

"It feels like someone's watching us," Jesse whispers to Irvin. Scanning the field, he sees rows upon rows of graves sticking up out of the grass in the afternoon haze, like men ready for battle. But he doesn't see anything *alive*.

Then suddenly, a branch breaks.

The boys freeze in their tracks. Loud and heavy sounds are coming from a clump of trees. *It's too large to be a squirrel. Is it a dog?* Jesse whirls, breathing hard. He's heard of feral dogs hanging around graveyards, digging up bones.

Then, *ZING*! Out of the trees springs a creature.

"EEP!" Irvin shrieks, jumping back.

"What in the wor—" Jesse mutters.

A blur of hair and feet—*it's not a dog; it's not a bear* —comes whizzing toward them. Its fur is brown and matted. Its padded feet are webbed. Gripping the dirt, it throws up clumps of earth as it races. The creature scampers past the boys, back into the woods, and then disappears.

Irvin and Jesse remain rigid.

"Whoa. That was crazy!" Jesse howls.

"It was some kinda mutant!" Irvin yaps, gaping. "Like a bear got together with a beaver and *that* popped out. That thing was *freaky*!"

"Let's get the drone and get outta here," Jesse says, scanning the woods for signs of the animal returning.

Together, the boys dart for the drone. Grabbing it, they run for their bikes, watching the woods as they go. Jumping on his bike, Jesse crams the drone into his bag. Feeling the familiar push-pull of his pedals, the cemetery grows small behind him. He glances over his shoulder every few feet, searching for clues as to what the creature might've been.

"Maybe it was like, uh . . . umm . . . a really hairy child," Irvin stammers, wide-eyed. "You know, like in *The Jungle Book.*"

"Er, yeah. Or it could've been a Sasquatch," Jesse says, still looking around, scanning for movement. "People swear by those things."

Irvin whistles through his teeth. "Whatever it was, it was fast," Irvin guffaws.

Jesse shakes his head, not wanting to accept the image of the creature running through his head on repeat as reality. In truth, the thought of explaining what he saw to anyone else seems laughable—*a hairy beast lurking around a cemetery? A wild creature that's never before been seen. Yeah, right!*

"Oh, *stop,*" he scoffs lightly to Irvin. "Maddie probably would've thought it was cute and tried to bring it home to feed it treats."

Irvin chuckles. He, too, knows Jesse's little sister is always trying to bring home stray animals: three-legged dogs and one-eyed cats or birds with their wings missing. *Seeing the hairy man-thing, she'd probably try to coax it home with her to keep it in her bedroom.*

"Maddie would invite it to a tea party." Irvin howls.

Only when the boys arrive at Irvin's house, a split-level with a built-on addition, do they finally stop laughing.

"Whoa." Irvin spits, listening to the cries of his family erupting from the house.

Jesse swallows hard. "It sounds like a war's going on in there."

Irvin's the second youngest in his family—he has two older brothers, an older sister, and a little sister; and every one of his family members gets into it, especially his eldest brother and his dad. There's not a laid-back bone in the McMurtry family tree. According to Irvin, family meals are like training for the Marines. A door slams, and the windows on the little house shake. *No wonder Irvin's always over at my house.* Jesse longs to leave but stands his ground next to his friend.

Slowly, the boys make their way onto Irvin's doorstep. Opening the door, Irvin misses clipping his three-year-old sister by mere inches. The toddler scuttles across the tightly woven carpet of the living room with her bare bottom hanging out and her pants dangling down.

"Come here now, Shiriki!" Mrs. McMurtry yells, chasing Irvin's baby sister and wielding Shiriki's tiny underpants in her fist like a warrior clutching a bludgeoning stick. "Ya can't run around *naked* all the live-long day, child."

Catching hold of Irvin's sister, Mrs. McMurtry stops running. And as she does, her eyes light on the boys, frozen in place at the entrance like two statutes.

"Good ta see ya, Jesse," Mrs. McMurtry pants. Then steeling her gaze on Irvin, she belts, "Irvin, clean out the shed!"

Irvin shoots Jesse a desperate look.

"I'll be back tomorrow," Jesse promises, hurrying back out of the house, down the stairs, and onto his bike before Mrs. McMurtry enlists him to do chores, too. *Better to get out quick.* Jesse's learned some things about Irvin's ma over the years—he knows better than to get between Mrs. McMurtry and Irvin's chores.

Try as he might to not think of it, the image of the creature in the cemetery haunts Jesse the whole ride home. *Why was it there? What could it have been? Why did it run at us?*

Finally, rounding the bend of the gravel drive to his house, he relaxes. All the lights in the house are on. His dad's SUV is parked in the driveway. Noni's blue Cadillac is pulled in behind it. No menacing creature is following him. *All is as it should be,* he thinks. Perhaps that's why he doesn't notice the quiet movement.

He walks his bike behind the house to the shed. Jesse hates the shed. Belongings from the people who lived in the house before him are still in it, decaying next to his family's things. The whole cave-like shack smells of mildew and mothballs and rot, like an old person's closet that hasn't been touched since the day they passed. Jesse muscles his bike in. He wedges its tires in between a corroded lawnmower that hasn't worked since the day his family moved in and a rake. Then backing out, trying to see where he's stepping, he walks straight into a cobweb. Swinging, he tries to get the sticky spindles off him, but the cobweb's thread clings to his damp skin.

"Gross!" Jesse groans, rubbing his face and arms, hoping the spider didn't come with its thread that's plastered to him. Jesse stumbles out of the shed. And as he does, deep in the woods—not close, but close enough that he hears it—a branch cracks. *Oh, no, it's the thing from the cemetery.* Jesse starts, glancing up just in time to catch a glimpse of its fur. Then in a flash, it's gone again.

Jesse runs for his house, his hair standing on end. *Did it follow me?* His heart thuds in his ears. "Why on earth would it be following me? I'm seeing things. I only saw a shadow sprinting away; I can't be certain what I saw," he mutters to himself, angry at being so frightened.

Would a Navy Seal be scared, shaking like a leaf, barely able to breath because some animal in the woods is running away from him? Jesse forces himself to stay on the steps standing guard, surveying the woods.

Birds flutter in the branches, looking for insects. Squirrels scamper along the ground, chasing each other up trees. And the blistering Alabama sun beats down, smothering the world in its heat. Nothing's out of the ordinary that Jesse sees. But then, Jesse isn't seeing as clearly as he could.

Giving up, Jesse goes inside.

"Jesse!" his father calls from the kitchen. Coming into the foyer, his dad grabs him in a hug. Normally, Jesse finds it annoying when his father treats him like a child, cradling him in his oversized arms like he did when Jesse was young; but at this moment, Jesse doesn't mind as much as he normally would.

"Wow," his father quips. "So, you've got a whole weekend in front of you."

Jesse lightly shoves his father away. He wants to tell his dad what he saw in the cemetery. He wants to tell him what he saw outside just now. But Jesse stops himself. *A man wouldn't whine about being scared, would he?*

"You should've heard the lecture Mr. Armstead gave us," Jesse says instead. "Thank goodness I won't have him for a teacher again next year."

Jesse flinches at the sound of Noni's heels on the hardwood. She pushes through the kitchen door, her arms crossed and her lips pressed tight. She doesn't have to speak for Jesse to know that she's heard him slag off his teacher. *Noni has bat-like hearing; nothing gets by her.*

"Tut-tut," his grandmother starts in, furrowing her brows. "Show Mr. Armstead some respect. I'll admit from your stories, Jesse, he does sound . . .

different. But that doesn't give you the right to be disrespectful. He's still the adult. And you, my dear, are still the child." She sticks out her hip.

Bark. Bark. Bark. Lecture. Lecture. Lecture. Jesse feels like everybody's always barking at him, lecturing him like he needs to hear it—Mr. Armstead, his dad, Noni. *Noni really ratcheted it up after Mama died. Like she's worried Dad's raising me to be a hooligan.* Jesse rolls his eyes. *Noni stepped in to fill those shoes and picked that flag right up, like she was born to be the angel in my ear, yapping about what I should be doing and about what I should be thinking.*

"But, Noni," Jesse says in self-defense, desperate to get out from the old woman's glare, "Mr. Armstead basically said he failed us because we're 'subpar material.'" Hearing his little sister calling from down the hall, he slips out of the room before his grandmother has time to tell him what else he's done wrong.

Smiling, Maddie waits for Jesse at the doorstep of her bedroom, cradling a painting in her arms. "I made a gift for you," she announces as Jesse nears. "It's a present for your room."

"Oh really?" Jesse hums, taking the painting. He holds the artwork up to the light and then *oohs* and *ahhs,* though truth be told, he can't tell if it's meant to be an elephant or a rocketship. The colors blend together, turning from pink to a brownish orange before running off the page. But there's a swoop in the picture that makes Jesse think Maddie's painted an elephant. *It's hard to say. Maddie's artwork leaves a lot of room for interpretation,* Jesse thinks without vocalizing a guess at what it could be. He's made that mistake before.

"Dinner in twenty," Jesse's dad calls down the hall. "Grandpa's at Rotary, and Noni's staying for dinner."

"Okay," Jesse calls back. "So long as we're not having what Sophia made."

"What? Why not? What's wrong with it?" his dad asks, peeking his head around the corner into Maddie's room.

"Umm, for starters, it's not edible—" Jesse sticks his finger down his throat. "Irvin took one bite of that gnarly soup when he came home with me after school. I don't think he'll ever be the same." Jesse cringes, remembering the look on Irvin's face.

His dad scrunches his face like he's trying to sort out a plan B for dinner.

"*Blech.* I don't know *why* you ask her to cook for us, Dad. She doesn't make food; she makes science experiments," Maddie chimes in.

And all the way up the hall from Maddie's room, through the foyer, and in the kitchen, Jesse hears his Noni interject, "I'll agree with that!"

Five pieces of pizza from Graffitti's Pizza Joint later, Jesse rolls over in his bed. He rubs his overstuffed belly with the palm of his hand.

His dad flips off the light. "Sweet dreams. I'll see you in the morning."

Jesse hears the door of his bedroom click closed. "It's not even dark yet. Why do I have to be in bed?" Jesse mutters beneath his breath. He blinks into the evening light. Yes, his dad's rule is that he and Maddie be in bed by nine o'clock, no questions asked. *But I'm twelve years old, and it's Friday.* "Will I be doing this when I'm twenty?" Jesse isn't so sure that he won't be.

He pounds his fist on the bed in frustration. He's hot. His legs itch. He's achy. He's so uncomfortable.

"When I'm older, I'll leave here. I'll get out of Alabama." *It's not that I hate it here. There's some things I like about Eufaula, at least.*

Jesse likes riding his bike to Noni and Grandpa's house, steering around the bumps that riddle the road. He can wander the woods and explore the town's streets that connect through a network of dirt and gravel alleys. He likes the laid-back attitude a small town offers. He doesn't mind that the stop signs are worn and that they're no longer meant to be read so much as recognized by their shape. And Jesse loves the lake. He loves to watch the frogs with the tiny horns sticking out over their eyebrows. He marvels at the schools of fish swimming in the eddies. Watching the cranes hunting for fish and the beavers piling up their sticks reminds him that there's life outside of this place. There's a world that's bigger than he and his problems.

Jesse's mama used to say, "God's power is clearest in nature." And Jesse agrees. The uniformity of flower petals, patterns on a moth's wings, and the symmetry of a bug all can't have happened by accident, Jesse knows. "Nature's order is God's order," his mama would say. She's right. Being outside, he feels it.

But sometimes, Eufaula feels so cramped. I want to meet people with different stories than me, people full of life who don't wake up feeling sad. Jesse shakes his foot, feeling the bed jiggle. *I want to do things! I want to feel the desert sands under my feet. I want to wander the streets of New York and San Francisco. I want to live!*

Jesse wipes the tears from his face as he mulls over his last thought for a moment.

"Can I make myself into someone else?" Jesse wonders aloud. *Can I re-create me? Can I imagine a new world—somewhere far, somewhere beautiful, somewhere there is no pain and where all is lovely?* Jesse wonders. "Nobody would be sick. Nobody would die there."

Closing his eyes, he tries to shut out his life. He tries to push himself into a new one, an imaginary one. But instead of crossing into a new existence in someplace different, thoughts of how he came here flood his mind. He can't stop them from coming. He can't push himself to pretend.

Before Jesse's family moved here, all he knew was Atlanta. He remembers his family's house on Virginia Avenue. Its smells, the layout, and the feel of that house are as familiar as the back of his hand. When Jesse woke up there in the early morning, he could walk down the stairs past his parent's room and into the kitchen without ever opening his eyes.

That house had loads of problems. The basement collected water; the insulation wasn't done right; the windows were drafty. In the summer, his room was too hot; and in winter, his room was too cold. Jesse's mom was always having somebody over to fix the plumbing, the roof, or the fridge in that house. His dad was always complaining about how he wanted to knock the whole thing down and rebuild. But Jesse's mom wouldn't let him. She was happy knowing that other families had laughed in that house. She liked that the house was lived in.

Sometimes, when Jesse closes his eyes and thinks of it, he imagines everything as it was when his family still lived in the house on Virginia Avenue. Everything changed when his mother, Lillian, got sick.

One night in the middle of the night, Jesse's mama woke with stabbing pains. Over the next week, she got worse. She was tired. She couldn't eat. Her belly filled with bloat, and her back ached.

Before she got sick, Jesse's mom had always walked him to school. He remembers the warmth of her hugs when she said goodbye in the mornings. He can picture her smile when she picked him up in the courtyard of the school in the afternoon. Sometimes at night, when he's alone, Jesse can almost feel the touch of his mom's skin, his hand in hers walking down the sidewalk. But when the illness set in, his mom could hardly move. Time with her came to a halt.

Her pants began to sag. Her collar bone bulged out from under her neck. A purple rash started on her knuckles and spread to her elbows, her chest, and her knees like Spanish moss spreading on a tree. Next, the rash covered her cheeks and her eyelids.

His mother waged war on the disease that was taking her. She set her mind to living, and she fought. She took all the drugs that the doctors gave her. She forced herself to go to chemotherapy, even though she was tired. She tried herbs and acupuncture, anything she thought might keep her here with her family longer. But despite all of it, one Friday morning at 7:12 a.m., Jesse's mama left him.

When Mama had first got sick, Jesse remembers being angry. The boy had pounded his fists. Like a distant dream, he remembers his knuckles swelling, streaking the brick wall with his blood, yelling, "Why her*? Why's it got to be* my *mom who's sick?" But no answer came. No voice thundered from the sky in reply. No angel appeared.*

Then after the rounds of drugs, the anger left Jesse as quickly as it had come. It was with the drugs that his mom started showing signs that she was losing her grasp on reality. She started talking about crazy things. In the hospital, she'd ask to see Jesse alone. When Jesse's dad and Maddie were gone, Lillian told her eldest son about a far-away land—"another world," she claimed, where her brother was the king. She told him about battles between good and evil, and magical books, and animals who could speak.

And Jesse wasn't angry anymore. He didn't have the energy to be angry. His mom didn't even have a brother— or so he thought.

Jesse stopped going to the hospital. He didn't want his mom cornering him, telling him strange tales of the Land of Miriam, making him more uncomfortable than he already was. Instead, the boy sat for hours in his room not moving, staring at the ceiling, watching the clock tick.

When his dad came home from the hospital, he'd make Jesse get up. Then came the emptiness. Jesse felt as though there was nothing left to him when his mama died. The boy didn't want to be reminded he was living. He felt like a maggot, not worthy of life. I want to crawl in a hole and rot alone so that animals won't smell me, he had thought more than once during that dark time.

A wound grew inside of him all that time. He felt it first when his mama fell ill. It grew with her sickness; it ground itself into him with her death. It hasn't left. It's with him now. He doesn't know where in his body the hurt lives—it's just with him, a part of him. The ache, the yearning—a sore emptiness as real and alive as his spine or his heart or his spleen is in him, breathing. He doesn't know how to make it stop. He doesn't want to make it stop. In some way, the pain keeps his mom with him. It reminds him that he was her son. She was his mom. She was real. She lived. She loved him.

When school was over that May, less than a month after Jesse's mom passed away, Jesse's father left his job at a bank in Atlanta. His dad packed up the family's things in the house on Virginia Avenue. They moved in with Noni and Grandpa in Eufaula. Then his father found this house. He bought it, and they all moved to 105 Cherokee Lane.

CHAPTER 6

EONIA

Despite the grueling heat, a coldness rushes in, chilling Eonia to the bone. King Angus in the flesh is more horrifying than Eonia could've ever imagined. *How could anything so disturbing be real?* The princess bristles.

Angus' face, split down the middle as it is, belongs in nightmares, not in the conscious world. One half of his face, the left half, brims with life and love and hope. It is beautiful. But the other half is mangled and distorted. His right eye, three times the size of a normal eye, drifts close to his nose. His right lip, swollen and fat, droops. Teeth, some jagged and others thick and round, jut out in every direction, making it impossible for him to close his mouth properly. Consequently, a steady stream of drool slips from his lower lip and dribbles down his neck. And there, atop his head, sits a ring of leaves and twigs—it is the crown of King Angus, king of the Gors.

Waves of fear ripple through Eonia. Still, she raises her eyes to meet King Angus' gaze. She keeps her eyes trained on his, refusing to break his stare. She holds her neck, thick for a fourteen-year-old girl's, rigid with defiance—to her intense consternation, Eonia's never had her mother's long, lean, graceful neck. Eonia's always been stocky; it seems she was born with muscles rippling up from beneath her skin. Rather than thin, Eonia's frame is sturdy, with broad shoulders and a bulky strength that is not traditionally coupled with the physique of a princess.

Amused by the girl's daring, King Angus doesn't flinch. "Welcome to your home, Princess Eonia," he says in a voice that's otherworldly.

Beneath the sing-songy, high pitched ring of his voice, though, his tone hints at what the Gor king is *really* thinking. It's the same as when a person says something seemingly nice and lighthearted, but understanding the backstory, it's clear what's really being said. That's how it is for Eonia now, standing before Angus, trembling beneath his cold hard glare. The shock of her understanding cascades through her like the chop on the sea vibrating up through a boat moored to a buoy. She understands what King Angus means quite well. He means for this to be Eonia's home *forever.*

Will I ever leave? Will I ever get off this island? Or will this awful place be my home, where I'll live out the rest of my days until God mercifully allows me to die? Eonia quivers. But Eonia's strong. Even as fear grips her, the girl keeps her eyes locked on the Gor king.

King Angus, tiring of the princess' refusal to cower, cocks his head at her. His voice, darker and deeper than he had begun but still melodious, booms, "Princess, I have been waiting for you."

Eonia stiffens and pushes up through her boxy frame. "Why have you brought me here?" she demands. "What do you want with me?" Without waiting for an answer from Angus, she says quietly but clearly, "The Light will find me. You won't get away with this."

King Angus smiles, and the drool trickling down his neck quickens. Without opening his mouth to speak, Angus' melodious voice rings in her head. *Oh, but, Princess, we already have gotten away with your kidnapping. And you should know, we know your little secret.*

Eonia gags. King Angus spoke to her! How? He didn't speak out loud. He invaded her thoughts; he communicated in her head. King Angus has the gift of telepathy! No wonder he's risen up to be Gor king. No wonder he's recruited Kelptars to help them. And he knows about the book! He knows Eonia can open it!

Overwhelmed, Eonia crumples to the ground. She presses her face into the earth and hears King Angus sigh, triumphant. "Ahhh, yes!"

Having sufficiently terrorized the poor princess and dispelled of the girl's bullishness, Angus directs his attention to Schlom and Ben kär, who have remained silent up until now, listening. After being so vulgar and boastful the whole journey here, they're left cowering at Eonia's side, seemingly afraid to speak. In his presence, they're too frightened to even look upon the Gor king directly.

"So, tell me, brethren, how did you find the great Land of Miriam's kingdom?" Angus asks them. "I received word of your success through the crawlies. But do fill me in on the details."

Crawlies? Eonia blinks. Crawlies are akin to worms, but they're *much* bigger. Through their network of underground tunnels and channels, they communicate with each other. *Given that King Angus*

is telepathic, I suppose he can speak with the crawlies, too.
Eonia scowls.

Eonia doesn't know that much about crawlies at all, really. Up to this point, she's never given a thought to them; they've seemed relatively inconsequential to the whole order of things, albeit that they're an especially unattractive species. *Are crawlies spies for Darkness?*

Ben kär grumbles and stares at his boots, avoiding King Angus' eyes. "It was nothin'. We'd do anyding fer yer almidey Highness. The Light didn't stand a chance against yer humble servants, Schlom an' Ben kär. Dey didn't even know wad hid em."

"Is that so? And how did you find the newly crowned Lord Tenebris Letch to deal with?"

Schlom speaks up. "He was steady, m'lord. There's no doubting that he's Dark through an' through. The only thing is"—Schlom glances away from the Gor king, weighing how much he should say to him—"the only thing is ye might want ta watch out fer him."

"*Oh?* Do tell us more, Schlom. Whatever do you mean?" King Angus smirks as though he knows very well what Schlom means, but he wants Schlom to say it out loud to him.

"Well, m'be I shouldn't've, um, ye know . . . m'be I shouldn't've said anything to ye, Yer Greatness," Schlom stammers. "It's jus', uh, ye know what I mean, I gather. I git the sense that Lord Letch sees *hisself* ruling over the Land of Miriam when this is all said an' done."

"Indeed," King Angus answers, serenely. "Tenebris Letch does exude a certain level of naivety. It's apt of you to notice, Schlom. I commend you." King Angus' eyes narrow, and his mouth twists. "You needn't worry, though. I will correct Tenebris Letch of his thinking when the time comes. But for now, let's allow Tenebris Letch to maintain his delusions. His ambition will help us. And for now, at least, the Almighty Below is pleased with him. By and by, that will change."

CHAPTER 7
JESSE WALKER

Eufaula, Alabama

"Dad?" Jesse whispers into the darkness.

Quiet, yet loud enough to hear over the hum of the HVAC whirring, the steady rise and fall of an unmistakable *huh, huh, huh* pants in Jesse's room. Rapidly it comes, not unlike the sound of a dog's breathing, but Jesse's dog doesn't sleep in his room.

Something's breathing in my bedroom. Jesse starts, recognizing the panting for what it is—the sound of a living being that shouldn't be in here breathing near him.

"I have to get up," Jesse whispers. But oh, he dreads leaving the safety of his covers. *Is it actually in my room, or is it coming from outside,* he wonders, hoping it might sound closer than it really is. Then there's rustling, and the floor creaks, leaving no doubt that whatever it is, it is in here.

Jesse senses it. Something blurry and bulky is on his floor.

He struggles to remain calm enough to think.

He resigns himself. Forcing himself from his covers, Jesse wills himself out of his bed and stands. He reaches for the light switch.

"Ahhhhh . . . " Jesse gurgles, his voice catching. No matter how many ideas he could've conjured up, he wouldn't have been prepared for the sight that's before him.

Crouched in front of him is the strangest creature he's ever seen. It's not human; it's not an animal—it's unlike anything he's ever seen in this world as he knows it. But then he *has* seen it before. *It's the creature from the cemetery.* And given that it's here in his bedroom, there's no more questioning that it's what was outside of his house earlier this evening, lurking. "I wasn't imagining things. It stalked me!" he yelps.

The creature backs away.

At least, it's not as big as it looked in the woods, he observes, noting that it can't be much taller than his little sister, Maddie, who's just shy of four feet.

Jesse's pretty sure if it comes to it, he can take it. And it's old. It looks ancient and worn. Deep wrinkles line its green eyes. Its whole body, except for its face, is covered in fur that's run through with gray. The creature has no clothes. But a single gold medallion hangs from its neck.

"Despite its freakish appearance, it doesn't seem to want to hurt me." Jesse breathes. *There's a softness to its face*, Jesse notices as he stares at it, and it stares back at him. Then the creature smiles, and its human-like eyes twinkle.

"Hello, Jesse," the thing says in a voice that's calm and civilized.

Jesse stumbles. *It talks?* Jesse's whole world begins to spin. He feels as though he's coming unhinged. *Is it real? Is it an alien?*

"Umm . . . hi. What are y—" he starts, then pivots. "Er, uh . . . rather, uh, who are you?" Jesse's voice cracks. "That was you I saw earlier. You followed me. Why? What do you want from me?"

The beast—or is it a hairy man?—ventures a step forward. "Forgive me, Jesse. I didn't mean to startle you. Yes, that was me you saw earlier when you were with your friend. And indeed, I was outside of your home again this afternoon. Sorry I ran away, but that wasn't the place or time for us to meet. I needed to speak with you privately."

"So, you broke into my house in the middle of the night?" Jesse sputters, inching closer and closer to the door.

"Didn't you get the note I left for you in your backpack? I tried to warn you that I would be coming."

"That was *you*? You put my mom's note in my backpack?" Jesse's mouth drops. He steels a glance at his dresser where he'd tucked his mom's letter bearing the words, "The Land of Miriam needs you."

With a sweeping gesture, the beast bows so low that the hair on his head touches the ground. "Yes, indeed. I left you the note. It wasn't easy for me to sneak it into your backpack, either. You're nearly always toting that luggage around with you." The creature wriggles its nose. "I had to sneak into the locker room at your school gymnasium to deposit the letter in your pack. The smell of that place . . . " It shakes, as if shaking off the scent of the boys' locker room.

"In any event, allow me to introduce myself," he says with a wink. "My name is Barrington, and I am a Thwacker from the Land of Miriam. I have come to take you with me to Miriam, Jesse."

"You've come to take me with you?" The boy shrinks, not believing his ears. *This furry beast thinks that I'm going with him?* "I'm not going anywhere!" His head spins with this realization.

Stranger, though, than the fact that this creature is in his room and that he'd go with him in the middle of the night to some far-off land is a sense of familiarity that Jesse feels creeping in. Like hearing a name for the first time in years, the boy realizes he has heard "Thwackers" before. *Where would I have heard of them,* he wonders. *Was it online? Was it at the zoo?*

Then it hits him. "Mama told me about them!" he exclaims. He remembers it now. And what's more, Jesse's nearly certain his mom had talked about a Thwacker named Barrington specifically. *And here he is, standing before me in my bedroom.* Jesse blinks, recalling the name that's been tucked away, hidden but not forgotten from years ago, etched into the crevices of his brain.

"Now, it makes sense," Jesse mutters, dropping his shoulders. "I'm in a dream. I'm dreaming of the stories Mama told me." *It's happened before, plenty of times.*

It's true, Jesse has dreamed of the stories his mom told him from time to time. It's just that up until now, all of those dreams haven't been this detailed. Up until now, none of those dreams seemed real.

Barrington huffs. "I must remind myself, Jesse, that you don't know me. You don't know the Land of Miriam. Did Lillian not tell you anything about us at all, though?" He rolls his eyes at Jesse as though he's disappointed.

Jesse doesn't know what to say. He's troubled that a figment of his imagination, a component of his dream, would refer to his mom by her given name. *That's strange for a dream*, Jesse notes, as he himself would not refer to his mom as "Lillian." Not to mention, dreaming or not, he doesn't want to have a heart-to-heart with this creature. He doesn't want to rehash all the stories his mom made up when she was dying.

"I'd rather not discuss it," Jesse answers. *I don't owe this beast anything*, he decides. *He tracked me down. He came into my room. He's pushed his way into my dreams.*

In truth, Jesse's mom had told him lots about the Land of Miriam while she had been in the hospital. "And I told you, I can't go with you," he says to the creature. But even as the words come out of his lips, he knows he doesn't sound convincing.

With a wave of his hand, Barrington dismisses him. "We have pressing business, Jesse. Trust me, I will explain everything to you later. But for now, there's no time. We must fly from here!"

"Fly!" Jesse gawks, leaning up against his bedpost. *Mama never mentioned anything about flying. This dream is getting weirder than weird.*

Barrington crosses the bedroom. Reaching the window, the Thwacker whistles. *THUD.* There's a sudden bump on the glass. Jesse's window is ten feet off the ground. *What's tall enough to reach that?* Jesse thinks, staring wide-eyed out at the darkness on the other side of the glass pane, trying to make sense of what could be out there.

Again, a thud sounds at the window and something brushes up against the glass.

Barrington unclasps the window. Opening it, he motions for Jesse to come and look.

What should I do? Should I go to Barrington and see what's waiting outside? Or should I scream to wake up Dad?

Barrington's eyes flash. The Thwacker looks at Jesse with an aliveness that beckons. Jesse's thirst for adventure is too great. He lets go of his bedpost and sighs. "Fine. What've I got to lose?"

And just outside, so close that he might reach out and touch it, a white horse glistens in the moonlight.

"Is that a horn on its nose?" Jesse stammers. "What could it all mean?" he wonders, trying to reconcile his dream with reality. And as he squints through his window, considering, the horse raises feathered wings.

Jesse falls back from the window, struck numb by the creature's beauty. Landing on the floor, he gasps. "An alicorn!"

Barrington smiles at Jesse like one would smile at a child taking his first steps. Pulling Jesse up to his feet, Barrington steadies the boy and motions toward the beast.

"Jesse, I would like you to meet Drakendore."

Jesse remains inert, dumbstruck.

"Drakendore's the fastest flyer in all of Miriam," Barrington continues, glossing over the boy's bewilderment. "And dare I say, she's the most magnificent alicorn that's ever lived. You're in luck. She's agreed to take us to the Land of Miriam. Come along now." The Thwacker gestures toward Drakendore matter-of-factly, motioning for Jesse to climb on.

Without another word, Barrington crawls out of the window. He propels himself off the ledge and leaps onto Drakendore's back. Then turning to Jesse, the Thwacker holds out his hand. "Let's go, Jesse!" Barrington quips.

"None of this is happening," Jesse tells himself over and over. *An alicorn and a Thwacker aren't outside my window, waiting to take me to a far-off land, the Land of Miriam . . .* "I'm dreaming. I must be."

Yes, Jesse feels awake. "But that's impossible." He shakes himself. "I'm asleep." *And if this is a dream (as it certainly is), I can go with them. If this is a dream (as it must be), I can live out this fantasy. Isn't that what I wanted—an imaginary life? An escape from what's real?* "There isn't any risk in any of it if this is a dream," Jesse tells himself.

He climbs onto the window's ledge. Outside the house, the air is damp on his skin. The crickets' singing rings in his ears, punctuating the otherwise-still night with the melody. Crouching, he grabs hold of Barrington's hairy hand and jumps. He launches himself from the window. As he does, the boy's toes catch the splintered wood of the windowsill, and he teeters, dragging his foot across the window's ledge. Unbalanced, he plunks down atop of Drakendore with a thump.

"Umph!" Jesse grunts. Drakendore's ears twitch. She turns to Jesse as if to say, "You. Go easy on my back!"

"That wasn't very dreamlike!" Jesse chortles. The feel of Drakendore's hair is soft and defined. In front of him, Barrington wiggles, and the Thwacker's fur rubs against his bare legs.

Barrington, Drakendore, the bugs, the trees, the moon, the stars . . . "Everything seems so real!" he grumbles. *None of this feels like make-believe!* "What if I'm wrong? What if this isn't a dream?"

He pinches himself to wake up. "OUCH!" he cries. "This isn't a dream!" he squeaks. "I'm bleeding! This is happening! I shouldn't be here! I need to get off. I need to go home. I need to get back to my family!"

But Drakendore's moving. She's spreading her wings. The ground is getting smaller beneath him. Jesse is flying.

CHAPTER 8

EONIA

Isle of Mires, Land of Miriam

Biting down, Eonia tastes blood. Cracked and sore, clinging to her skin, there's barely any nail left on Eonia's finger. Yet still she rips at it. She's always been a nail-biter. It's just one of a long list of less-than-ladylike habits of the princess.

Of course, King Angus watches her. Hour after hour, day after day, he sits in this hut, watching. He's waiting for her to come undone, it seems. And she *is* coming undone—he has not been starved for amusement there. The princess is different than she was when she first came here. Alone with these creatures, she can barely remember her hopes and dreams.

Covered in filth, she blends in like an animal, camouflaged against her surroundings. Her attention is short. She's on pins and needles. And she hears *everything*. She hears the guards outside of the hut now, conferring in grunts and dribble. It sounds like they're arguing.

There's a knock at the door.

"Ugh, we're sorry ta interrupt ye, Yer Highness. Bud id seems we have a bid of a situation out h'ere."

"Come in," King Angus answers. The door opens. Standing at the threshold, the guards peek in, too hesitant to enter. "Well, what is it?" Angus demands.

"Apparently, m'lord, one of the Kelptars ate Grog."

"It ate him? Why? What did he do to it?"

"We're not sure, m'lord." The guard shakes his head. "As best we can tell, based on da Gors who saw id happen, da dragon was upset dat Grog didn't move out of ids way fast enough. So, it fried him up ta a crisp, an' id devoured him. Like I said, we're a li'l fuzzy on da details, m'lord . . . "

"Those horrid dragons!" King Angus grunts, standing. "I told them not to eat us! I'll have a word with the Kelptars. And while I'm at it, one of you should come with me. I want the remains of Grog's body tossed into the sea, so the other Gors don't see him rotting. I don't need it out in the open, scaring everybody."

"Uh, der's no remains remaining fer us ta toss, sir."

"Very well," Angus growls, seemingly put out for the first time since Eonia's been here. "Then both of you stay here in this hut and stand guard over the princess until I come back."

King Angus starts to leave, but as he does, he glances in Eonia's direction. *What're you staring at, Princess?* His words ring in her head. *Do you find this amusing? Is it funny that one Dark agent has gone off and eaten another?*

Feeling uneasy under King Angus' glare (as, in actuality, he's quite right that Eonia was enjoying the scene), the princess, without thinking, feels for her necklace, an amulet that was a gift from her parents, the king and queen.

The stone's cool, smooth finish makes Eonia think of her mother's smile when Queen Marakee had given it to her. On Eonia's fourteenth birthday, her mother had snuck the present onto Eonia's plate at breakfast. Oh, how Eonia had giggled, pulling off the silver paper. And nestled there within it was a wooden case embossed with an image of a flowering cross, a marking for Life in the Land of Miriam. Inside of it, Eonia's amulet had glistened. Eonia remembers the warmth of her father's hug after he clasped the necklace around her neck. Strong and safe as she felt then in her father's arms, it seemed as though nothing bad could ever happen to her, as though nothing could ever come between them.

That wasn't long ago, really. Eonia's fourteenth birthday was only a month ago, but everything's changed since then. On that day of her fourteenth birthday, Eonia was still innocent, carefree, and giddy. *Will I ever be that way again? Will I ever go back to the way I was before all of this happened?*

She steals a glimpse at her amulet between her fingers, shining against her dirt-crusted skin. It's only been a few days that she's been here, imprisoned with the Gors on this island; yet each day and night, seemingly an eternity, changes her. It may as well have been forty years since she came here. Distressed as she is, Eonia doesn't notice King Angus' narrowing of focus.

"Aah!" King Angus blurts aloud, catching sight of the amulet.

Up until now, Eonia had done a good job hiding it, tucking it away in her dress. Angus rushes for her; and Eonia knows she's made a mistake. She feels his thick, sweaty fingers close around her neck.

It takes only one tug for the delicate chain to break. The necklace snaps, and the amulet thumps to the ground.

"Nooooo!" Eonia cries out.

King Angus' lips curl into a grin, reveling in his ecstasy over her agony. He covers the amulet's shimmering light with his boot.

"Don't do it! Don't smash it! I'll give you anything. Please don't break it!"

Shifting his weight onto it, he grinds his heel in. The amulet bursts into a thousand pieces.

Eonia falls to the ground, sobbing. Shimmering and beautiful, her necklace was her last tie to her home, to the people who knew and loved her. It was her reminder of what life was like before all of this. And now, it's gone. All that's left to her now from the kingdom, from the life that she knew, is a dirty, torn nightgown. And even that is breaking apart, disintegrating even as she wears it.

Again, she hears King Angus' sing-songy voice from within, chiding her as he likes to do.

Was it important to you, Princess? Was it a gift? You've no use for such things here. If I'd noticed it before, I would've gotten rid of it earlier. But then, you were hiding it from me, weren't you? You were trying to keep it to yourself. The voice pauses, but only for a moment. The silence is almost worse than the voice. But as if on cue, it continues. *You will learn, Princess, that there's nothing you can hide from me. You belong to Darkness now. There's nothing we do not see.*

And with that, he walks out. His guards hover in his stead, keeping tabs on Eonia for him.

Poor, dear, sweet, kind Eonia. Before she came to this place, she awoke with the sun, eager for each passing day. She danced in the moonlight, humming the tunes of funglebugs. She smiled at the clouds and opened her mouth to catch drops of rain. "I was alive." She spits. "I shouldn't be here with these monsters, left to die with them."

And she's right; she shouldn't be. Other Magi walk through life shrouded in drudgery, caught up in minutia. They don't turn their faces heavenward, praising God for life's blessings. They don't notice that they have any blessings at all. Eonia was never like that; she loved living. "Shouldn't it be they who are here, not me?"

Crumpled on the floor, pressing her face into the ground, feeling the grit of the earthen floor in her teeth, Eonia convulses. She has claim to the throne of Miriam. "I don't want it." She pounds her fists. *I want to be an ordinary girl. I want to run in a field. I want to pick flowers and eat ice cream. I want to have friends.*

Of course, yes, she is her parents' daughter. Her position was not a choice. Her path was predetermined. She must bear that weight. She must carry that burden. And yes, she knows it. But is it too much for her?

"I don't want to die here," she whimpers. *Please, God, don't let me die here in this desolate place, alone and lost among these monsters, far away from everything I know, lightyears from everything I love.*

Poor, sweet, lovely Eonia. If only the Light knew that she's here.

CHAPTER 9

JESSE WALKER

From Earth to The Land of Miriam

"Hold on!" Barrington calls out. Jesse strains to hear the Thwacker seated in front of him as the wind whooshes past his ears.

"Hold on to what?" Jesse scowls. There's no saddle or reins. *What is there to hold on to?*

Jesse clasps his arms tighter around Barrington's middle as they soar. Higher and higher, they go. The street, the neighborhood, the town spread out beneath them. Everything's getting smaller and smaller. Trees lining Eufaula's streets, so big in person, look like bushes from up here. Then, shrinking into dots, they completely disappear.

Meanwhile, Jesse wants answers. He's tired of playing the part of an unwitting fool. Why is Barrington taking him to the Land of Miriam? How will he get home? "Hey! What will Dad and Maddie do when they find out I'm missing?" he shouts.

Out of nowhere, Jesse hears a voice. *They won't know you're gone,* the voice says assuredly.

It's Barrington's voice; but Barrington isn't talking, and Jesse didn't talk to him.

"What's going on?" Jesse asks aloud.

"Your thought control is working," Barrington calls in response. Then without speaking again, Barrington tells him, *We're nearing the Land of Miriam, and your power is getting stronger.*

"Power!" Jesse blurts. "What power?"

Again, Barrington's voice comes from inside of him. *You have Lillian's gift. Your mother was telepathic, too, you know.*

"Telepathic? This is *nuts!*" Jesse guffaws, feeling as though he's been tricked. "I thought I was in a dream when I agreed to come with you, Barrington." Jesse's heart pounds. "Now, we're flying, and I've got voices in my head." If he weren't up so high, he'd jump down off Drakendore this minute and make a run for it.

Barrington yells back, "I did not trick you." Then telepathically Barrington tells him, *You chose to come. And as soon as we've completed our mission, I'll return you home. Like I said, we won't be gone long enough for your father and Maddie to know that you've been gone. So, put your mind to rest about that.*

"Why won't they know?" Jesse asks against the whipping wind. "And how do you know about my dad and Maddie?"

"Of course, I know about them." Then, without speaking, Barrington tells him, *Your mother talked of you, your father, and Madeline many times over the years. That's nothing. What saddens me, though, and what I do find appalling is how little you seem to know about yourself. I didn't anticipate having to explain everything to you from the beginning, Jesse.* Barrington sighs. *Of course, you were so young. And Lillian was so protective. She didn't want to overwhelm you, I suppose.*

"What?" Jesse sputters.

Barrington steels a sideways glance. *As for your question regarding the passage of time, Jesse, Miriam has a time all to its own. Many things are different in the Land of Miriam, not least of which is how time passes. However long you stay in the Land of Miriam won't take up the same amount of time as it would in your world.* Barrington pauses for a moment, letting the impact of his thoughts sink in. *We'll return you to your home before your father and Madeline know that you've gone missing.* "You have my word." Barrington quips.

Jesse's head hurts. Disoriented from Barrington's telepathy and the flying and all that's been said, he pictures his mom in the hospital when she was sick. He tries to remember all the things she'd said about the Land of Miriam. He thinks back to when she told him about Barrington.

She was especially unwell when she'd asked to speak to Jesse alone in her hospital room. Sitting in her mechanical bed with all its lights and buttons, his mom's skin had been as pale as the white sheets themselves. She'd had an unnatural glow under the room's fluorescent lights. Her gray eyes, usually full of energy, had been dull with pain. Still, she'd smiled at Jesse and straightened herself up for him.

"Jesse, there's something I need to tell you about," she'd said to him. "It's before your time to know, but it appears we've little choice in the matter, my dear."

Jesse had started to cry, and Lillian had held his hand. "Don't cry. Everything will be okay. You'll see. There's another land, Jesse. It's a beautiful land, full of magic. I have family there—*you* have family there, my love, as does Maddie. It's called the Land of Miriam."

She had continued to tell Jesse about her brother, the king; and good and evil forces; and a magical book. She had told him about Barrington, the Thwacker, and that he was like family to her. Jesse had thought she was delirious.

But she didn't mention that Thwackers aren't like people. She didn't tell me that they're hairy animals.

"I beg your pardon," Barrington interrupts his thoughts. "I am not a hairy animal!" He glances at Jesse and raises his eyebrows.

"It's bad enough I've got to hear your voice in my head!" Jesse screeches. "But it's absolutely *not* okay for you to hear my thoughts, too. How's this happening? I didn't give you permission to break into my head and listen to me think."

Barrington nods. "It's as I said, Jesse—you're telepathic." Then, switching to nonverbal communication, he tells him, *You control it, not me. I don't have the gift of telepathy, unfortunately. Not many do. You can shut me out and let me in.*

"But how am I supposed to do that?" Jesse protests.

I'm not exactly sure. Barrington frowns. *Frankly, there's little instruction I can give you. You're just going to have to experiment with it and figure it out for yourself. The more you utilize your power and practice with it, the more it will become second nature for you, I presume.*

Jesse strains to keep from screaming. "This is ridiculous!" he cries. "You've made a mistake, Barrington! I'm not gifted. I don't have telepathy. That's the dumbest thing I've ever heard!"

Undeterred, Barrington continues, drilling in his point. "You most certainly do, Jesse," he says imploringly. *As I said, you inherited the gift from Lillian. Moreover, it's rare, indeed, for someone to have the gift as powerfully as she did. And best I can tell from what Lillian told me and from the conversation we're carrying on now, you have the gift just as powerfully as she did.* "Dare I say, yours may even be stronger than hers was."

Barrington pats Drakendore on the mane. *I know this may be unsettling for you. But it's important that you understand, this is a blessing you've been given. Telepathy allows you to speak with everyone. Through thought, you can communicate with all the species in the Land of Miriam, regardless of their language.*

At that, Barrington turns fully around, facing Jesse as best he can as the two of them dart through the night sky on Drakendore. "And soon, boy, very soon, that ability may prove itself critical."

Jesse braces himself, scrambling to adjust for Barrington's movement so as not to fall off. "Barrington, please face forward," Jesse barks. "I don't want to end up splat on the ground. You may be used to flying on an alicorn, but—"

Before Jesse can finish his sentence, a wall of light surrounds the trio. It's as though they are flying through the sun. Jesse bends his head into Barrington's furry back, shielding himself from the brightness. They're flying through the light barrier, crossing through light years, passing from one world and on to the next. Deep down inside, on a subconscious level, Jesse notices the difference. The moon and stars hang the same as ever they did, but the smell and the feel of the air have changed. They're different than they were when Jesse left his home. It's subtle. But if he really delved into it deeply, Jesse would notice his body isn't having to work as hard as it had before to breathe. The atmosphere is different. The air, energized and light, tingles on his skin. Even the light itself has changed. It's crisper.

When Jesse opens his eyes again, blinking into a new world, they're swooping toward a meadow, barreling toward the ground. He holds his breath as Drakendore hits the earth. "We're moving too fast! I can't hold on! I'm slippin—" Drakendore stops, and Jesse is sent flying with nothing beneath him.

THUD! Jesse's head hits the grass. Pain shoots through him. He rolls and comes to rest.

"We're here!" Barrington calls down merrily from above.

Jesse cradles his knees to his chest, kneading his arms and legs with his fingers, probing himself for injuries. *It's as though he hasn't a care in the world,* Jesse thinks of Barrington, hearing the lightness in the Thwacker's voice. Still seated atop Drakendore, Barrington beams.

And indeed, Barrington is overjoyed that he has arrived safely here with the boy. Jesse, on the other hand, is blissfully unaware of all that could've happened on his journey here and of the danger that still awaits him.

CHAPTER 10
EONIA

"I have to use the washroom."

"You *just* went," King Angus snarls at the princess impatiently. Angus stabs at the princess with his words like an icy dagger hurled through the air.

And yes, of course he's right. *But I'll do anything to get out of this hut that I'm stuck in.* Eonia smirks. *I'll use the washroom a thousand times if it helps me escape from here.* If she has any hope of getting off this island, no doubt, Eonia needs to survey the Gor village. She needs a better understanding of her surroundings. It's not possible to understand anything trapped in this hut with the Gor king like she is. She needs an excuse to go outside and look around.

"I have to go again," Eonia says resolutely. "You don't want me messing up the floor, do you? It smells bad enough in here as it is."

"Fine, but make it quick." King Angus stands and slides the door of the hut sideways, opening it.

Eonia walks out of the hut and into the evening. Laden with moisture from the swamps and from the sea, the air is warm and thick. After another long night of debauchery, the Gors are waking and mulling about the village like vermin. Gors, you see, stay up all night drinking and fighting. Then they sleep into the afternoon. *It's practically their morning*—Eonia rolls her eyes—*and already the sun will be setting soon.*

Eonia tries to get a closer look at them as they scurry around the village. Haphazard and hurried, they look like insects scattering to avoid a swatter.

"That's far enough," King Angus booms. "Don't go any farther."

Eonia retreats into some bushes and squats. Then, feeling Angus' eyes on her, she flushes red. *I can't have any privacy.*

As quickly as she can, the princess pulls her nightgown back down over her knees. Mud-stained and damp, the once-white nightgown clings to her clammy legs. And as she stands, a lapo races by, its long ears and bushy tail bobbing behind it. After seeing the princess, the lapo stops hopping for a moment and stares at Eonia. Terror-stricken, its heart beats wildly. Then, hearing the Gors drawing near, the lapo darts away and scampers into the swampland. Moments later, from the same direction that the lapo had come, several Gor children bound in, chasing after the animal.

There are five children in all, four boys and a girl. They have sticks in their hands. Eonia squints, trying to decipher what their motive is. *Are they trying to kill the lapo, or do they want to eat it?*

Lapos aren't good to eat. Even the hungriest of scavengers, young and naïve as they may be, will soon discover that lapos are far too boney. And they don't taste good. They're earthy and gamey with a hint of dirt to their meat. No one's palette (not even a Gor's), is so undiscerning that he'd want to eat a lapo. Plus, there's no question that it's not worth the energy it would take to catch the thing. Lapos are fast.

The children stop in their tracks when they notice Eonia. Wielding a stick like a sword, the smallest child snarls, and the glint in his eye tells Eonia everything she needs to know about his intentions toward the lapo.

"Yer da princess King Angus got wid a'em, ain't ye?"

Eonia doesn't answer.

"We've heard 'bout ya. Rumor is we're gonna burn ya."

"I see," Eonia mutters, not moving. She understands now these children aren't chasing the lapo to eat it. "You're running after the lapo to torture and kill it. Aren't you?" she asks them. "It's a game." She shakes her head. "I should've guessed it already."

The small child smirks, his black eyes growing darker, and Eonia stumbles. The Gor children laugh.

Eonia knows that Gor children don't have an easy way of it. There are no role models for the Gor young. There are no examples of greater good for them to aspire to. Unloved and unwanted, they're tossed aside and left to fend for themselves. From birth, Gor children are exposed to sin after sin until they're practically swimming in duplicity and fear. With nowhere to turn, most Gor children eventually acquiesce to the Darkness that surrounds them. They gradually embrace evil to excel within the confines of the Gor structure. They learn to lie, cheat, and steal. Through nurture rather than nature, they learn that there's no one to care for them, no one to love them. Anything they need or want, they must do for themselves, even if it's to the detriment of others.

Even still, not every child caves to Darkness. For some, goodness is so innate that try as it might, the Dark can't completely stomp out the Light that's in them. To account for this, the Gors have a ritual—King Angus has already highlighted it for Eonia several times since she's been here. Each year, the Gors hold a bonfire in the middle of their village. If a Gor child hasn't pledged himself to Darkness by the age of fifteen, they burn him.

The Light knows the bonfires happen, of course, and the Light tries to stop them. It tries to figure out when such ceremonies will be held, so it can save the innocent. And the Light does have success in this. But the Gors are covert. King Angus calls for the bonfires on a whim to prevent Magi from meddling. And for obvious reasons, once the ceremony has transpired, all is too late. The damage has been rendered.

Clearly, these children think Eonia's fate is to be burned in a bonfire like the Gor children. They're wrong, of course. Eonia knows it well. She's aware of the Dark's plans for her. She frowns. *It's not a bonfire.*

"Are you having a nice chat?" King Angus booms at Eonia for all to hear, his voice dripping with sarcasm. "Hurry up. This isn't meant to be an all-day affair."

Eyes wide with fear, having not noticed King Angus was standing there, the Gor children turn and run with the smallest—and seemingly, the most heartless—child in the lead. Watching them scuttle, sliding this way and that in the swampy sludge, Eonia shudders. "Are *all* the Gor children chasing the lapo to hurt it?" Eonia whispers. *Could it be that one of them is running to save it?* Eonia wonders. *And if so, will the Light manage to save that child before the Gors identify his allegiance and burn him?*

Eonia's like that. She cheers for the underdog. She rescues the wounded funglebug whose wing has torn loose. She picks the lonely child to join her team. She's always been like that. Ever since she was a young child, she's acted as though it is her duty to care for the things around her. She doesn't know any other way to interact with her world, aside from taking up the responsibility to make it better.

Don't make me come and get you. King Angus' voice flashes through her mind, startling the princess.

Eonia huffs, angered by Angus' sudden breach of her train of thought. "Even in my own head, it seems I'm not safe from him," she mumbles. Thankfully, though, Eonia knows a thing or two about telepathy. Eonia doesn't have the gift herself, of course, but

Lillian did; and her aunt taught her the basics of how the gift works. Eonia is aware she has to *want* to convey a thought to allow the gifted (in this case, Angus) to hear her thoughts. She can close herself off from him by blocking him out and ignoring him. It makes it particularly hard for him, she knows, if she refuses to look at him. And so, she does her best to not even look his way.

CHAPTER 11
JESSE WALKER

A Field in the Land of Miriam

"We're here," Jesse repeats. His voice is muffled and faint through the ringing of his ears.

Where is "here"? Jesse wonders. He glances around at the landscape surrounding him. "Um. Where are we?" he asks Barrington.

Barrington climbs off Drakendore and steps down. "We're in Miriam."

The three of them—Jesse, Barrington, and Drakendore—appear to have landed in the middle of a run-of-the-mill field. "But is it the morning light?" Jesse mumbles. *There is something off about this place.* The grass is too green, and the flowers are too bright. All the colors are more vibrant than seems natural to the boy. An airy mist blanketing swaths of the land moves from place to place as though guided. The sky, the leaves, the droplets of dew reflecting the dawn's pinky hue pulse with an energy as though the scenery itself is alive and listening.

Jesse struggles to stand. His legs, sore from squeezing around Drakendore's middle, wobble. Barrington steadies Jesse, and he brushes the dirt off the boy's elbows and knees. "We should start walking," Barrington tells him. "Tanglewood is a good distance from here on foot, and Drakendore needs to leave. She has to take a trip."

"No!" Jesse cries, surprised by the sound of alarm his own cry carries as he wraps his arms around the alicorn's neck. Jesse buries his head into Drakendore's fur, hiding himself from the cold reality of her upcoming departure like an ostrich hiding its head. "Drakendore can't leave!" he pouts. "What if something happens to her? We won't be able to fly back. I could be stuck here forever, Barrington!"

"Stop being dramatic," Barrington replies. "Drakendore has to leave. She needs to explore. She needs to gather intelligence."

Refusing to budge as though his life depends upon Drakendore, Jesse keeps his arms woven around the alicorn's majestic neck.

"She's going to take off, Jesse. I suggest you step back." Barrington rolls his eyes, shaking his head.

And with that, Drakendore thrusts out her wings, pushing Jesse away. "Don't go!" Jesse gurgles, his throat raw from lack of sleep and yelling.

Drakendore dips her head toward Jesse as if to say, "It's all right; I'll be back." And then she flies up and away, spiraling out and over the meadow. She soars toward the rising sun, and in only a moment, Drakendore's a dot on the horizon. Then she's gone. Barrington and Jesse remain alone in the field, as though only seconds ago, Drakendore wasn't right there with them.

Barrington takes Jesse's arm in his. "Drakendore is scouting our path for tomorrow. She's flying to the Isle of Mires," he says gravely. "In the morning, she'll return, and the three of us can travel together again." Barrington's face brightens. "Until then, let's get to Tanglewood with you. We have a party to get to."

"A party?" Jesse murmurs. "A party with whom?"

"Thwackers, Jesse!" Barrington's eyes sparkle. "Tanglewood is where the Thwackers live. Every Thwacker in Tanglewood is excited to meet you."

The boy nearly trips over himself. "Thwackers! You mean there're *more* creatures like you?"

Mama didn't mention there are more *of them,* he thinks, hurriedly. She didn't mention any Thwackers besides Barrington. She didn't tell him there's a whole village of them. *Will the other Thwackers be friendly? Will they be as hairy as Barrington is? Will they have his ginormous vocabulary?* Jesse worries, gaping at Barrington, trying to imagine what a whole village of Barringtons could be like.

"Of course, there's more Thwackers. There's no cause for concern. We're a friendly lot," Barrington tells the boy. "Although, I am uniquely loquacious." He winks.

"Please stop doing that," Jesse pleads, realizing Barrington's eavesdropped on his thoughts again.

And even now, skipping in their direction, a furry beast scurries across the field toward them looking very much like Barrington.

From afar, the thing shouts, its voice pressing and shrill, "Welcome! Welcome to Miriam! We've waited so long to meet you, Jesse!"

Barreling toward them through the grass, it's getting closer in leaps and bounds. Reaching them, the beast throws itself into Jesse like a dust devil. Its hairy arms engulf him. Jesse feels as though he's being swallowed, smothering in its fuzz.

Is it attacking me? He shrinks, wrestling to get away from it. *No, no. I think it's hugging me.*

Holding Jesse, pulling him in closer still, the Thwacker starts babbling again. "I've been waiting so long to meet you, Jesse. And here it is in such awful circumstances. It's unfortunate that it has to be like this. Has Barrington caught you up on everything? Do tell us what you think of it all."

The Thwacker—*is it a girl?*—speaks in a high-pitched voice and has girly features (as much as a hairy beast could). Jesse decides that, yes, it is a lady Thwacker—if there is such a thing.

Catching his look, the girly thing stiffens. She stops. She's letting him go.

Did I say something? Did I offend her? Jesse starts, wondering if the lady Thwacker can hear his thoughts, too. She's looking at him like he's got three heads. Jesse blinks, concerned. "Oh!" he cries. He wasn't trying to offend. "I'm doing the best that I can!" Jesse croaks. *She ran up to me. She grabbed hold of me. What was I supposed to do? How was I supposed to act?*

Barrington, who's remained quietly on the sidelines watching them until now, pipes up in Jesse's defense. "Millie, you'll have to forgive him. He doesn't know us. Lillian hardly told him anything about Miriam. He didn't even realize that he has powers until we were flying here." Barrington gives

Millie's shoulder a squeeze. "He's coming around. But he needs time to process it all. It's a lot for him to digest."

Millie takes a hard look at Jesse. "All right, very well," she clucks in a taunting tone but with a kind glance. "Wipe that ghastly look off your face, Jesse. I'm not an alien. And yes, I am a girl."

"Agh!" Jesse blurts. *She hears me, too!*

She pulls on the boy's arm like she's leading a cow out to pasture. "Lillian used to not look at you when she didn't want you to hear her thoughts. Of course, she exercised her thought control quite well." Millie squints. "Now, tsk-tsk, to the tree hut with you," she admonishes him. "You need time to settle. We'll have a proper visit before you leave us again in the morning. You have a dangerous adventure ahead of you, I'm sorrowful to say. A very dangerous adventure, indeed. The least we can do is to have a nice visit before you must leave us again to save the princess."

"Save a princess?" Jesse jumps at Millie's words. Bouncing on the field, the blades of grass straighten up beneath him, boinging him like a trampoline. "Nobody said anything about saving a princess!"

Millie purses her lips. "You haven't told him about Princess Eonia?"

Barrington sighs again. His shoulders slump like a dog that's gone through the trash. "Well, we've had a lot to cover, Millie. I didn't want to overwhelm the boy."

"Excuse me," Jesse interrupts, "but I'm standing right here. Can one of you *please* tell me what you're talking about?"

"Mhmm. Yes, yes, of course we can." Barrington nods briskly. "I'll tell you all about it while we walk."

And without another word as to where they're going, or what they're doing, or how Jesse is involved in any of it, Barrington and Millie turn and walk into the woods.

Springing across the moss, the Thwackers push their way down a close path and into the forest. Jesse struggles to keep up.

"I suppose, Jesse, I should start at the beginning," Barrington says. "Princess Eonia is a Magus, and Magi maintain order and harmony in the Land of Miriam. Without the Magi, the Land of Miriam would crumble. It would fall into Darkness. Everyone knows this."

Darkness. Jesse's mama had talked a lot about Darkness when she was sick. *If what Mama said is true*—the boy shivers—*the Land of Miriam exists in a neverending state of war between good and evil.*

Barrington stops to watch a bird flutter. Struck by Barrington's attention to it, Jesse wonders, *Are the birds here evil? Is Darkness watching us now?*

Dropping his voice to barely above a whisper, Barrington continues, "What is not known is that Princess Eonia is not just a princess. She is the key to the *Book of Good and Evil*, as was her mother, Queen Marakee, and her mother before her, and her mother before her—all the way up to Queen Adira.

"You have heard all this before, haven't you? Lillian must have told you about the book, at least. Didn't she?" Barrington pauses, waiting for the boy to answer.

"Yeah." Jesse nods. "She told me stuff."

Truthfully, Jesse's mom had talked about the book a fair amount. But Jesse had thought she was losing her mind. He had thought she was affected by the drugs, imagining things. In addition to the book, you see, she'd told Jesse that she could talk to animals and that her brother was a king. But Jesse's mom had never had a brother of which he was aware, let alone one that was a king. What was the boy supposed to believe—that his mom was a fairy tale princess and his nonexistent uncle a handsome prince?

And if all Mama said was true, Jesse finds himself thinking, *why didn't she tell me about her life before she was dying, before she knew she was leaving me forever? Didn't she trust me?* Jesse scowls, wondering what it all could mean.

"She told me about the book," Jesse finally concedes, deciding—for the time being, at least—that it's best to be forthright with Barrington. After all, Jesse's in a strange land with nowhere else to turn and no way to get home. What other choice does he have? "Mama said she'd sworn to protect it," he admits.

Barrington's eyes light up. "Good," he booms. "As Lillian might've said, then, the book is a collection of secrets and spells—a textbook of sorts, compiled over twelve hundred years ago.

"Originally, the book was designed to protect the Light from Darkness," Barrington comments. "A long time ago, though, fearing the book would fall into the wrong hands, Queen Adira, a powerful Magus, cast a spell on the book. She locked it, and no one has laid eyes on its words since.

"Over generations," Barrington continues, "the Magi have passed the book's good secrets down by word-of-mouth, while knowledge of the book's evil has died away. The book itself is thought by most to have been destroyed."

Another bird flutters by. Jesse ducks, and it narrowly misses his head. "What's with the birds? Shouldn't they fear us?" Jesse interrupts, wondering again if the birds are listening.

"They're funglebugs." Barrington narrows his eyes, waiting until the bird disappears. "I'll tell you about them later." Then he lowers his voice even lower. "As I was saying, the legend of the book is well-known. Less known is that the book still exists. Moreover, certain Magi can unlock it. They can break the spell; they can make the invisible words become visible again."

Barrington glances Jesse's direction, raising his eyebrows. "The ability runs along Queen Adira's descendants—they're known as the Keys. The power passes from mother to eldest daughter. It lies dormant in the girl until her fourteenth birthday when the power comes alive. It activates."

Jesse is speechless.

"Only one key exists at a time, though. When the power in one key activates, power in the prior key goes away." Barrington makes eye contact with Jesse, waiting for him to comprehend what he's just explained.

It's happening again, like it did on the way over when they were flying on Drakendore. Barrington's stopped talking. His lips aren't moving, and Jesse doesn't hear him like he normally would. Yet his voice is sounding inside of him.

Clear as day, Jesse hears Barrington tell him without speaking, *From that point forward, if the girl's eyes grace the* Book of Good and Evil, *Queen Adira's spell will be broken. The book will fall open. The words, spells, and secrets will be exposed for all to see—the righteous and the sinister.*

Barrington pokes his walking stick at the base of a tree, his face ashen, his voice solemn. *And so it goes, Jesse, if Princess Eonia so much as looks upon the book, then Queen Adira's spell will be broken. Once unlocked, if the book falls into the hands of the Gors—or any other Dark agent, for that matter—the Dark may harness the secrets set forth therein to rule over the Land of Miriam.*

Jesse rubs his temples. His mom and Barrington's stories coincide. His mom had told him about Queen Adira. She'd told him everyone thought the book had been destroyed.

Barrington continues, *Three days ago, Princess Eonia disappeared from the kingdom. The funglebugs have news that the Gors have her. They are holding the princess on the Isle of Mires. We must go to her. We must save her.*

Jesse shivers at Barrington's intensity.

"Jesse, this is important," Barrington says, finally speaking in his normal voice again. "The princess' life is in danger, as well as the future of Miriam. It upsets me to put you in this position, but you must use your powers to rescue Princess Eonia. Miriam's very existence depends upon it."

Jesse has a gazillion questions, not least of which is what Barrington expects *him* to do about any of this. Before he can ask Barrington, though, Millie calls out from ahead, "We've made it!"

Millie's stopped. She's standing in front of the biggest tree Jesse's ever seen. Next to it, she looks shrunken, like an ant next to an eighteen-wheeler. The trunk of the tree is wider than a school bus. It reaches up higher than Jesse can see. Its branches spiral out, twisting and turning, like the arms of a former heavyweight champion, still burly and forceful and keenly aware of their power and majesty.

Millie raps on the tree with the heel of her hand; and before the boy's very eyes, a door appears. As Jesse moves closer, he sees the sign "B & M" engraved

on the door. *This is their house. They live inside of a tree!* He's gleeful at this realization.

Once inside, it's clear to him that this is no ordinary tree. It's not dark and gloomy the way the inside of a tree might be. It is filled with light. Jars glowing with liquid shine through the tree's interior, lighting the hut with a homey glow. And it's got a woodsy scent, like a Christmas tree that's still fresh and sparkling. Jesse must admit, Barrington and Millie's tree hut is cheery.

Furrowing his brows, Barrington clears his throat. "Jesse, one more bit of business before we can relax for the evening."

Jesse gazes up into the darkness of the tree trunk above him, marveling at how far the tree goes as he listens to Barrington.

"Centuries ago, we determined it too dangerous to house both the *Book of Good and Evil* and the book's key in the Land of Miriam," Barrington says solemnly. "We hid the book in your world. We stationed a Magus among humans to guard it there.

"When your mother was young, Magi moved her to your world to be raised as a human." Barrington rubs his hairy knuckles as though remembering a painful memory. "As you may know, your mother served as the book's last guardian for the Magi of Miriam."

Eyes glistening, Barrington trains his eyes on Jesse, drinking in the boy's presence. "You're to be the next one, Jesse. Did you know that?" His eyes shimmer, widening, as though he's announced Jesse's in line to be the future king of England.

Jesse, on the other hand, does not feel like any of this could be a good thing. The dear boy is confused. Yes, his mom had told him he was meant to be the next guardian for the book. But Jesse didn't understand what she meant, and he didn't believe her. He still doesn't have a clue what it all means. Lillian didn't want to weigh the boy down with such baggage. She didn't want to trouble him with obligations from her homeland at such a young age.

"How am I supposed to guard a Boo—" Jesse starts to ask Barrington, desperate to understand how he's meant to fit into all of this.

RAP. RAP. RAP.

A knock on the door reverberates through Millie and Barrington's tree hut. Barrington hops up and scuttles past Jesse to answer it.

"That didn't take long." Barrington chuckles, opening the door.

And past Barrington on the other side of the door, there are more—many more—Thwackers. There are Thwackers of all ages, shapes, and sizes. Each of them is short. Each of them is hairy.

A kid Thwacker yells, "He's here!"

"Jesse!" booms another voice.

And another one yelps, "Open the door wider, Barrington. We want to come in!"

The Thwackers push their way into the tree hut, barging past Barrington. Jesse jumps back but is unable to make a getaway and hide from the horde before they swarm him. Caught in a wave of Thwackers, tumbling, Jesse can't extricate himself from the jumble. They're patting his back. They're kissing his forehead. The boy giggles, unable to hide his glee. A carefree happiness that he hasn't known since his mom was alive bubbles up from within him. But then, there's also a very real need he has to *breathe*.

Wrestling himself out from the pile of Thwackers, Jesse breaks through to the surface, searching for air, gasping. "Oooh!" He explodes joyfully at the sight of food.

Thwackers weighed down with goodies are piling plates of food on the table. There's vegetables and bean dip, rolls with nut butter, and muffins and honey. Millie, who's carrying a fruit basket, sets it down on the table. Inside the basket, Jesse sees fruit of all different shapes and colors. There are apples that have hair like peach fuzz, instead of being smooth and waxy. There are bananas that are red when they should be yellow. And there are melons that look like grape-sized cantaloupes. Beside the basket is a bowlful of salad piled high with lettuce. Unfortunately, the lettuce just looks like lettuce, Jesse notices of the salad, disappointed.

Millie, sensing the boy's hunger, drooling as he is at the very sight of the delicacies, calls out to him, "Dig in!"

Jesse grabs a plate. Spooning food onto it, he loads it up until it's heaping, trying some of every dish. Then sinking into a chair, he sits down with his plateful of food. And amidst the din of Thwackers that hums around him, he shovels in the food.

Jesse's never tasted anything this good. Or has he? The bean dip, earthy and rich, reminds him of a dip his mom used to make for church banquets. And like his childhood lovey (a faded and worn stuffed bear, long since discarded but well-remembered), the muffins are comforting to him. "I've had muffins like these before," he comments. After seconds and thirds and loads of pie, his stomach puffs out, bulging like a football. He unbuttons his pants. Then finally sitting back, he relaxes into the afternoon.

Throughout the rest of the day and into the evening, Thwackers arrive at Barrington and Millie's tree hut. Each time the door opens, another Thwacker steps in. Jesse meets Morton and Drumbell, Haverton and Alyse, Sylvia, Karley, Albert, and Snivel. They all ask about Maddie. They all ask about Jesse's dad and how life's been for him. They tell Jesse how honored they are to meet him and how much they miss his mom's visits to Miriam.

Outside of the tree hut, the Thwackers play music. Dancing, Millie and Barrington swing around, twirling each other on the padded moss. Merriment rings out through Tanglewood for hours until the sun begins to set.

Eventually, Thwackers say their goodbyes with handshakes and hugs. One by one, they go back to their arborous abodes that are scattered throughout the village, hidden in the trees. Finally, the gathering dwindles until only Barrington, Millie, and Jesse are left alone and exhausted. Millie shows Jesse to a bed in a room that's off the kitchen.

Pulling the sheets back, Jesse crawls in. He's a foot taller than the tallest Thwacker, it seems, and his feet dangle off the edge. Still, it's comfortable, and he's tired. It seems his head doesn't hit the pillow . . .

An hour can't have passed. Jesse's awake, sweating. He's been dreaming. He feels himself shaking.

In his dream, winged beasts spewed fire from their mouths, setting the brush near Jesse aflame. Barrington and he were running and running . . . trying to get away, trying to save the princess. A huge man with black eyes, half a face, and a crown on his head bore down on them. The man's eyes, like marbles, drilled holes into Jesse as the boy raised his fists to defend himself so he's not pummeled out of existence.

It was just a dream, Jesse tells himself. "It wasn't real."

Even still, Jesse passes the rest of the night in fits of sleep and tortured wakefulness, trying to forget the terror of it.

CHAPTER 12
EONIA

Isle of Mires, Land of Miriam

A guard sets a plate of food and a cup of water down on the hut's dusty hearth. Without looking up, Eonia crawls over to it. Her stomach growls. A trickle of blood runs down the meat and congeals at the base of it. "Ick!" she groans, steeling herself so as not to vomit.

Two times a day, a guard brings a meal to Eonia— if one can call it a meal. The food, mostly meat, is bloody and barely seared. On two occasions, Eonia's found crawlies squirming, drilling their holes into it, tunneling their way through the flesh.

The first two days, Eonia didn't touch her plate. On the third day, though, feeling herself growing weak and dizzy in the head, she tried to eat; but she threw up instead. On the fourth day, holding her nose and swallowing hard, she forced the mushed meat down her throat and managed to keep the food down.

Sooner or later, I'm going to escape from here, Eonia tells herself, eying the plate on the ground. *I need my strength. I must eat.*

The guard who brought in the food stays in the hut, watching. He grits his teeth. "Well, are ye gonna eat id already, or are ye gonna let da crawlies do yer job fer ya?"

Eonia brings her eyes level with the guard's and immediately regrets it. Gors, she has come to learn, live on the edge of starvation. *This food must look like a feast to him.* Foam collects at the corners of his mouth. Malice glints in his beady eyes. He wants her food. *If Angus wasn't near, he'd probably be willing to kill me for it.* Eonia reflects on the guard's desire for her food and the dangerous predicament she's in.

The guard twists his face in a sneer. "Nod up ta snuff fer ye, is id, Princess? Not wad yer used ta eatin' in da kingdom, eh?"

The guard's face, like King Angus', doesn't look real. He, too, looks like he's popped out of a nightmare. Grossly distorted, it seems his face is a mask that's made up to frighten children, rather than made of flesh and bone and sinew. Eonia blinks at the apparition in front of her. *He must've sinned some serious sins to look like that.* She shakes her head in horror.

It's well known that a Gor's appearance is a manifestation of his sin. Each heinous act a Gor commits, his features grow more and more distorted from their prior version. An evil deed may cause one side of a Gor's lip to droop; an eye may drift to the middle or off to the side; or an ear travels down, and the other travels up. Perhaps a nostril becomes bulbous and flares. And unlike Magi—as well as people in the other world, who have hairs on their heads—Gors have thick bursts of hair all over them. A Gor may have no hair at all, except for a patch that erupts from his forehead. Regardless of what form the manifestation of sin takes in a Gor, the more distorted a Gor's appearance, the more heinous his acts must've been.

Make no mistake now—nobody's perfect. Every creature has flaws; even the most impeccable specimen admittedly has some characteristics that fall short of perfection. This isn't like that. A Gor's mangled features are not imperfections—far from it. A Gor's distortions don't occur in nature. Rather, a Gor's mouth may turn vertical; an ear may end up on a chin; an eye may land in the middle of a cheek. A Gor's appearance reflects the evil, the rejection of God's goodness and order, that blooms inside of him.

He thumbs his nose at God's beauty and grace. And over time, he becomes a monster from the inside out.

Eonia picks the meat up off the plate. Closing her eyes, she bites into it. Like teaching herself to walk again, or to breath, or to blink, or to do any action that should be automatic but now requires more focus than seems natural, she chews, willing herself to grind down through the gelatinous slab of red. And as she does, she tries not to think about what type of meat she might be eating. But as the blood spreads on her tongue, she can't help but think of Grog, the Gor that the Kelptar seared. *I hope there really was nothing left of him.* She grimaces, imagining the guard who told King Angus that Grog had been eaten. *I hope I'm not eating Grog,* she thinks, trying to push the idea from her mind.

I want to live. I want to live. I want to live. Eonia reminds herself of that one truth as she chews, ripping the meat apart and swallowing.

The guard stares, a puddle of spit collecting on his chin, watching her chew. Eonia picks up the plate and carries it to the corner of the makeshift hut in which she's trapped, moving as far away from the guard as she can. His hollow eyes follow her every move.

"Enjoy id, Princess. Da tides are turnin'. Id won't be long before we have da keys ta da kingdom. And when we do, I'm gonna eat up all yer Magi food— fruits an' sweets an' all da rest of it. Ye can keep yer crawlie meat."

With that, he leaves. Outside of the hut, Eonia hears him laughing with another guard; and she swallows, fighting to keep the meat down.

CHAPTER 13

JESSE WALKER

"Chirp diddley-dirp. Boom-boom cachoom. I see you!"

Jesse shoots upright and looks around the bedroom. *Did it just say, "I see you"?*

"Chirp diddley-dirp, Boom-boom cachoom, I see you!" It chirps again.

Barrington had told Jesse that the birds in the Land of Miriam talk. He'd said that they are called funglebugs and can speak. Barrington told him that the Light uses them to spy on things, to relay what's happening in the Land of Miriam to and from the kingdom.

Is that what's happening now? he wonders. *Is one of them spying on me from the branches above? Was it watching me while I was sleeping?* The funglebugs, and their consistent presence, have befuddled Jesse since he first arrived here in this strange land.

"They're so weird," he says quietly of the talking birds. Bleary-eyed, he rubs his forehead, still throbbing from a terrible night's sleep, trying to "clear out the cobwebs," as his mom used to tell him, so that he can think straight. All night long, he tossed and turned, dreaming a terrible dream.

The funglebug continues to sing.

"Be quiet!" Jesse shouts, desperate for peace so he can think. If only he could see the pesky funglebug, he'd be tempted to pelt it with a pillow. Nothing harmful. It's not like he wants to injure the funglebug or anything. He'd just greatly appreciate it if it was quiet already.

And surprisingly, the funglebug stops chirping.

"Umm, thank you," Jesse says cautiously through the lump in his throat, unsure what to make of the sudden silence. The funglebug was indeed listening to him, it would appear. And standing by the bed in a seemingly empty room with an unseen funglebug listening in, Jesse decides it's best to leave.

In the kitchen, he finds Millie cooking. "Yoohoo! Good mornin'," she crows cheerfully. "How'd ya sleep?"

Jesse shrugs, not wanting to admit that he's hardly slept a wink for fear of monsters chasing after him. "What're you making?" he asks her instead, breathing in the smell of sweet dough frying on the stove.

"Kettle cakes." Millie flips the dough on the griddle. "Your mother used to love them."

"Mama stayed *here?*" Jesse jumps as her words run down him like an icy shower, leaving him awake and sputtering.

"Oh, yes. Loads of times. Before Lillian had you and Madeline, she used to visit us often in Tanglewood. And whenever she stayed here with us, she was always asking me to make her kettle cakes!"

Since Jesse arrived, he's longed for more information about his mom's life here in the Land of Miriam. The night before, a number of the Thwackers mentioned how much his mother had meant to them and what a wonderful leader she had been. Jesse didn't know what to say, and they'd seemed reticent to share details. Now, it seems, though, the opportunity has presented itself on a silver platter to learn about her life here, but Jesse is hesitant to ask Millie more questions. He doesn't want to hear about the life his mom had without him. And what's more, he doesn't know why he feels this way. *Is it jealousy?* He feels his cheeks redden, and he looks down to block Millie from intruding on his thoughts. *Am I scared she loved the people here more than she loved me?*

"I've never seen a table like this before," Jesse says, avoiding further conversation about his mom. He rubs his hands along the length of the table, feeling the grain of the wood. "Where did it come from?"

"Right here in Tanglewood," Millie chirps happily. "Thwackers are excellent woodworkers, you know. We're the best craftsmen in Miriam."

"Oh, that's cool," Jesse mumbles, wondering how Thwackers whittle wood with such thick, hairy hands.

Finally, after what seems like a long time, Millie places a plate of kettle cakes down in front of Jesse. Syrup oozes down the sides of the cakes, drips onto his plate, and gathers in a sticky pool around the cake's edges. *It's understandable that Mama loved these,* Jesse thinks—the smell alone is making him weak in the knees. He wasn't hungry at all until he smelled the kettle cakes on the stove cooking, and now, it seems he's never been this hungry before for anything in his life. Anticipating the gush of sugar, he raises his fork to his mouth—

BANG!

Barrington slams the door of the tree hut closed behind him and enters. Without so much as a greeting, the Thwacker crosses the room, scowling and clenching his fists. Jesse hasn't seen him like this. Taking a plate of kettle cakes, Barrington sits down beside Jesse. He doesn't even say hi before he begins.

"Your armor is ready," Barrington tells Jesse. "Sckabor is gleaming."

"Armor? Why do we . . . " Kettle cakes catch in Jesse's throat. He's caught-up in a coughing fit, unable to finish asking why in this vast world, he'd need armor.

Patting him on the back, Barrington continues. "Drakendore is safely returned from the Isle of Mires. She didn't see Princess Eonia firsthand, but she did survey the Gor village. It appears the funglebugs are correct."

"F-f-funglebugs?" Jesse stammers, clearing the kettle cakes from his throat, remembering the chirp diddley-dirp, boom-boom cachoom from this morning.

"Yes, the birds, Jesse. Funglebugs are somewhat akin to the birds in your world," Barrington says quickly.

"I remember. It's just that they . . . well, they woke me up this morning. It's like they were spying on me."

"Right. They do that from time to time. Now, as I was saying"—Barrington heaves, waving his hand—"per Drakendore's surveillance, the Gors are holding somebody up on the Isle of Mires. It must be the princess." Barrington pauses, letting the information sink in. "In fact, I gather King Angus is guarding Princess Eonia himself—which presents an unfortunate challenge."

"King Angus, the Gor king?" Jesse asks, picturing the monster with a crown on his head running after him in his dream, sensing that the two are related.

"Yes." Barrington lowers his eyes. "King Angus is the king of the Gors. And there is yet another challenge of which we were not previously aware." Barrington scowls. "It seems, based on Drakendore's surveillance, that Kelptar dragons are guarding the Isle of Mires."

"Ah!" Millie groans from the kitchen, dropping a pan. Clanging, the fallen pan reverberates through the tree hut.

"Did you say *dragons*?" Jesse shivers, raising his voice above the clanging pan, thinking he must've misheard Barrington's words.

To Jesse's chagrin, Barrington nods.

"We can't march into a den of dragons, Barrington!" Jesse yells, disbelieving.

"I'm afraid we don't have a choice."

"But it's absurd. I can't fight dragons!" Jesse's eyes are bulging.

It's true, Jesse wanted adventure. But he didn't want adventure like *this*! *I'm not interested in risking my life!* He shakes. Jesse simply wanted a change of pace. He would've settled for climbing a mountain or taking a balloon ride or horseback riding in the woods. *Never in a million years did I wish to be riding around on alicorns, fighting dragons, and saving princesses!*

"This is crazy. I'm just a kid, Barrington. I don't have powers. I'm not from this land. There's been a mistake, a misunderstanding. Don't you see? I don't belong here! I should be home. I should be with my dad and Maddie!"

Oh, how the boy craves the company of his father. What he wouldn't give for the feel of his father's arms around him, wrapping him in one of his bear hugs. The boy longs to hear his father say, "It's all right, Jesse. It's all going to be okay." Of course, Jesse is aware by now that his father can't ensure everything will work out in the end. This particular observation was painfully confirmed when his mother passed away. Even still, there's a sense of safety his dad instills in him. Perhaps it's knowing that his father will do anything in his power, no matter what, to fight for him.

And it's not just his father the boy misses. He wishes he could see his little sister, too. In contrast to the need for change that he felt so heartily on the night he departed with Barrington, Jesse longs for the normalcy of the mundane. He imagines tickling Maddie's armpits till she falls to the ground laughing, snorting to the point of hysterics. He thinks of Noni barking at him to tuck in his shirt and take off his muddy shoes. He thinks of his dad, frustrated he left his bike in the driveway.

Will I ever get back home to them? Will I ever see Noni and Grandpa again? Will I ever know how things turned out for Irvin after I last saw him, when his ma was yelling at him about chores?

"*Pfffh.*" Barrington sighs with a wave of his hand, dismissing Jesse's protestations. "Jesse, you couldn't be more wrong. You aren't just a kid; you're a Magus yourself. For crying out loud, not only are you a Magus, you're also kin to the throne. Princess Eonia is your cousin. King Mor and Queen Marakee are your uncle and aunt. Child, God made you for this!"

"What does God have to do with any of it?" Jesse juts out his chin.

Barrington raises an eyebrow. He looks at Jesse as though he sees through him. And in as civilized a tone as anyone could imagine, given the situation, Barrington answers calmly, "God has everything to do with everything, Jesse. Surely you know that."

Without further explanation, the Thwacker turns and begins to pace. "Don't you see? You're an agent of Light, Jesse. You're one of us. You fight for good. You fight for what's honorable and pure. Your heart doesn't know any different."

But he doesn't know me! Jesse trembles. "It's not that I don't want to help," he cries. "I do. It's just I don't see how I can. Why *me*? Why am *I* here? What is it that *I* can do?"

Barrington knits his brows. "Perhaps, Jesse, I should give you a better understanding of your background," the Thwacker says. Squaring himself off with Jesse, he crosses his hands like a professor about to recite a treatise.

"Your mother, as you now surely appreciate, was from here. She danced between your world and ours for years and years." Keeping his arms clasped, Barrington resumes his pacing. "Then, after meeting your father, she came to the Land of Miriam less often than she had before. And after she had you and

Madeline, her trips became even more seldom. She feared she would be waylaid in Miriam, I believe. She was concerned she would be unable to return to you."

Barrington turns on his heel. "And all that time living in your world, Lillian never spoke a word of the Land of Miriam to your father. She was worried, I gather, that it would be too much for him."

"Too much for him?" Jesse gawks. "That makes no sense at all!" he huffs. "Dad loved Mama more than anything. Knowing about the Land of Miriam wouldn't have changed any of that. Why didn't she trust us?" Jesse snarls, his temperature rising like one of Sophia's soups on the burner beginning to boil over.

"I don't know the answer to that." Barrington tilts his head thoughtfully. "Only your mother would be able to answer you. My guess is, though, that she was worried that Darkness would somehow find you and take you from her—or something to that effect. I don't really know. I can't speak for her." Barrington shakes his head.

"What I do know is that toward the end when the severity of her illness was clear, we pressured your mother to return to Miriam, but she wouldn't hear of it. She was resolute, insisting she spend her remaining time with you, your sister, and your father. Even when she was in pain, dying, she loved you too much to leave you."

A sense of dread Jesse has always felt when talking about his mom is rising up within him like a giant serpent preparing to strike his heel. He's mad at his mom for not telling him about the Land of Miriam sooner. Worse even, he's mad at her for leaving him. Deep down, he knows his anger isn't justified. She didn't *want* to leave him. She didn't *want* to die. Indeed, she did everything in her power to try to live. She fought for her life. But Jesse can't keep himself from feeling betrayed. He can't rationalize away his thoughts.

"Before she got sick, I was normal," he mutters. "I was happy."

After his mom passed, Jesse balled up his frustration. He banished the anger he felt toward her, and he buried it deep inside. As is to be expected, the boy tried to hide his feelings from himself as much as he tried to hide them from everyone else. *How can I be upset with her? She's dead*, he told himself over and over. But like a furball that refuses to stay down, all this talk about his mom is bringing his torment back to the surface.

"Lillian would be furious if she knew that we have you here in Miriam, facing what we're facing." Barrington plants himself in front of Jesse and heaves. "But what choice have we got? We need you, Jesse. We need your help."

"But why me?" he shouts angrily. "Maybe Mama knew this land. Maybe she understood it. Maybe she was even from here. But not me. This isn't my place to be."

"You are gifted!" Barrington booms. "How many times do I have to tell you that? You are telepathic, Jesse. You have a gift. You are your mother's child through and through. How do you think you were talking to me on the way here?" Barrington snorts.

"I don't know how I was talking to you. I don't know anything about it. It just happened. I didn't control it. I wasn't trying to make you talk in my head. I wasn't trying to let you hear my thoughts as I think them."

Barrington's eyes shimmer. "And that's just it, isn't it? It just happens." He nods enthusiastically. "Lillian said if you think a thought to anyone—any species, regardless of their language—then they will hear you, and you can understand them. The key is that you have to want to communicate with them, and they must want to communicate back. And you're getting the hang of it; I can tell. At least, I'm not picking up on your private thoughts like I was before."

"Similarly, if they speak out loud, you will understand them for the same reason." Barrington takes a deep breath, hoping he's explaining it correctly. "Regardless of whether it comes in words or flashes or in pictures, you can understand them," Barrington concludes as best he knows how.

Jesse pushes his plate of kettle cakes out from in front of him. "All right, if that's how it works, how come I haven't noticed it before? I'm twelve years old, Barrington. Wouldn't I have discovered this *gift* before now?"

"The power isn't as prevalent outside of the Land of Miriam." Barrington shrugs, not caring to admit that Jesse has a point. "Surely, you have noticed *something*, though." He squints at the boy. "You have to have had *some* sense of your ability, have you not, Jesse?" Barrington presses.

Barrington's right, of course. There are many times Jesse's understood what others have thought without the need for words. The boy's great misunderstanding, however, is that he thought he was like everyone else. He thought it was like that for everyone. Flying the drone with Irvin, Jesse knew Irvin was worried he'd crashed it and wouldn't be able to pay for another. And Jesse knew what Noni would say when he was slagging off Mr. Armstead before she'd said it. Then there's his dog, Jerry. Jesse nearly always knows what Jerry wants. It's as though he can hear the dog when it wags its tail to go outside or to be fed, or Jerry wants to be patted behind his ears.

Just because I know what Jerry wants, though, doesn't mean anything, Jesse thinks to himself.

Jesse's operated his whole life under the mistaken impression that everyone possesses this level of "intuition," as his mother had called it. Lillian didn't want Jesse to be self-conscious that he's different. She put off explaining his power to him. She told herself she'd explain it to him later, when he's older, when he's more grounded and could handle the news and utilize his power more effectively. But she ran out of life before she could set him straight. In the hospital, Lillian had tried to explain Jesse's power to him.

"How many dragons did Drakendore see guarding the princess?" Jesse asks, not wanting to talk about his so-called "gift" in more depth.

Barrington muffles his answer. "Four, but there may be more."

Millie groans. She shuffles off toward her bedroom.

The pit in Jesse's stomach swells. "And what *exactly* are these dragons like?"

Barrington wrings his hands, and his face pales. "Kelptars are no good, Jesse. Of all the dragons in Miriam, Kelptar dragons are the worst. A Kelptar's power grows and flourishes with each Light force it crushes."

"Thankfully, though, Kelptars are lazy and slothful and, dare I say, not very intelligent," Barrington says with a mild smirk. "Pea brains, in fact. Literally, a Kelptar's brain is no larger than the size of a pea. Left to their own devices, they're not very dangerous because they're too dim-witted to present a real threat. But used as a tool, they may prove lethal."

Barrington sighs as though he feels the weight of the world upon his shoulders. "And that's the problem. The Gors have enlisted the Kelptars. They've joined together. At the direction of the Gors, Kelptar dragons, I fear, can kill us."

"Great." Jesse's insides churn. "How can you and I get through them, then? If the Gors are directing the Kelptars and the Kelptars are helping to guard the princess, how will we survive?"

Barrington tilts his head, weighing the alternatives. "The Kelptars' involvement is not ideal," Barrington admits. "Our best hope, it seems, is to enlist dragons of Light to help us."

"There're dragons that're good here?" Jesse asks, feeling slightly better about their chances if they have dragons of their own fighting for them.

"Oh, yes." Barrington nods assuredly. "Kelptar and Snapjaw dragons are Dark agents; but Morgan, Rainbow, Dogfish, Firefly, and Butterfly dragons are all good dragons. Like us, they're agents of Light, working to maintain harmony throughout the Land of Miriam. We can recruit them."

"So, the good ones can come with us?" Jesse ventures, taking a bite of his kettle cakes.

Barrington presses his fingertips together. "Well, it's not that easy, I'm afraid. Of the seven dragon species in Miriam, only three can fly, and only three breathe fire. Unfortunately for us, Kelptar dragons do both. That's what makes them so dangerous. Firefly dragons, I believe, are our best hope."

Jesse swallows. "Because Firefly dragons can fly and breathe fire?"

"Yes," Barrington answers. "Morgans and Dogfish are powerful fire-breathing dragons, but they can't fly; and the Isle of Mires is a remote island in the Sea of Sunderway. We have no way to get them there. Fireflies, then, seem to be our best answer to the Kelptars."

Jesse takes a sip of water. As calmly as he can, he lays out Barrington's plan. "So, you want me to recruit good dragons to help you save a princess, who's supposedly my cousin and is being held by evil men and evil dragons on an island?"

"Right on, my boy." Barrington levels his gaze on Jesse. There's not even a glimmer of a hint that Barrington's being humorous about any of this. Doing his best not to scoff, Jesse remains silent. He wolfs down the rest of his kettle cakes. They may be his last meal.

CHAPTER 14
EONIA

Isle of Mires, Land of Miriam

Angus steps onto the stage. Flames from torches lick the black night, casting an orange hue onto the crowd's faces.

"Good evening, Gors!" Angus belts, straightening himself up to his full height. He flexes his bulging muscles. Sweat glistens on his skin—even in the dead of night, it's humid on the island.

"It's *our* time!" King Angus raises his arms above his head, gesturing toward the heavens. "I'm assembling an army to take over the kingdom."

The crowd shrieks with evil glee at his pronouncement. King Angus grins and continues, "Not only are the Kelptars with us, but we're also gathering others who've been waiting in the wings, biding their time to rise and serve us."

The crowd trembles with bloodlust and chants, "Darkness is rising!"

Looming over them, King Angus wipes the drool from his chin.

Eonia, who's tied to a chair on the stage behind the Gor king, looks down into the sea of Gors that are before her. *The whole village must be here.*

Gors, filthy and half-naked, study Eonia with a curiosity that's laced with a dull hatred. The princess searches the crowd's faces for the Gor children she saw before, chasing the lapo in the woods. But in the dim light, she can't be certain if they are here now. Eonia does, however, note the Gor women. With wiry hair that's never seen a brush and faces creased beyond their years from hard living and poor nutrition, the women before her bear a silent look of resignation. *There's nothing but fear and pain and death for them to look forward to,* Eonia surmises.

Meanwhile the men, who keep the Gor civilization grinding forward in no particular direction, swing their clubs impatiently.

"We will wipe out the Light!" King Angus cries, beating his chest. "One by one, we will destroy them until they beg for mercy. In the end, they will serve us. They will bend to *our* will."

Never! Eonia longs to scream but is silent, fighting the urge to make the situation more perilous. *He's wrong! He has no idea!* Eonia reaches into the depths of her core, grasping hold of who she is and what she stands for. Withdrawing into her own world, Eonia finds solace in the face of the Gors.

The travesty of this pathetic kidnapping—the Dark's bid for Miriam—will amount to nothing in the end, she promises herself.

Eonia has to be right—the alternative is unthinkable. *Darkness will forever exist as scavengers, picking off the remains thrown from the Light, acting on impulse, feeding their minute-to-minute desires.* Eonia chews her tongue. *Dark agents don't understand selflessness.* "It's beyond them," she murmurs beneath her breath. *They can't grasp the depths of my soul. They don't know that I'll never do their bidding. They can't understand that I have a higher calling to save the Land of Miriam. No, Dark agents will not use* me *to unlock the book for them.* "Never!" she whispers. And the idea that she would let them is suddenly funny to the girl.

King Angus, twice my size, will never get what he wants. "I won't let him." She spits. *The fate of Miriam doesn't turn on King Angus—it turns on me, the lonely girl Magus that I am! I'll never unlock the book for them. I'll stamp out my own beautiful life to salvage the fate of*

Miriam before I allow them to use me. I'm the powerful one, not them! Eonia starts to laugh at the irony.

King Angus, sensing movement, catches a glimpse of the princess behind him, and he glares. "We'll see if you laugh when your kingdom falls," he hisses, silent to all but for her to hear.

Angus is angry. He doesn't understand that Eonia's laughter is steeped in greater pain than her tears. And this thought—that he thinks that she can be happy here, that he thinks that she can make gleeful sounds here *with him*—makes her laugh even harder. "He's angry because he thinks that I'm happy!" Eonia snickers. *He doesn't know what happiness is!*

But then, there's the question of how many Light agents must die to defeat the forces of Darkness that are mounting. Lord Letch will not give up. And King Angus has power. Indeed, he's speaking with Eonia now, using telepathy. He's gifted. There's no one Eonia's known who has the gift of telepathy besides Eonia's Aunt Lillian. And she's dead. Eonia's cousin, Jesse, is said to have the gift that Lillian possessed, but Eonia's never met him. Nobody in the Land of Miriam has met Jesse—or at least, that's what Eonia's been led to believe. He lives in the other world, not here in Miriam.

Of course, some Light agents besides Magi can communicate with other Light species. Funglebugs can speak languages besides their own, and Thwackers can understand many. But that's different from having the ability to communicate with everyone—Light or Dark, no matter what the species—that full-blown telepathy gives. And it's clear, King Angus has the gift of full-blown telepathy.

King Angus is the link bringing Dark agents together, telling them about the book. Eonia grimaces, considering the cold, hard facts at hand. *He secured the Kelptars. He can speak to them. He can motivate them. I must warn the Light. But how can I when I'm stuck here?*

A guard brings King Angus a mug of drink to the stage of the dirty, ragged amphitheater. Raising his cup, King Angus chants at the crowd as though singing a lullaby, "Magi, Magi, holier-than-thou Magi. Their smugness makes me want to hurl! I despise them to their very core. Do-gooders, they are lovers of others and their infantile, self-righteous society. They live for their forsaken cause in the name of God, the Enemy."

King Angus takes a sip of his drink and hurls his mug, smashing it. He shouts even louder, "They're always praying to God and asking for His favor and begging for His forgiveness. *Weaklings!* That's not for us. Who is God? Who is He that He should lord over you and me?" King Angus asks the crowd, raising his arms to the heavens and clenching his fists.

"Magi think since they are close to Him—God, the 'Enemy,'—that He will protect them. He does not!" Angus quips. "They sing. They pray. They hug. They take care of each other. They feed the poor. They take care of the sick. Why? What does any of it do for them? I'll tell you what—*nothing!*" he shouts, spreading his fingers and stretching his empty hands toward the crowd dramatically. "He doesn't *love* them. God doesn't protect anyone. He won't shield them from evil. No, dear Gors"—Angus pauses for effect—"He won't protect them from *me*."

Angus grimaces, spreading his lopsided lips. "It's time to show the Land of Miriam a real king—a king who has power, a king who can rule!" Angus yells, flexing his arms.

The crowd roars. Plugging her ears, Eonia can't hide from their deafening screams.

"The justice of Hell is about pragmatism." Angus nods sternly. "It's concerned with results, take or be taken. The Almighty Below expects results." He spits. "That, I understand. The Almighty Below wants a track record of success. That, I aim to deliver." Angus plants himself before the cheering crowd. "From Hell's corridors, I have risen to blot out the Magi. From Hell's noise, we will bring down Miriam!"

Eonia closes her eyes and prays.

CHAPTER 15

JESSE WALKER

A knock at the door makes Jesse nearly fall out of his seat.

"Come in," Barrington calls.

The door swings open to reveal a hefty Thwacker with a beaming smile. Jesse instantly recognizes the Thwacker from the party. *What was his name again? Dumdum? Drumblum? Dumbbrell?*

He was especially friendly, Jesse remembers. But he had a thick accent, and it was hard for Jesse to understand him when he spoke. The Thwacker had asked Jesse all about his home—about his dad and Maddie and Noni and Grandpa—as Jesse had strained to understand his jolting speech. He'd told Jesse that he loved Jesse's mom and that Jesse looked just like her.

"Good morning, Drumbell," Barrington announces, greeting the sizable Thwacker at the door. "How'd you make out with Jesse's bow?"

Ah, that's right. Drumbell! That's his name. Jesse nods a greeting to the Thwacker from last evening.

Drumbell holds up a bow and smiles at Jesse even more brightly. "It's ready fer ya, Jesse. Cleaned an' tuned!" Drumbell booms. Then he tilts his head as though considering; and as he does, he uses the bow to scratch an itch on his hairy neck. "The bow was off-kilter," Drumbell says, waving the bow in the air again, evidently having satisfied his itch. "So, I centered it an' tuned up the string fer maximum momentum.

"Prayers it never fails ya. I understand yer headed ta the Isle of Mires with Barrington ta rescue the princess. I only wish there was more I could do ta help ya, though." Drumbell punctuates this thought with a friendly wink.

With two great steps, Drumbell reaches Jesse. The Thwacker extends his heavy, furred arms to pass Jesse the bow and a bag with arrows. Taking them, Jesse wonders, *What am I supposed to do with these? I don't know how to shoot a bow!*

"They're just a precaution, Jesse," Barrington interjects, noting Jesse's alarm. "Hopefully, you won't need them. But if you do, they'll be good to have."

Jesse reaches out his hand to shake Drumbell's to thank him, but instead of shaking Jesse's hand, Drumbell pushes it away. "Aw, handshakes are fer strangers," the Thwacker grumbles.

And Drumbell *hugs* him! With the Thwacker's arms around him, Drumbell squeezes. Like two weights, he's dragging Jesse down. The boy's eyes bulge. Drumbell seems big-hearted, but he's also just plain big. And he's *strong.*

I feel like I'm wrestling a bear. Jesse quivers, fighting to breathe.

Drumbell's squeezing the boy good-naturedly, but he's compressing his chest. Jesse wheezes, pulling back from the Thwacker to the extent that he can. *There's too much hugging in Miriam! They hug to say hello. They hug to say goodbye. It seems as though they even hug when the wind blows. Stop! I want out! I need air!* Jesse's desperate to put some space between himself and the Thwacker.

Finally, Drumbell releases him. Doubling over, Jesse sputters on the ground, gasping. Drumbell doesn't even seem to notice. The Thwacker appears blissfully unaware that Jesse's on the ground, fighting like a beached whale to suck in oxygen.

Doesn't he know he was strangling me? He's like a grizzly!
Jesse gapes, still unable to speak.

Drumbell crosses the treehut's threshold to leave, mumbling again to Barrington about how he wishes there was more he could do to help them. *I've got an idea*, Jesse thinks, still gasping on the ground, fighting to fill his lungs. *Next time, don't suffocate me! That would be helpful.*

From behind him, Jesse hears Barrington's voice. "Drumbell, would you like to come with us?"

Jesse looks up with inexplicable horror as Barrington's words sink in. He watches Drumbell's face light up like a Christmas tree.

"There's room for the three of us on Drakendore," Barrington tells Drumbell, assuredly. "Drakendore's strong."

"Room . . . on . . . Drakendore?" Jesse manages to squeak, willing the air back into his lungs so he can form the words to speak. "There's no room on Drakendore! There's barely even room for you and me, Barrington. How will we fit Drumbell? He's as big as a tree!" Jesse shakes, clutching his chest and gazing at Drumbell's legs that are planted in front of him like two monster-sized trucks.

Paying no heed, Barrington insists, "It will be a huge help to have you join us, Drumbell. We're planning to leave this morning. Can you dress and meet us back here as quickly as possible?"

Drumbell beams. "Of course, I can! I'd be honored ta join ya." Drumbell hurries off to collect his things.

Barrington closes the door. With Drumbell out of earshot, Jesse huffs. "Is it really necessary for Drumbell to come with us? For starters, how are the three of us going to fit on Drakendore?" Jesse rubs his forehead. "You know very well that you and I can barely fit on her. Secondly, I don't think I'll survive another of Drumbell's hugs. Don't you mind that he nearly just *killed* me?"

"There's plenty of room on Drakendore," Barrington quips. "And to your point, Jesse, you're a big boy. You'll survive. Maybe tell Drumbell to lighten up on his greetings a smidge? He's not always conscious of how strong he is.

"In any event," Barrington assures him, "Drumbell will be a huge help if we have to engage in ground combat. He's the most renowned archer in the Land of Miriam. If anyone can help us on the

Isle of Mires, he can. And I, for one, am grateful for any help he has to give."

"Ground combat?" Jesse mutters, suddenly queasy.

"Yes, ground combat. There's always a chance it will come to that," Barrington admits without making eye contact. Then more brightly, he says, "Let's find your armor, shall we? Millie's tucked it away in the bedroom, I believe." Barrington begins walking away before he's even finished speaking.

Turning the corner from the kitchen, Jesse follows Barrington to a large room in the tree in an area Jesse has not yet been. In the corner of the room, Jesse sees there's a bed much larger than the one Jesse had slept in. *In Thwacker terms, it's gotta be a king*, Jesse surmises. And there's a lot of furniture in the room, including chairs, two night tables, and an ornate dresser.

Millie peers out from under the covers of the bed as Jesse and Barrington enter. Upon hearing the news of the Kelptars, Millie had crawled under the covers to sulk away her fears. Hearing them now, though, she pokes out her head.

I'd like to crawl under the covers and hide from all this, too, Jesse thinks, noticing Millie's whiskers peek out from under the sheets. And there, beside Millie on the floor, stacked in loose piles, glistening, is the armor to which Barrington had been referring. Atop one of the piles, a sword with a silver blade shimmers.

"It recognizes you," Barrington comments, as the sword shines even more brightly.

"It recognizes me?" Jesse sputters. "How can a sword recognize somebody?"

Barrington squints at the boy, a hint of agitation etched on his face. Jesse gets the sense that he's disparaged a phenomenon that Barrington considers to be great. "Sckabor has been passed down through generations of Magi to you, Jesse," Barrington announces solemnly. "In fact, at one point in time, it was your great-grandfather's sword. It's simple, really. I think the sword smells your blood and recognizes you as its rightful owner."

"Umm . . . it can smell my blood?" Jesse startles, not convinced that a sword smelling his blood is a very good thing. And on top of that, he's unsure what to make of all this talk about his unknown dead ancestors. Jesse's never even known his grandfather, let alone his great-grandfather. He understood from his mom that her father, Jesse's grandad, had died long before Jesse had been born. The thought of Jesse's great-grandfather raises even more questions for the boy, who is already struggling quite hard to get his head around his changing family landscape as it is.

"My guess is that Sckabor smells your ancestors' blood in you and recognizes you for who you are," Barrington says nonchalantly, so as not to scare the boy further. "Go ahead. Pick it up," Barrington tells Jesse, pointing to the gleaming sword.

Jesse stands over it, and the sword glows more fiercely. Jesse's heart flutters. He grasps the hilt. The blade, sparkling, casts its glow across the room.

"It fits my hand perfectly," Jesse stammers. And holding the sword, feeling its solid weight in his hand, a surge of energy runs through him. A vibration, like tiny waves of electricity, travels through Jesse's body like a breeze blowing through trees, rustling their leaves. In a flash, Jesse senses maybe he *was* born for this.

Maybe I am meant to wage war against the Dark. Maybe it is possible that I—Jesse Walker—am meant to save a princess. "Can I save Miriam?" He shivers with excitement. Like waking from a deep sleep, the boy feels realization dawning. Wielding the majestic sword, he feels light, vibrant, and free—as he surely was created to be—for the first time in forever. His limbs move fluidly. His thoughts come clearly. *I feel so alive.*

Barrington and Jesse dress the remainder of the time in silence. Jesse slips on a garment Millie calls a "tunic," and he puts the rest of his armor on over it, which consists of a belt to hold Sckabor and short-sleeve chain mail that stretches to his knees. Dressed, he looks like an action figure.

"I feel ridiculous," Jesse murmurs lightheartedly to no one in particular, reflecting on his attire.

Barrington, who's been quiet, looks at him approvingly. "Let's get going, shall we? The journey to the Fireflies' lair is a long and strenuous one. There's no time to waste."

Leaving the tree hut, Barrington nearly trips over Drumbell, who's waiting on the other side of the door next to Drakendore. It takes a while for the three of them—Barrington, Drumbell, and Jesse—to situate themselves on top of the alicorn. As it turns out, mounting Drakendore in chain mail isn't easy.

And it's no help at all that we've another rider with us. Jesse shakes his head, frustrated. He notices, too, that Millie, who's watching, seems to oscillate between tears of concern and tears of laughter, watching the riders try to organize themselves. *We're like a comedy routine.* Jesse rolls his eyes as he wriggles, trying to make more space for himself, wedged in the middle between Barrington and Drumbell like a slice of salami.

Finally, though, they get situated. Millie waves goodbye wildly as the three of them trot off into the woods atop Drakendore. As they trot, Barrington calls over his shoulder to her, "Don't worry, Millie! We'll be careful. I'll pass on your regards to Malacor."

Malacor? Who's Malacor? Jesse wonders, wanting to ask but too busy dodging trees to form a sentence.

"We have ta find a clearing," Drumbell grunts in Jesse's ear from behind him. "The tree coverage in Tanglewood's too thick. If Drakendore tries ta fly with us through this, we'll be battered ta bits."

Jesse sees a break in the woods. Light shines through the trees, bathing the path ahead in warm sunshine. Reaching it, they gallop out of the woods and into a clearing. Jesse realizes it's the same clearing where he and Barrington had landed yesterday when they'd first arrived in the Land of Miriam.

Without a moment's hesitation, Drakendore stretches her wings. With one powerful flap, they're airborne.

"Next stop's the dragon's lair." Drumbell hoots happily.

CHAPTER 16
EONIA

There's rustling, and the door slides open.

It's him! What is he *doing here?* Eonia wonders.

Lord Letch stalks over to where the princess crouches. Like a crawlie, he hisses, "Ssss, sss, sss, holier-than-thou princess-s-s-s. I was just chatting with King Angus about you. Do you knows the joy it brings me to see you here? What an honor it is to have taken King Mor's el-dess-t daughter from him."

Eonia glares at Lord Letch from where she sits, but she doesn't get up.

Sneering, Lord Letch paws at her hair. "Day after day, I sssit with your father, at banquets and in boardrooms and at dinner. He mopeses and bemoans his beloved daughter's kidnapping. He sobs on my shoulder, crying, 'Where isss she? Where is my angel, my daughter, my baby girl? Oh, where is Eonia?'"

As though she's been hit, Eonia falters and cringes, recoiling from Lord Letch's touch. "They still don't know!" Eonia croaks. Even now, her father doesn't understand that Lord Letch is evil.

She was thinking Lord Letch was found out. She thought he'd be imprisoned by now. *But no, he's not in prison. He's here!* She nearly vomits. "You've come to check on me, have you?" she spits out.

All this time, while Eonia thought he'd been discovered, Lord Letch has been roaming the Land of Miriam freely. Confronted by Lord Letch's now-vapid face, Eonia recalls first meeting the lord. "You weren't this pompous when you first came to the kingdom, groveling on your hands and your knees." Eonia juts out her chin.

It was five years ago. Tenebris Letch showed up in the kingdom, begging for work and for food. It was autumn when he came—September, if Eonia recalls correctly. It was one of the first days that felt like fall that year. Eonia's governess, Mildred, had ended Eonia's lessons early to sneak off with her boyfriend. Eonia pieced together that Mildred was running off, shirking her responsibilities to

meet a boy in the woods, unchaperoned. Eonia didn't care in the least. She was grateful for the free time.

The sky was a crisp blue, and the breeze blew through the leaves. The air smelled of squash and spice and wood-burning fires from homes outside of the kingdom. Eonia, who was eight years old at the time, was playing catch in the quad when Lord Letch came. She was digging out a ball that had fallen in some bushes when she first saw him. His clothes, tattered and torn, hung from his frail body. His eyes, a clear blue, had a purpose to them. His skin was still as smooth as driftwood. Tenebris Letch couldn't have been much older than maybe sixteen or seventeen.

His parents, as the story went, had died, and his grandparents had abandoned him. Lord Letch, as he told everyone, had traveled from beyond the High Bogong Plains of the Land of Miriam to beg for the king's mercy. And Eonia's father (being the King of Miriam), felt sorry for him and made him a page boy at the capital. At the time, Eonia had liked him. She even thought he was good-looking. But that was before she knew him.

As time went by, she watched Tenebris Letch. Eonia saw what he said versus what he did. And he knew it. She soured on him and he on her. Of course, he's never kissed-up to Princess Eonia the same way he does to her

*parents and to the other lords. Why would he? She's just
a girl. She has no power—not yet, anyway.*

His eyes like slits, Lord Letch gurgles as he sucks
in a deep breath, eyeing Eonia. "That was before I
understood what a sad lot Magi are," Lord Letch
snarls. He palms the princess' head. "King Mor, the
sop. I can hardly believe, Eonia, dearsy, that your
daddy still hasss no idea." He snickers. "He doesn't
knows that it's me who hasss takens you from him.
He doesn't knows that it isss I who sss-stole you out
from under his nosey.

"Oh, Princess, you're with a different kind of a
kingsy now, aren't you?" Lord Letch gleams, lips
spreading in a keen smile. "A king who has power—
King Angus, king of the Gors! Never againsy will
your daddy sssee his darling girl."

Eonia pictures Lord Letch walking the halls
with her father. She imagines him sitting next to
her mother at the dining room table, eating in the
Great Hall. All this time, while she's been stuck
here in the Mires, Lord Letch has been moving
around the kingdom, biding his time, waiting for an

opportunity, plotting the moment to kill her parents so that he may take over the Land of Miriam.

Surely, he wants them dead. Eonia grimaces. *He doesn't want Father and Mother lurking around the kingdom. He doesn't want them inspiring Magi to revolt against him. With the power of the book, he aims to rule the Land of Miriam in Darkness. He won't want transgressions of the past hanging around the kingdom, haunting him.*

Seeing Lord Letch here—imagining him sipping wine next to her mother, chatting at council meetings with her father's advisors, acting like he's one of them, like he cares—while she's stuck here with these monsters because of *him* is more than Eonia can bear. She's in agony! She longs to sink down through the ground until she's covered in dirt, hidden from the cold reality that Lord Letch is here and *free!* She knows, too, that after satisfying himself that all's well here, he'll head back to her parents in the kingdom. *And there's nothing I can do about it!* Eonia groans.

She longs to scream *Traitor,* expelling her lungs of all oxygen. But instead, she just looks at him, her gray eyes dipping into his. *His eyes are darker now,* she notices. It was in the dim light of her bedroom she last saw him. Still, she's sure of it. It's ever so slight, but she sees the Darkness growing in him, evidencing its first manifestations. "Your eyes are becoming black like a Gors," she comments.

Lord Letch twitches at this. *He's always been vain.* Eonia raises an eyebrow. *Soon, he'll look like a monster inside and out.*

"Poor, poor, s-s-sad Letchy," Lord Letch slithers. "Hypocrisy thrown in my face each day, I tried to be likes the other Magi, Princess. Humph. My naivety shames me!" he quips. "I knows well now, Magi are a sham—always praying, whimpering for God to have mercy and forgive them. Lily-livered sssissies, each one of you are!"

"Mind you, princess-sss, it's not that I ever doubted God's existence." He spits, wagging his finger at her. "That's not the issue. I'm not daft. Did the sky paint itself blue? Did funglebugs make themselves sing? Of course not! It is His *love* that I nevers believed. Why would God love precious Letchy, Princess? Why would God love *you*?"

Eonia's heart aches. Oh, how she longs to strangle him. Violently, she shakes. *I must keep my anger in,* she thinks. *For Miriam's safety, I have to be calm. I can't give Darkness a foothold. I can't let my heart darken, not here, not surrounded by Dark agents as I am.*

Yet her longing is so strong, she can't squelch it. A hatred she's never felt pulses through her veins like a poison. She wants *revenge*. Every beat of her heart screams, *Kill him! Kill him! Kill him!*

Eyes glinting, Lord Letch growls, "God doesn't *love* you. He didn't *love* me, did he, precious Letchy? No!" He bristles. "And I nevers expected Him to! I know that the only one who loves me is me. God doesss-n't protect anyone. He won't shield you." Lord Letch crouches and peers at Eonia, his face so close to hers that he almost touches her nose with his. Eonia smells his foul breath as he hisses, "No, dearsy Princess, He won't protect you from *us*. He can't squelch outs the Darkness."

Standing, Lord Letch gesticulates with flicks of his fingers like they're tongues of a lizard. "'Free choice,' God calls it. He lets you *choose* good or evil. He lets you *choose* Darkness or Light. And Darkness I chose!" Lord Letch bellows. "I needed steady-handed execution, not emotional drivel! The justice of Hell is about pragmatism." Lord Letch cranes his neck. "The Almighty Below has expectations. I'm a bureaucrat versed in regulations. I can work within that structure. I knows how to manipulate the inner workings of Hell to get what I need. *I*, my dearsy Eonia, am no dumb-dumb."

"I have no delusions," he announces with another flick. "I have no romantic glances at the rose-colored past. At times, I will admitses, I skirted the edge of the Enemy's party—*your* party, Princess—repeating my prayers like a simpleton." He scowls. "For a while, I even praised God, the 'Enemy.' Blessedly though, I nevers developed those blasted habits of yours fully. I never religiously went to church or prayed or gave monies to the poor. Occasionally, when my will was weak, yesss, I tossed in some coins at the altar or gave my unfinished sandwich to some sop on the kingdom's streets. But those were aberrations, not the normsy, I'm proud to report." He steels his eyes on her.

"S-s-still, Princess, I spent so long with you pitiful Magi—King Mor, your father, the imbess-cile, being the absolute worst of them." He snuffs. "How I kowtowed to him, showering him with affection and false admiration. I wasted so much energy on him! To thinks that I thought *he* could lead *me* to power!" he blubbers. "What power does your father have, Princess? God's power?" Lord Letch raises his arms toward Heaven mockingly.

"It pains me that I thought I could climb up the rankses under him. What ranks does King Mor have beneath him?" Lord Letch howls. "Simpletons, that's who!" He waves his finger. "Lets me be the first to tell you, Princess, your father is a God-fearing idiot; and he runs the Land of Miriam accordingly. If it's ranks of idiocracy you wants, then yes, King Mor is the king! But beyond that, he's nothing to offer.

"I seethe, thinking how foolish I was," Lord Letch rues. "Years of my precious life have been wasted pandering to him—King Mor, the sop, the dunce, the idiot." He caresses Eonia's head with his spindly fingers, catching her straggly, unbrushed hair in his manicured nails. Eonia springs away, wincing at the touch of his skin.

Lord Letch laughs as Eonia scampers. "If you know what's best for you, Princess-sss, you will join us-sss." He chortles. "What will happensy to you, you should ask yourself, dearsy Princess, when we defeat him? What will happen, Eonia, when Magi no longer hold the kingdom?"

CHAPTER 17

JESSE WALKER

Drumbell's arms wrap around Jesse like a straitjacket, grounding him onto Drakendore's back as they fly across the sky. *At least, I'm not as likely to fall off,* Jesse thinks smugly of Drumbell's grip.

Seated behind him, Drumbell hollers in the boy's ear, "Firefly dragons live high up in the snow-capped mountains o'er the Rickenbacker River Gorge. I bet ya haven't seen a dragon b'fore, have ya, Jesse?"

"No," Jesse mutters, his voice muffled by the wind.

"Of curse, ya hadn't!" Drumbell hollers to him, hearing Jesse just fine. "Dragons don't live where ya live. Anyhoo," Drumbell continues, "I haven't neither! I've read loads 'bout em. But I haven't seen a dragon in the flesh, breathin' in front o' me!"

That's what I need to see. Jesse shivers, a chill running down his spine. *A dragon in the flesh, breathing in front of me. This is a terrible idea!*

170

"The route ta Rickenbacker River is dangerous, fer sure," Drumbell bellows, not picking up on Jesse's growing concern in the least. "Thankfully, though, Drakendore an' Barrington have visited the Firefly lair b'fore. They know the way—it's ta the west. And ta access it, we'll travel along the High Bogong Plains o' Miriam," he tells him. "Then we'll ascend like a rocket ta climb the Rickenbacker Mountains."

The route to the lair is dangerous. Jesse repeats Drumbell's words to himself, noticing, too, that Drakendore seems anxious. The alicorn's wings cut the air as smoothly as always; but her head is high, and her ears twitch back. Looking past her twitching ears, Jesse gazes down into the grasslands below, wondering how worried he should be. And as he does, he sees animals running beneath him.

"What are they?" Jesse asks, thinking to himself that the animals look a lot like deer.

"Kooboo," Drumbell answers him.

The kooboo scatter irregularly, running this way and that. From the air, Jesse sees why—a pride of large cats is encircling them.

"Oubré are movin' in fer the kill," Drumbell hollers, noticing the cats moving in the grasslands as well.

But before Jesse and Drumbell see the fate of the kooboo, Drakendore sails on past them, past where the kooboo run on the ground, past the oubré preparing to feast on their meal—and now, Drakendore is carrying the Thwackers and the boy toward a flock of birds approaching from the opposite direction.

Barrington points at the birds. "Swandocks," he identifies. "Lovely creatures. Swandocks mate for life and live up to three hundred years. It's rare to see so many together. Most often, they travel in pairs."

Spreading their wings, the swandocks glide side by side. Their giant, birdlike forms look like seesaws, teetering back and forth in the wind. Then the swandocks are gone, and Barrington's pointing to the ground, his voice sounding again. "The High Bogong Plains are home to many of the Land of Miriam's creatures. Below us now, you can see the buffaloon frolicking," he tells Jesse, and he points to a group of large animals on the ground, playing in a stream.

Like kids in a water fight, the buffaloon suck up the water in their elephant-size snozzles and spew out the spray, soaking each other with their high-pressured streams. Sunlight catches the spray as it travels through the air, and the water sparkles.

Crossing over the plains, Jesse sees many more animals. Barrington and Drumbell take turns telling the boy about each of them. Then eventually, the plains end, and shadows from the Rickenbacker Mountains appear. At first, the mountains look like distant clouds, far away and of little concern. But as they draw nearer, the mountains become clear. Rickenbacker's peaks stand proud and menacing.

With a jerk, Drakendore's body tilts up. *She's taking on Rickenbacker.* Jesse tightens his grip to keep from slipping.

Slowly and carefully, Drakendore climbs with Barrington and Drumbell and Jesse. She climbs and climbs and climbs. Without ceasing, the rock shoots up toward the heavens. Barrington's hands, normally a creamy brown, are ashen from gripping Drakendore's mane. Jesse's whole body quivers in pure exhaustion, as he fights the urge to cry out while the rock beneath him, unforgiving and mocking, glares. *The mountain is waiting for Drakendore to flounder. It's waiting for us to fall.*

But Drakendore bears down. She doesn't falter. Her body works to the extreme. Steam rises from her hot, sweaty fur. And gradually, the tree line thins. Then advancing toward the top, the trees disappear completely. Gray snow blankets the earth beneath them. Jesse gulps at the air. "There's not enough oxygen; I can barely breathe," he huffs. His eyes bulge at the realization. Yet Drakendore moves on, ever steadily.

"We're almost there." Barrington calls. "Just a little further."

Finally, there's a break in the rock. Rickenbacker stops.

Drumbell howls, "We're 'ere! We're at the top! Hallelujah! We made it!"

The horizon, clear and infinite, spreads out before them. Squinting against the sun, Jesse sees for miles and miles. He looks out over the distance from where they've come. "It's like looking at one of Maddie's jigsaw puzzles from up above," Jesse observes.

He sees streams crisscrossing the flatlands. He sees the wetlands where the buffaloon frolicked. He sees the grasslands where the oubré stalked their prey. And farther still, ever so far away, Jesse makes out the treed woods of Tanglewood, where Millie awaits Barrington's return.

Crossing the mountain's crest, Drakendore swoops down into the gorge. Breathing in air crisp with the smell of evergreens, Jesse's stomach flutters, and his arms tingle. Jesse feels as though the weight of the world's been lifted from him.

"Woooohoooo!" Drumbell hoots.

And Jesse shakes—not from fear or because he's tired but with gratitude. "Thank You, God, for my life! Thank You for the beauty of this place!" He revels in the majesty of the moment.

Then Drakendore lowers. She touches down along the burbling river.

"Ahhhhhhhhh." Jesse sighs, sliding off Drakendore, savoring the feel of solid earth under his feet. Without talking, Jesse, Barrington, and Drumbell linger in the peace—for mere seconds.

The Thwackers and Jesse barely have time to catch their breath and get their legs, wobbly and spent from the long journey, up and under them once again before a blood-curdling *SCREECH* shatters the quiet. Jesse stops moving. He stops breathing. Squinting into the mountains, he spies three dragons perched on top of one of the mountain's crests, peering down.

Big as they look from here, they must be the size of bulldozers up there. Jesse trembles at the thought.

"Stay still," Barrington orders him.

The dragons watch for a moment, then launch.

"They're flying for us!" Jesse shudders.

The dragons thunder through the air. Deafening screams ring out over and over and over. Out of the corner of his eye, Jesse sees Drumbell train his bow.

"Talk to them, Jesse!" Barrington yells. "Use your telepathy!"

Desperate, Jesse focuses all his energy. *We've come in peace. We've come to ask for your help. Don't hurt us! We're agents of Light. Don't hurt us! Please!*

Like lightning, the dragons are on them. Their mouths open. Their talons reach. *They're coming in for the kill!* Jesse quivers with fright, unable to tear his eyes from the horrific beasts.

Overcome with terror, drowning in a sea of adrenaline, Jesse's mind fogs. It's as though moments last forever. Overwhelmed by fear, Jesse disconnects, as though taking a step back from himself, stepping out to watch the dragons swooping in at him from afar. Everything slows. The boy feels as though he's floating, disconnected from himself, disconnected from his fear, watching the dragons hone in on him like a hawk swooping in for a squirrel.

Jesse feels the breeze from the dragons' wings. Then their shrieks soften. Their wings slow.

"Did they hear me?" His heart leaps. The boy emerges from his trance-like state like a bear waking to the first signs of spring. The Fireflies lower to the ground. Whether they heard him or not, Jesse hears the dragons. *It's as it is with Barrington,* he thinks. He doesn't know how it's happening; it just is. "I understand them." He realizes with shock and disbelief. "They recognize Drakendore. They're remembering Barrington. Their anger is melting into joy!"

"You've done it, my boy!" Barrington swacks his back heartily. "I told you, you've got the gift!"

On the ground, the dragons suddenly seem timid. Like ducks, they waddle toward Jesse. Situating themselves nearby, they wait for Jesse to clarify his thoughts that he'd sent to them before when they were spiraling toward the earth.

Only moments ago, the dragons had seemed terrifying to Jesse, shrieking across the sky. But on the ground, the dragons look out of place, almost silly to him now.

They're different than they seemed in the air, he thinks to himself. *These dragons don't seem scary. Are these really the great Fireflies that Barrington had talked about?* He studies them, surprised by the dragons' suddenly docile nature on the ground.

The largest dragon sways its neck. It catches Jesse's eye. The words, *Yes, we are,* ring in the boy's head, clear as a bell.

"Umph." Jesse stumbles, caught off guard. "I, uh . . . *sorry,* I didn't expect him to hear me think that." Jesse stares, wide-eyed with embarrassment.

"Greet them, Jesse. Tell them we need to see Malacor," Barrington says.

Jesse twitches, stepping toward the dragons. Scales ripple down their skin. Pointed claws extend from their feet. The dragons fan out their wings behind them as he comes near. "They don't seem mad, at least," Jesse reflects, thankfully. *There's a softness to them. There's warmth to their eyes,* he notices, grateful for the dragons' patience as he approaches.

My name is Jesse Walker, the boy starts.

The dragons crane their necks. *You want to walk to where?*

What? No. My name is Jesse Walker, Jesse tries again.

The smallest dragon, who had been preening itself, stops and nods, narrowing its eyes.

Forming the words in his head, Jesse focuses on each word as he thinks it. *This is Barrington and*

Drumbell and Drakendore. We've come to ask for your help, he explains. *Something bad has happened, and we need to meet with Malacor, please.*

All three dragons look at the boy expectantly. The closest Firefly, the largest one, responds. A throaty voice rumbles inside Jesse's head, *Welcome. We are honored to meet you, Jesse. I am Sprinter, and this is Luna and Gloria.* The dragon gestures to the other two dragons. *We are sorry if we frightened you. We thought you were intruders. But then we heard your pleas. We recognized you as a Magus. We recognized Drakendore and Barrington from past meetings between Magi and the elders.* Sprinter bows in Barrington's direction.

Of course, we will take you to Mala . . . The dragon drops his head, scratching its leg, its voice trailing off.

Jesse squats down to regain eye contact with the creature, struggling to understand what's being said.

Oh, sorry, the dragon responds at Jesse's overture. *I had an itch. As I was saying, we will take you to Malacor. If I may ask you though*—it hesitates—*what happened in the kingdom? Travel to Rickenbacker River Gorge is difficult for anyone, let alone a Magus and two Thwackers on an alicorn.* He squints. *It must be something very important that's brought you here. What is it? What's happened in the kingdom?*

As best he's able in broken thoughts and restarts, Jesse tells the dragons about Princess Eonia and the Isle of Mires and the Gors and the Kelptars. When Jesse mentions the Kelptars, the dragons get antsy. They start squawking like a gaggle of geese.

Barrington interrupts amidst the squawks. "Jesse, we really need to meet with Malacor."

"Okay, okay, I'll ask again." He shrugs, not knowing how best to calm the squawking creatures.

Eventually, though, the dragons quiet down. And realizing how tired Drakendore must be after the long flight, they offer to fly the Thwackers and Jesse to the Firefly lair, so Drakendore may rest on the ground.

"Um, I'm not sure we want to do that," Jesse answers in response to their offer, not wanting to ride a dragon in the least. But when the boy relays the Fireflies' suggestion to Drumbell and Barrington, the Thwackers shout yes enthusiastically; and Drakendore whinnies and lays down, as if to say, "I'm done."

CHAPTER 18
EONIA

Isle of Mires, Land of Miriam

Lord Letch is gone. King Angus came to get him, and they left. Even still, Eonia hears the two of them talking outside the hut.

"I see whatsy you've done with her, King Angus," Lord Letch says. "Very impressive! There's a separation bubblingsey up inside of the princess."

"Good of you to notice, Lord Letch," King Angus booms, indulging himself in Lord Letch's flattery. "Indeed, Princess Eonia's thoughts are running inward. Her anxiety is wearing her thin. The princess holds a mistaken belief, it seems, that she should be happy," King Angus prattles on. "And that's been quite useful to us. She's distraught that she's so miserable here; her burgeoning unhappiness is making her weak."

Eonia can't see King Angus through the walls of the hut, but if she could, she'd see him beaming.

"Why should a creature be happy?" Angus snarks, mocking the mere concept. "Wherever do they get that idea from? That's not a thing!" He snarls with contempt. "We want creatures *worried*. We want them living for tomorrow. We want them to focus on the stress of uncertainty. Lust and ambition and fear—*these* are the things of the future," he exclaims. "And we want them eating at her. It's the future where the imagination runs wild, Tenebris Letch. It's the *future* that is the Dark's playground.

"And yes, you are correct, Lord Letch." King Angus chortles, reveling in his success. "Eonia is spending more and more time worrying about the future. She's concerned about her parents. She's worried what will happen to her should we find the book and win."

"Might it be then, Angus—me hopesy you don't mind if I call you by your first namesy, dearsy Gor king"—Lord Letch bows ever so slightly—"that Eonia is becoming ss-so desperate that she'd turn to the Almighty Below to ss-saves her mealy-mouth parents? I can hardly think of the favor it would garner me if I could deliversy the Princess of Miriam into the handsies of Darkness!" He blubbers on excitedly, unable to stem the words before letting them slip from his lips.

King Angus' enthusiasm, stoked by Lord Letch's flattering remarks, wanes. He squares his shoulders with Lord Letch, his face dropping like a curtain. "I beg your pardon, Lord Letch. You mean the favor *I* would garner for delivering the princess into Darkness, don't you?" Angus asks, his melodious voice dripping with disdain at the lord's blatant attempt to circumvent him.

"And I caution you, Tenebris, that it's in desperate times like these that the Enemy Above often asserts Himself the most. Even when all hope is lost, God's urchins have been known to look around, wondering why they've been forsaken, and yet still obey Him," Angus says scornfully.

"That said, we've done our best to separate Princess Eonia from Him, the Enemy Above. We've done our best to weed God out from being near her—at least, seemingly so for the girl." King Angus gazes upward. "The Enemy Above, as you'd appreciate Lord Letch, wants the princess living in the present. He wants her finding beauty. He wants her thankful for the things of today, like her 'daily bread' and the beauty of a child's smile." He frowns. "It's through beauty and thankfulness, of course, that God so often calls His children to Him." Angus shakes his head, trying to shake off his discomfort at the thought of God's authority. "On the contrary, we want Princess Eonia living in the *future*, worried about *herself—her* needs, *her* worries, *her* pain," he snarls.

"Look around, Lord Letch." Angus waves his arm, triumphant, gesturing at the scene that surrounds them. "Do you see much beauty *here?* I should think not!" Angus scoffs. "And I know for a fact, the princess' 'daily bread' isn't what it used to be." His eyes glint. "We haven't given her anything to be *thankful* for since she's been on the island with me," he boasts. "Still, I'm not certain we'll win the girl over. The Enemy has a strong hold on her," he laments. "What matters most, as should be obvious, is how much we manage to cordon her, God's creature, off from Him." Angus makes a cutting motion, as though severing a plant with a machete. "We need a separation to happen—at least, a separation from the girl's perspective." Angus levels his gaze.

"I'll continue working on her," he concludes. "We are making progress, it seems."

Listening from inside of the hut, Eonia seethes. *Calm down, Eonia. Miriam needs you. You must think. You must be reasonable,* she repeats to herself silently, playing the part of her mother in an attempt to introduce rational thinking; but Eonia's patience is dwindling. She's too furious to calmly evaluate the situation. Lord Letch and King Angus are talking about her as if she isn't even in here, capable of making decisions. They're talking about her pledging her allegiance to Darkness, of all horrific things!

Eonia wants to storm out there. She wants to throw open the hut's flimsy door and scream, *Traitor! Traitor! Lord Letch, you're a murderous traitor!* She wants to grab hold of him. She wants to pull him in close, look Lord Letch in the eye, and *see* his downfall. She wants to watch him hear Light's triumphant horns. She wants to see him realize how insignificant he is.

Instead of rushing outside, she must sit here idle in this hut, listening, while Lord Letch and King Angus meet. She can't tip her hand to them that she's stronger than they think she is. She can't give away her cognizance.

"And what is the purpose for their meeting, anyway?" Eonia whispers. "Has Lord Letch come all this way just to taunt me? They can't have found the book." If they'd found the *Book of Good and Evil*, Eonia would know it. The key (Eonia, in this instance) always knows where the book is. It's part of the spell. If the Dark finds the book and it's near, the princess will be able to tell. Eonia knows very well that the book isn't here. *It's still in the other world.*

For many years, Eonia's aunt Lillian served as the book's guardian. Until her death, Lillian served as a loyal servant of the Land of Miriam, keeping the book safely hidden at her home. The Land of Miriam wasn't ready for Lillian's passing, unfortunately. She became sick and died too soon for the kingdom to make proper adjustments. The Light hadn't prepared anyone else in the other world to guard the book before Lillian was gone from them. They had thought Jesse, as her son, would take over Lillian's role as the book's guardian when Lillian passed. But the boy was just a child when she died. Jesse wasn't ready. And besides, he didn't even know about the Land of Miriam then. His mother hadn't told him anything.

Upon Lillian's death, and even before her passing, the king and queen had considered sending one of the lords or Barrington, who's always been close with the crown, to the other world to bring Lillian's children, Jesse and Maddie, to visit the kingdom for a time. But they didn't want to go against Lillian's wishes. Plus, they were concerned that they might overwhelm the children at a time when they were already grieving.

While Lillian was sick, King Mor decided it best to move the book from Lillian's house. The king himself traveled to the other world to kiss his sister on the forehead. He visited Lillian and said goodbye to her for the last time. And he took the book with him. He found a secluded cabin high in the Grand Tetons in the other world and hid the book there.

"Verinsy well," Eonia hears Lord Letch speak. "I will workensy on the queen."

"Mother!" Eonia whimpers at Lord Letch's proclamation. An implosion of grief besets the princess. A pain as sharp as a knife stabs her in the abdomen. Having stood by the door to hear Lord Letch and Angus more clearly, Eonia falls to the floor. Her insides, spasming, throb as though she's consumed poison. Poor princess Eonia—she's either going to get sick or soil herself, it seems.

CHAPTER 19

JESSE WALKER

Firefly Lair, Land of Miriam

"I can't get a grip!" Jesse shouts from where he's landed on the ground, having fallen for the umpteenth time.

Luna's back is slippery, and Jesse's hands, wet with sweat, slip right off the dragon's skin. *Getting on and off Drakendore is tough enough,* Jesse thinks, wringing his hands. But Luna's twice Drakendore's size. Jesse throws a leg up onto Luna's side with no specific plan and lets his leg slide right back down again. He feels like a stinkbug trying to climb out of a toilet. The boy doesn't have the flexibility to work his way up and grab hold around the dragon's neck. Jesse picks at the skin beneath his nails and gazes up at Barrington and Drumbell mounted on top of Sprinter, the larger of the two dragons that are left before them to be ridden.

"You may be used to climbing trees, swinging from limb to limb, and mounting beasts," Jesse complains, "but I am not."

"Hmm, ma'be take the chainmail off?" suggests Drumbell, who's seated behind Barrington on Sprinter.

"I don't wanna fly to the lair in my underwear!"

"They're dragons, Jesse." Barrington chuckles. "They don't care what you're wearing."

Resisting the urge to talk back, Jesse peels back his chain mail. The cool breeze from the river ripples over the boy's skin. Goosebumps bristle on his arms and legs, pocketing his smooth skin like speckles on a sparrow's egg. Shivering, wearing only the tunic Millie had given him, Jesse climbs onto Drakendore's back, using her like a stepstool. Then working himself into a crouched position, Jesse pushes off Drakendore; and he launches, spread eagle, like a squirrel jumping between trees.

"Ooomph!" He crashes face-first onto Luna. Floundering, Jesse grabs hold of the dragon as quickly as he can, doing his best to avoid slipping back down to the ground again. *Nothing about this is pleasant.* He shivers, smooshing his face against the dragon's slithery scales, considering what he wouldn't give to be home, lounging on his family's polyester sofa, eating chips and playing video games with Irvin instead of riding a dragon up a mountain.

Barrington shouts over to him, "All right, hold on, Jesse! This won't be an easy flight, but it'll be a short one. The entrance to the Fireflies' lair is just up and under the waterfall."

Taking off quickly, Jesse hears Drumbell and Barrington on Sprinter laughing with glee in front of him as they shoot across the valley. Jesse, sorely wishing to be atop Drakendore rather than on Luna, plasters himself to the dragon's neck, battling to hold on through a stiff wind. Closing his eyes against the wind, he prays. And when he opens them again, there's a waterfall across from him, cascading from a peak. *That must be the waterfall Barrington mentioned.*

Red, orange, yellow, green—the gushing stream looks like a rainbow rushing, flowing down the colorful rock and running into the valley. Awe blooms in the boy's chest as he marvels at its beauty.

Then in an instant, Sprinter swoops down, around, and under the waterfall's stream. Luna follows on Sprinter's heels, catapulting through the air behind Sprinter with Jesse. Above them as they fly, the waterfall gushes out and over the lip of the mountain, out and over the dragons carrying the Thwackers and the boy. Tiny droplets of water from the waterfall's stream float in the air, forming a mist that glints around the flying caravan. Sunshine catches the droplets mid-air, and the mist glows as though the droplets themselves have been set aflame. *It's like a thousand lightning bugs dancing.* Jesse smiles, mesmerized at the sight of it.

They climb between the mountain and the waterfall. The water's so close to them now that Jesse could reach out and touch the waterfall's stream with the tips of his fingers. And up ahead, in the mountain and closer to where the waterfall begins, Jesse sees a hole.

"That's it!" Jesse hears Barrington call to him faintly through the roar of the wind and the gush of the waterfall. "That's the lair!"

Before Jesse knows it, they're flying into the hole. They're entering the mountain, and the pitch-black darkness weighs heavily on them. The boy blinks into the darkness, feeling as though a blind mole might feel, crawling through the darkness by touch. Aside from the sound of Luna's wings beating, it is quiet. Gone is the sound of the waterfall. There's no sound at all.

"Is this right?" Jesse shouts, breaking the silence, hoping Barrington and Drumbell are close enough to hear him.

Is this right? Is this right? Is this right? His voice echoes off the walls of the tunnel.

Barrington shouts back to him, "Yes!"

Yes. Yes. Yes.

"We're in the lair!"

We're in the lair. We're in the lair. We're in the lair.

Then Jesse's moving toward light. There's an opening. And he can see now, too, that the space between him and the rock around him is razor-thin. There are only three feet between Luna's wings and the walls of the tunnel that surround him as they thunder through.

It's getting easier and easier to see. Jesse blinks against the wind at the growing light ahead.

He flattens himself against Luna, so he doesn't hit the walls that nearly graze him. Then without warning, they spring out of the tunnel through an opening like a cork from a bottle.

From hundreds of feet above, light streams in from a crack, lighting the cave. There are dragons lounging everywhere. Some are sleeping; some are preening; others are visiting with each other. All the dragons have the same black and red striping as Sprinter, Gloria, and Luna. And in the middle of the lair, in the center of the dragons, is the largest dragon Jesse could've ever imagined. His feathers are worn; his skin is gray and sagging.

That must be Malacor.

The moment the Thwackers and boy enter, the dragons stop. A hush falls over the lair. Sprinter lands close to Malacor's perch. Luna lands next to him. Taking his time, the boy looks from dragon to dragon, his chest tightening, alarmed by the great number of dragons around him.

"Umm. Do ya plan on gettin' down anytime soon?" Drumbell grumbles up to Jesse from the ground, looking up with a quizzical stare.

Slowly, Jesse slides off Luna as carefully as he can. "Is that the elder?" Jesse whispers. "Is that Malacor?"

Barrington nods.

"How old is he?" Jesse asks, barely breathing.

"Two hundred and thirty-seven years old." Barrington smiles brightly, clearly impressed by Malacor's age as well.

Jesse gulps.

"The lifespan of a dragon's around three hundred years." Barrington winks, eyes twinkling. "But fire-breathing dragons die long before then. They catch themselves on fire and burn themselves out. The average lifespan for a fire-breathing dragon is more like fifty to one hundred years. Malacor is very old for a Firefly."

"Huh," Jesse mutters, thinking Malacor looks every bit his age. "How'd he get so old?"

"He's strong and smart," Barrington responds. "Now, Jesse, can you translate what I say for him? Can you put into thought what I say in words?"

Jesse brushes himself off. "I can try," he answers, having no confidence at all that he can.

Jesse takes a step closer to Malacor. Listening to Barrington, Jesse imagines the words Barrington says. He pictures each word in his mind to send to the aged dragon as he had done before with Luna, Sprinter, and Gloria. Jesse's not sure if this process will work to effectuate his telepathy, but he has a sense that it may. It seemed to help before when the dragons were thundering toward him to kill him, anyway.

"Malacor, it is good to see you, my friend." Barrington begins. Jesse maneuvers to make eye contact with the aged dragon and visualizes each of Barrington's words. "I am delighted to be in your land amongst the Fireflies again." Barrington pats Jesse's shoulder. "As in the past, I've brought some friends with me. The Magus communicating with you now is Jesse Walker, Lillian's son," Barrington tells them.

Malacor, Jesse observes, bends at the mention of his mom's name, as though bowing out of respect for his mom's memory.

Barrington nods, acknowledging Malacor's gesture as well, and he continues, "And this is Drumbell. Perhaps you've heard of him?" Barrington asks. "He's somewhat famous in Tanglewood." But Malacor shakes his head no, breaking Jesse's connection to him. Jesse is coming to learn there is a certain sensation he feels when maintaining thought contact. *It's not unpleasant—kind of like a brain massage.*

"In any event," Barrington continues as Jesse refocuses his energy on Malacor, "the three of us flew from Tanglewood this morning on Drakendore to see you." Barrington whistles through his teeth, thinking of all that's transpired to this moment. "Regrettably, an incident has occurred in the kingdom that has brought us to you," Barrington tells him, raising his outstretched hands toward the dragon. "We need your help, I'm afraid."

Jesse translates Barrington's words as best he can and then waits. Uncomfortable, he fidgets in the silence, hoping his telepathic powers are operating as intended.

Eventually, quietly, he hears the ancient dragon's voice reply, *It is a pleasure to meet you.* He looks at Jesse as though he sees through him. *I knew of your mom, Jesse. Condolences on her passing. And it's good to see you as well, Barrington. I trust that you and Millie are keeping well.* Malacor's yellowish-brown eyes scan Barrington before honing in on the boy again to communicate.

Gloria traveled ahead of you, Malacor tells them. *She told me of Princess Eonia's taking. She mentioned that the Kelptars and the Gors are holding the princess on the Isle of Mires.* His eyes narrow as he tilts his head. *There is much I do not understand; however, about the circumstances surrounding Princess Eonia's capture and her imprisonment. Could you clarify the details?* he asks.

Barrington nods his agreement. "Yes, of course."

Raising his eyebrows, Malacor continues with his thoughts that reverberate through Jesse's brain. *Why would Kelptars and Gors work together to capture Princess Eonia? In all my years, I've never witnessed two Dark forces working together for longer than a few hours. Is there more to the story? Is there something Gloria failed to mention?*

Malacor remains perfectly still, waiting for Jesse to finish translating for him. The only movement in the lair, it seems, is the steady rise and fall of the elder's chest with each cautious breath.

"You are correct, Malacor," Barrington says and begins to pace. "There is more to the story than we originally relayed. However, the details are sensitive." He catches Malacor's eye. "May we meet privately to discuss matters further?" Jesse dutifully translates for everyone.

At that, Malacor cranes his neck as if to acquiesce and releases a deafening *SCREEEEEEEEECH!* One by one, the dragons, who had been watching Jesse and the Thwackers curiously, rise and take off through the tunnel, exiting the lair. Jesse counts twenty-three Firefly dragons as they leave.

When the last one exits, Barrington pulls Jesse's arm and motions for him to move in closer. Huddling in the empty lair, Barrington whispers in a voice that's barely audible the words for the boy to tell.

"Yes, there are more motivating agents of Darkness to work together than we initially disclosed to Gloria," Barrington whispers. "I failed to mention that Princess Eonia is the key to unlocking the book," he admits, pursing his lips as one might when divulging a secret that's been kept quiet for centuries.

Malacor perks up. He flaps his wings, his razor-sharp eyes gleaming. His voice hurriedly flashes in the boy's head, quicker than Jesse can keep up with. Jesse struggles to relay his words to Barrington as Malacor sends them to him.

Why are you talking about the book? Malacor bristles uncomfortably. *It was destroyed centuries ago. And what do you mean that Eonia is the key? How can she unlock something that doesn't exist?*

Quietly, Barrington answers, "It's not entirely true that the book was destroyed," he answers with a shrug. "Um, it's not true at all, really," he admits. "The Magi spread the word that the *Book of Good and Evil* was destroyed. A Magus—Queen Adira, specifically—locked the book with a spell," he tells them. "Magi hid the book so no one would find it. Only a handful of individuals know where the book is. And only Princess Eonia has the ability to break the spell and open it." Barrington frowns at his own statement.

"If the book is found and the spell is broken, then the book will be unlocked, Malacor." Barrington sighs wearily. "Its secrets will be exposed for all to see. Anyone who gains possession of the book once Princess Eonia opens it can access the knowledge set forth therein." Barrington clasps his hands. "As I'm sure you understand, the book may be used for good or for evil then," Barrington mutters, appearing suddenly pale and wrinkled, as though aged with worry. "Our fear, as you can imagine, is that the Dark has determined that the book exists and that they know Princess Eonia has the power to open it," Barrington finishes, solemnly.

Where is the book? Malacor demands, holding his head high, arching his neck.

Barrington gazes at the opening in the stone above. "The book is hidden in the other world," Barrington answers, shifting uneasily. "We considered sending a Light agent to secure it, but then we'd risk being followed," he explains. "With Princess Eonia in the claws of Darkness, it seemed riskier to send someone and potentially expose the book's location than it is to keep it hidden." Barrington rubs the knuckles on his hands, dismayed at the weakness of the Light's position. "Once we secure Princess Eonia, we'll reassess the situation and perhaps send someone to get it," he grumbles.

Malacor trains his eyes on Jesse like two darts ready to fire. *How did the Gors, undetected, take Princess Eonia away from the kingdom?*

Barrington and Drumbell exchange glances, and Jesse once again notices how worried the Thwackers look. Barrington's forehead creases. His skin hangs. His usually bright eyes appear dull and distant.

"We don't know for certain." Barrington frowns. "The Gors took Princess Eonia from the capitol building that, as you may recall, is smack in the middle of the kingdom in the very heart of Miriam." Barrington presses his pointer finger into his palm, as if to convey that never should have happened. "They likely used Dark magic to capture her, and they came during the night. We can't be sure what they did or how they got in.

"At this point, unfortunately, we've more questions than we have answers." Barrington shakes his head as if to convey the seriousness of the situation. "We aren't sure what we're up against, which makes retrieving the princess that much more dangerous."

Malacor lengthens the folds in his neck and looks around the empty lair. His wrinkled lips turn up in a heavy-hearted smile. Malacor answers their plea. *You and I have a long, rich history, Barrington. I trust you implicitly. If what you say is true, then the Land of Miriam is, indeed, in grave danger. Of course, my friend, we will help you rescue Princess Eonia.*

He stretches his great, feathered wings.

As you know, though, Fireflies are not war-centric dragons. We're dragons of peace. Malacor's eyes burn with passion. *Since the book was destroyed—or locked away, as you say—we have not had much occasion for battle. The Light, led by the Magi, has kept the Dark at bay with little assistance from us. Even I am not trained to fight in outright combat.* He cranes his neck once again, looking around the empty lair.

I believe we have seven Fireflies, though, who may fare decently against Kelptars. They're not trained in the traditional sense, but they have the capability and the demeanor to fight and fight well. Malacor straightens through the length of his body, revealing his still-strong form. Although old, he is undeniably majestic. *I will send them into the Isle of Mires with you, Barrington. Together, we will stand with you against Darkness,* he vows, accentuating each word as he sends it to Jesse to ensure the boy understands him.

Then he becomes still. Narrowing his eyes, he peers at Jesse. *And how, may I ask, do you intend to handle the Gors?*

CHAPTER 20
EONIA

Poor Eonia. She's stuck here, unable to get out, while Darkness, led by Lord Letch and King Angus, go after her family. It's true, through the nit-picking and the fights, she's never felt she's measured up to her mother's expectations for her. But there has never been any doubt of her parents' love. Who would she be without her parents? How could she go on? She's not ready to be queen!

Her mind whirling, Eonia, confused and scared, thinks of a memory from when she was younger.

She was nine years old when her mother gave her a ring. It was a beautiful ring with her mother's family crest engraved into it, an image of an alicorn flying with a star emblazoned across its chest. Eonia loved the ring.

Sitting there with her mother, she studied the tiny detail on its band as her mother sat with her and lectured her on how to take care of jewelry.

"This ring is special, Eonia," her mother explained. "My mother gave it to me when I was nine. Your great-grandmother had given it to her when she was young, and her mother had given it to her. It's been in our family for a long time."

Her mother eyed her, trying to assess how closely Eonia was listening. "You may wear it, but take care of it," she insisted. "It's meaningful. If something should happen to it, we can't replace it. You understand, don't you?"

Eonia nodded at her mother eagerly. But Eonia isn't like her mother or her grandmother or her great-grandmother. She's like her father. Eonia roams the fields, rather than play dress-up. She romps in the woods, rather than sitting for tea or practicing her lessons. She's never taken to the training and education to make her a "proper princess," as her mother tells her quite often.

Eonia can almost hear her mother's voice shake, complaining, "Eonia, you're just like your father sometimes, arguing, parading around like a ruffian. Please, child, carry yourself with some dignity for the sake of the kingdom." And besides, she was only nine when her mother gave her the ring. She didn't know how to take care of jewelry!

Eonia took off the ring while she was playing. Or it had fallen off—she was not quite sure. It was only the day after she'd been given it, and already, she'd lost her mother's precious heirloom! The princess searched everywhere for it—her bed, the room, her clothes, everywhere she'd been. She re-traced all her steps, but she couldn't find the ring anywhere.

For a while, she tried to hide the fact that she'd lost it from her mother, hiding her hand behind her back or tucking it in her clothes whenever her mother came near. But eventually, her mother noticed the ring was missing.

"Where's your ring, Eonia?" the queen had eventually asked.

"I'm soooo sorry, Mama," Eonia had sobbed in reply, feeling as though her insides were twisting, preparing for the verbal onslaught that was sure to come.

But it didn't come. Her mother didn't lash out at her. The queen didn't berate her for not listening, or for being irresponsible, or for losing her ring. Rather, Queen Marakee took Eonia in her arms, cradling her like she did when Eonia was small.

"Oh, Eonia. It's my fault. I shouldn't have given it to you yet. I should've known. Don't cry, sweetheart. I'll help you look for it. You're so much more precious to me than a ring is."

Eonia had known from that moment on that no matter how many shenanigans she did, no matter how much she and her mother fought or how unlady-like Eonia might be, her mother loved her. And there was no changing that.

Eonia hears the grunts of Gors outside of her door, changing guard shifts.

What does Lord Letch aim to do with my mother? Eonia blinks at the hearth of the hut. Eonia's certain his end goal is to kill her.

Having finished meeting with Lord Letch, King Angus returns. "Get up, princess, we're taking a walk."

Eonia pulls herself up. She doesn't want King Angus to know how distraught she is. She doesn't want him to know that he's winning. As upset as she is, she doesn't want to allow him a foothold into her conscience. But Eonia's been longing for this opportunity. She's been racking her brains for excuses to get out of the hut to see the Gor village. She must seize the opportunity to explore the island, even if she is so disturbed by Lord Letch's visit that she can barely focus to move her feet.

Exiting the hut, Eonia fights hard to reign in her feelings and take in her surroundings as she follows King Angus into the Gor village. Everywhere Eonia looks, she sees pain. Gor women drag themselves around the village, looking hopeless and forlorn. Children, with hunger in their eyes, squabble and fight. Men amble around with no purpose, swinging their weapons and drinking.

What's to come of them all? What's to come of me? What will happen to my parents?

"You must've heard us talking, Princess Eonia," King Angus says. "I'm sure you were listening."

King Angus waits for Eonia to respond, but she says nothing.

"As you've probably guessed, Lord Letch is passing his time in the kingdom with your parents. He has unpleasant plans for them, I'm afraid."

The princess avoids Angus' gaze, wondering where he's going with this. Why is he telling her about Lord Letch's plans? Is the Gor king trying to make Eonia more miserable than she already is?

"Lord Letch, as I'm sure you are aware"—King Angus smirks—"has grandiose delusions that he is greater than he is." Angus draws his face so close to Eonia's that she is forced to look at him. "But

I will let you in on a little secret, Princess." He sneers. "Lord Letch is a pawn in the grand scheme of things." He gestures toward Eonia. "You, however, have the genes to rule the Land of Miriam. Think of it, Princess—you and I together would make a great alliance. Together, Princess Eonia, we could make history!"

It's as though she's being torn limb from limb as her rage over King Angus' deplorable proposal roils her. Shaking like a leaf, Eonia trembles from head to toe.

"I will *never* be partners with you!" she yells, her anger at a fever pitch.

Eonia looks into Angus' eyes, steeling her gaze on him.

I wouldn't be so quick to decide, King Angus' voice flashes from within. *You must think of yourself, Eonia. You must think of your needs. Will you stay here in this hut forever? Eventually, Darkness will win.*

If you join us, though, you can have your life back. You can return to the kingdom. Your parents can live. Yes, it will be different than it was before for you, but it is the only path forward.

If you help us find the book, Princess, I can help you, he assures her. *And together, we can do away with*

Lord Letch. King Angus smiles his ghoulish grin in obvious satisfaction.

Eonia feels the same chill on her skin that she felt when Lord Letch first appeared in her bedroom in the middle of the night in the kingdom. Like an ice pick, the cold is seeping into her bones, nestling itself in, infiltrating Eonia's defenses. "So, this is Darkness."

She's been waiting for it. She's been wondering when it would come. Dejected, she casts her eyes downward, marveling at the predictability of it. Darkness has waited until Princess Eonia is at her weakest to make its play for her.

CHAPTER 21

JESSE WALKER

Jesse bites his lip and watches Drumbell shuffle, shifting his hefty weight from one foot to the other on the dusty hearth of the Firefly lair like a truck tilting. Barrington, on the other hand, looks thoughtful, considering Malacor's question as to how the boy and two Thwackers should best handle the Gors on the Isle of Mires.

"Before Drakendore's surveillance yesterday, we thought only Gors were involved," Barrington responds. "Our plan was to enter into the Mires midday." He glances at Malacor. "As you likely know, Gors sleep during the day. Our hope, then, had been to rescue Princess Eonia while the Gors were still sleeping," he explains. "Conceivably then, we would have had to fight only those Gors awake and guarding the princess."

Barrington slouches and sighs. "Unfortunately, the Kelptars threw a wrench in that plan. Even if we do arrive on the Isle of Mires while the Gors are asleep, Kelptars may see us land. If a battle ensues, the noise from the dragons could easily wake up the whole Gor village."

Malacor peers out over his leathery snout. *Could more forces join you to support ground combat?*

Barrington shrugs. "We could recruit more agents to help on the ground, I suppose, but it would take time to recruit them. And then there's the added challenge of transporting non-flying agents over the Sea of Sunderway and onto the Isle of Mires."

Not a muscle on Malacor twitches as Barrington continues. "When we discovered the Kelptars' involvement, we came here immediately to seek your counsel." Barrington pauses. "We knew we couldn't succeed against Kelptars without the Fireflies' help. But beyond that, we haven't fine-tuned our strategy.

"Moreover, each passing moment risks further exposure of the book's secret. Each passing moment opens the door wider for Dark agents to join forces with the Gors and the Kelptars," Barrington adds hastily, as though conveying the need for action by the very tenor of his speech. "We must thwart Darkness' opportunity to access the book. We must close off the Dark's chance to take over Miriam,"

Barrington clasps his hands. "Time, I believe, is our most dangerous enemy, gentlemen."

Jesse thinks of his dad and Maddie. He thinks of Irvin. *If I were home now, Irvin and I'd be fishing.* The boy reflects, chewing on his cheek, longing for his friend's company as he stares wide-eyed at the scene that confronts him. He imagines riding his bike along next to Irvin's. Despite the chill of the lair, he can almost feel the warm sun on his back like he would at home, pedaling along the dirt road, headed back to his house after a long day of fishing behind old Mr. McNeal's house.

Jesse imagines a bag of fish slung over his handlebars, thumping against his knees. "I feel like one of those fish," Jesse whispers, raising his eyebrows. "Like I'm caught in a plastic bag with my eyes bulging, about to be face to face with Gors."

And the boy *does* look as bad off as a dead fish. His face, thin already, is drawn in and pale. His eyes are clouded and troubled. A vein that runs along his temple toward his brownish-black hairline pulses with the rapidity of a jackhammer against concrete. There's no doubting he is stressed. He holds his body tight.

Jesse's always been slender—not in the good-looking way, but rather in the stretched-out, lanky manner that makes him look like he grew too fast for his body to maintain pace. Despite his narrow frame, though, he has impressive strength. Without a doubt, his strength belies his fragile appearance. Jesse's far from fragile. For certain, he's not as strong as his friend Irvin, but Irvin's stronger than most boys by anyone's measure. After all, Irvin was the captain of the wrestling team last season. He's the proverbial bull in the china shop.

Ounce for ounce, he's the strongest kid Eufaula Middle has ever seen. Even still, Jesse holds his own with Irvin when the boys mess around, and Jesse rarely backs down.

"I've got it!" Drumbell yelps, startling Jesse, nearly making the boy jump. Whipped from his daydream, Jesse finds himself back in the cave, forced to focus once again on the dire situation they are in.

"What if the Fireflies travel ahead of us?" Drumbell offers. "One Firefly could act as a lure an' draw the Kelptars away from the Gors," he suggests. "Then all the other Fireflies'll be waitin' fer 'em, ready ta attack.

"Together then, the Fireflies can take on the Kelptars. And once all o' the Kelptars are dead, we can move inta the Gor village," Drumbell says.

Barrington and Malacor's eyes are glassy listening to Drumbell's idea. Without being dissuaded in the least, Drumbell forges ahead as though he's a drummer, rousing wary troops.

Jesse struggles to keep up with Drumbell's jumbled words, translating them for Malacor. "Kelptars aren't smart; they're jus' ornery, right?" Drumbell exclaims. "Ma'be Fireflies could repeat drawin' Kelptars away as many as . . . hmmm . . . five or six times till all, or at least most of the Kelptars, 'ave been dealt with," Drumbell offers hopefully. "The commotion might wake up some of the Gors, but it wouldn't be nearly as disruptive as a full-blown onslaught of 'em would be."

Barrington stares at the ground. Malacor remains still, considering. Only Drumbell remains animated, propelled by his desire to explain his plan. Enlivened, the Thwacker jumps back and forth along a sideways trajectory, displaying his miraculous athleticism despite his generous girth.

"BAH! We have ta have some kind of a plan!" Drumbell grumbles. "We can't very well walk straight inta the Mires an' risk wakin' up an entire village of Gors, can we?"

Like heat rising, Jesse senses Barrington and
Malacor's intensity as they consider their options,
tossing and turning strategic possibilities over in
their nimble minds, weighing them.

Finally, Barrington speaks. "Each second that
passes allows Darkness a chance to recruit more
forces. Each moment that ticks by is more time for
Dark agents to find the book. Yes, it would be helpful
to have more help on the ground. But at this late hour,
how and who? We've no time to debate. We've no time
to formulate tactics and maneuvers. For the moment,
at least, Drumbell's plan is the best that we have."

Like a thin film, an airy sand covers the rock of
the Fireflies' lair, having collected over centuries.
Bending, Barrington uses his finger to draw on the
dusty ground.

This place could use a cleaning. Jesse wriggles his
nose. He watches Barrington draw a map in the
dusty sand, imagining what Noni's face would look
like if she saw this much dust in one place.

"The Isle of Mires is three miles long." Barrington
points to the drawing in the sand. "And the Gor camp,
per Drakendore's surveillance, is on the southeastern
edge. We should land on the island's northernmost
point to give us the best chance to sneak up on the

Gors without waking them." Barrington points at the top of the map, marking his words.

"We'll have a better sense of what we're up against once we get to the Isle of Mires," he says seriously. "And we can adapt our plan then. For now, though, we must go. The fate of Miriam is in our hands, gentlemen. We must make haste for the Mires. May God help us, and God bless the Land of Miriam!"

A sense of dread like a thick morning's fog weighs on Jesse as he watches Malacor leave the lair. Even from here, through the walls of stone inside the cavernous lair inside the heart of the mountain, he can hear Malacor summon the other dragons in the valley. Malacor's cries echo through the mountain. They ricochet through the gorge. Anyone hearing those sounds knows that something's afoul in the Land of Miriam.

Barrington, who's whiter than usual, grasps hold of the boy's arm. "Mhm, Jesse." Barrington squeezes. "King Angus and his Gors are stronger than us. We must out-strategize them. We need to outthink them." Barrington's face softens. "In the Mires, it's imperative that we get the princess' attention before the Dark detects our presence," he directs. "Princess Eonia needs to know that we've come for her. Once she knows that we're there to help her escape, she can help us."

"How am I meant to do that?" Jesse asks. Having successfully convinced the Fireflies to help them, Jesse was hoping (rather wistfully) that he'd fulfilled his primary purpose for being brought on this mission. He was hoping that he could serve as a simple bystander from here on out—an "observer," as one might call it.

"Use your telepathy," Barrington tells him, dashing the boy's hopes with a wave of his hand. "Princess Eonia will hear you. Mmhm, uh . . . " Barrington looks at his feet. "It's important you understand, too, Jesse," Barrington says more quietly, "if we're in danger and if I'm injured or need to serve as a distraction, you need to leave me." He squeezes Jesse's arm even more tightly, conveying the gravity of his words. "I'm old. I've lived a long, happy life. Nothing would make me prouder than to die saving the Land of Miriam.

"You have your whole life ahead of you." Barrington shakes his head. "Miriam needs you. Your dad and Madeline need you. I'm past my prime. If someone must serve as a sacrifice in furtherance of our effort, let it be me."

"Stop!" the boy shouts. "Just stop!"

Jesse shoots Drumbell a pleading look, begging the Thwacker to intercede to make Barrington stop talking. Barrington doesn't say anything more. He doesn't have to. Jesse understands very well. *We might not make it out of this!* The boy swoons, spinning. *Barrington might die. I might die. I haven't ever seen live combat. I've no idea what to do!*

"Can't someone else help us?" Jesse shouts, hoping against hope that the answer is yes.

With sadness, Drumbell answers him. "Oy. The thing is, Jesse, since the Magi were given the book, the Dark hasn't mounted much of a force against the Light. There 'aven't been any real battles in the Land of Miriam ta speak of. There aren't any Light agents tried an' true in live combat that'd serve us much good in the Mires—even if we did have the time ta get 'em and bring 'em with us."

The Fireflies, returning, gather near the opening of the tunnel to the lair. The dragons clump together in groups looking anxious.

"They know something's up that's not good," Jesse observes.

Swooping through the entrance, Malacor settles down next to his brethren. Then one by one, the Firefly elder summons his warriors, calling each of them forward. With each squawk Malacor issues, a dragon steps up. When he's done, seven Firefly dragons stand on alert, awaiting further orders.

Malacor releases the remaining Fireflies. All but the seven shoot back out through the tunnel, exiting the lair. Then working his way down the line of the remaining seven dragons, Malacor introduces each one by name.

This is Yardley. He's a well-built, steady flyer. For a Firefly, he's adept on the ground. He'll be a resource for you in the air and in ground combat. Meet Firebomb. He's athletic and capable and houses awesome fire power. He'll prove a formidable opponent in the air as well as on the ground.

Malacor pauses a moment, as if allowing the impact of the moment to sink in, then continues. *This is Breeze. She's swift and agile. She's an asset in the air. Gloria—there's so much to say about my Gloria. She's clever. She possesses excellent aim with her fire.* With a mild smile, Malacor adds, *In general, female Fireflies have better aim than their male counterparts.*

Gloria squawks, *Thanks, Dad,* and Malacor's breath quickens. His eyes mist.

He's sending his own daughter into battle! Jesse winces at the realization.

Malacor struggles to remain calm. He closes his eyes. He turns to Sprinter. He moves on down the line.

Sprinter needs little introduction. He's loyal, and he's a commanding flier. Barnum, here, is fierce. He's a natural warrior. Be aware, though—Malacor raises his brow—*he's also young and impulsive. And lastly, there's Zena. Zena may be the most adept flamethrower in all of Miriam. She's a weapon, and she's clever. If you require strategic aid during your journey, Zena's counsel will prove invaluable.*

Having finished introductions, Malacor (with Barrington and Jesse's help) briefs the Fireflies on the state of Miriam. Malacor tells his dragons about the Gors and the Kelptars. He tells them about Princess Eonia and the danger that awaits them on the Isle of Mires. When he mentions Eonia, Malacor asks permission to divulge the secret of the book.

"Yes." Barrington nods. "These dragons are risking their lives for the Land of Miriam. The least we owe them is the truth."

As the facts unfold before the seven, Jesse notes their disbelief. There's fear in their eyes. *They feel like I do. The book, the princess, an evil coalition—it's too much to take in.*

Without further ado, Barrington hurries the group along. "We must go! There's no time to waste," he insists. "Jesse, ask the dragons which one of them we should ride," Barrington directs. "We need to get back to Drakendore, so we can get out of here. We need to get to the Isle of Mires as quickly as we can."

Unsure how to communicate with seven dragons at once, Jesse asks Malacor who should carry the Thwackers and himself back into the valley and to Drakendore. Malacor squawks; Gloria and Sprinter step forward.

Together, with Jesse on Gloria and Barrington and Drumbell on Sprinter, the haphazard entourage consisting of a Magus, two Thwackers, and seven dragons flies out of the mountain and into the valley. Lowering, Jesse sees Drakendore. Pristine and white, she is lounging on the shores of the river.

I know Drakendore. I trust her. He sighs, breathing easier. Seeing Drakendore again is like seeing a loyal friend.

Gloria lands by the river's edge. Jesse slides down off the dragon and runs for Drakendore. He wraps his arms around her neck and burrows his head into her fur. Close to her, the boy relaxes into the sense of security the alicorn lends.

CHAPTER 22
EONIA

The coldness has left Eonia, only to be replaced by an unbearable heat. King Angus had dropped off the princess at the hut. He left her there so he could "tend to matters" after he and the princess had finished their stroll through the Gor village. Directing his guards to keep watch over the princess from the hut's entrance, he had left Eonia to mull over his "proposition."

Alone with her thoughts in the hut's silence, Eonia replays her conversation with Angus over and over, rehearsing what her response was and what it should remain. As she does this, King Angus' words, together with those of Lord Letch, taunt her. It's as though they are laughing at the naivety of her beliefs. Never has Eonia wanted to hurt someone as much as she does in this moment. She wants to kill them both—but not in the ordinary way. Not in the peaceful, expeditious way that an execution might bring.

No, Eonia yearns for a much more sadistic manner of ending her rivals' existence. The princess wants to plunge a knife into King Angus' throat, bursting his jugular. She longs to watch his blood trickle down and pool at her feet. And lest she forget Lord Letch, Eonia has her desires for him as well. The princess wants to rip out his still-beating heart.

The heat. Eonia cringes, grasping around her throat. It's underneath her fingernails. It's crawling beneath her skin. A fire smolders inside her as her world comes crashing in. In a breath, everything she knows is threatened.

"I won't!" Eonia speaks in a raspy whisper.

You must think of yourself. You must think of your family. King Angus is right. Are you going to stay here in this hut forever? The voice slithers around her.

"I am thinking of myself! I am thinking of my family!" She groans at the walls.

If you join with the Dark, you can have your life back. You can save your parents. The voice is insistent and tempting. *It's true, you must serve yourself up to the Almighty Below to do his bidding, but it is the only way forward.*

Eonia pictures her mother with her throat slit, her face pale, and her body limp. She imagines her father on his throne, his robes soaked through with red, his eyes rolling. *Eonia, you can keep it from happening!* The voice is persuasive, guilting Eonia in ways even her worst fears never could. *You can stop Lord Letch from killing them! You can save them! You can be with them again! All you must do is agree,* the voice persuades her. *All you must do is join hands with Darkness. All you must do is pledge yourself to the Almighty Below forever.*

"But what would that mean?" Eonia coughs.

Then out of thin air, as though floating before her, her mother's face appears. Her mother's lips, out of sync with her words, ring in Eonia's ears, *Don't let them in, Eonia! Don't let the Dark get a hold of you! Once they sink their claws into you, it's not easy to break free.*

"I can't make it stop!" Eonia screams at the apparition. "I don't know how to!"

Her mother's face disappears. Then flushing red, all Eonia feels is anger and loathing and fear. The voice from before echoes in the girl's head. *Save her, Eonia. Save your mother. Help her.*

Eonia darts her eyes around the empty room. Desperate, she whimpers, "I know who you are!"

And Eonia understands, too, when she really asks herself, what she'd have to do to save her parents' lives. To join hands with the Almighty Below, she'd have to give up who she is—everything she knows and loves, everything she's stood for as long as she's lived. She'd have to forsake the I AM. She'd have to forsake Goodness itself. She'd have to take up God as her enemy.

"Nooooooo!" Eonia cries out. "I can't do it. I mustn't do it."

Some shred of her, still alive and thinking, buried deep within, remembers that her parents would never want that. They'd rather die than lose their daughter to Darkness. They could easily forgive her for forsaking their lives to save the Land of Miriam, but they would never forgive her for bowing down to him, the Almighty Below. Eonia, too, would never want it. She can't turn from Him! God arms her with strength. He makes her way perfect. He turns darkness into light! How can she desert Him?

Fortifying her own will as much as speaking to anyone else who might hear her, Eonia says, "I know what you want, Darkness. King Angus said so himself. You want fear to consume me. You want me to forget *everything*—the Light, who I am, what

I stand for. I won't!" she screams at the walls that hold her.

"God needs me here," she says with conviction, scanning the room as though speaking to someone. "He needs me present. How many times has Mother told me that? I'm not stupid! I feel Darkness eating at me."

The heat is easing. Again, the voice sounds, but it is weaker. *Think of yourself,* it hisses.

"Go back to Hell!" Eonia cries. "You can't have me."

The heat is gone. Eonia strains, listening for the voice, but no voice answers. All she hears is the sound of the Gors mulling around outside and the distant screech of Kelptars.

CHAPTER 23

JESSE WALKER

Crossing the shoreline to the sea, Drakendore and the dragons fan out beside each other. Together, they fly across the sky in the shape of a V, waves rolling beneath them as an endless stretch of murky water extends before them.

"Harumph, the Sea of Sunderway," Drumbell says.

Drumbell, Jesse and Barrington sit atop Drakendore in their usual formation. The scent of sea air carries the stench of something foul and dead. Through the afternoon haze, the sun beats down on Jesse, rendering him lethargic and uncomfortable.

Long gone is the crisp serenity of Rickenbacker River Gorge. Jesse cringes. The gorge's beauty seems no closer to him now than a far-off dream. "All I see now is a load of dirty water that's beneath us," he grumbles. His worries overpowering him and woozy from the smell and heat, he wonders what the Gors will be like. "Will they be as terrible as they were in my dream?" he whispers. He tries to think of home and his family, to stop the thought of the Gors from haunting him. He thinks of Irvin again. He thinks of his first day of school in Eufaula, when Irvin became his best friend.

Jesse rode to school that first day in Noni's blue Cadillac that smells of mints and leather cleaner. He had wiped his sweaty hands on his pants when Noni pulled into the school's parking lot with him. Noni had asked Jesse if she could come in to meet his teacher, but he only saw kids with backpacks going in. There were no adults, no grandmas around. There were no adults at all going into the school with the other kids.

Jesse had jumped out of the car before Noni could park to follow him. "Uh, no thanks, Noni!" he hollered back to her where she still sat in the driver's seat of the car's cab. "It's okay." His guts rumbled, despite his own reassurances. A chalky taste filled his mouth. He was going to be sick.

Jesse had gone to a small Catholic school in Atlanta. He had known everyone in his class since they'd been together since kindergarten. At Eufaula Middle, though, he knew no one. He was lost in a sea of strangers. Worse, he was lost in a sea of strangers who knew one another. Jesse was alone. Pain from his mama's death, a new town, a new house, and no friends came crashing in on him. He was sinking. Something tugged at his feet. His legs felt fat and heavy as blood from his brain rushed to his lower extremities.

Inch by inch, the boy dragged himself across the steamy blacktop of the parking lot toward the school that first day—until somebody bumped into him, hard.

"Where ya goin', kid?"

Relief washed over him. Jesse recognized the voice instantly. Jesse had met Irvin in the neighborhood and become friendly with him. Smiling, he looked up and met eyes with Irvin.

"Errr . . . Irvin, they let you go to school?" Jesse had asked, jokingly. "Are you sure you're at the right place? The juvie center is down the road I'm told. Um, aren't you meant to be there?"

Together on that first day of school at Eufaula Middle, the boys had walked into the school chuckling, enjoying each other's company and jabbing at the other as boys do. And after that, everything was all right for Jesse. That first summer, then his first day of school, and even still *today, Irvin's served as a constant for him. Nothing's the same for Jesse as it had been in Atlanta. His house, his friends, his school, the streets that he walks and the air that he breathes are all different than they were for him before. But Irvin's friendship has held steadfast.*

"I wish Irvin was here with me." Jesse sighs, breathing in the moist air from the foul sea. "He'd be making dumb jokes about the smell."

"The Mires are close now," Drumbell calls out to Jesse. "It should only be 'bout a kilometer er so more. Once we land, our challenge'll be ta remain unseen. Bah, with any luck, though, the Gors'll still be sleepin' at least."

Ahead, an island emerges. Like a swamp creature, it rises from the grimy water. *The island's overgrown; it's covered with brush,* Jesse notes, scanning the island's banks for movement. But squinting against the sun, Jesse doesn't see anyone. There's no movement at all on the island, except for the leaves that are blowing in the wind.

The Fireflies break their formation and cruise ahead. Minimizing their chances of being seen, the dragons skim across the sea. Jesse watches the Fireflies glide across the water's surface in front of him. Stealthy and forceful, they look like jets moving in.

Then the breeze dies. Everything becomes still. It's quiet.

WHOOSH. The first Firefly, Firebomb, touches down. Nothing stirs. Seconds later, Gloria lands. Then Sprinter. Then Breeze. As Yardley lowers, a chilling scream erupts.

Drakendore throws it into reverse. Backing away from the island, Drakendore, carrying the Thwackers and Jesse, distances herself from the scream.

"Where did it come from? Who screamed?" Jesse scans the shoreline wildly.

Then he sees it. A dragon is rising off the banks of the island. *It must be a Kelptar!* The boy blinks as he watches wings grab at the air. Even from here, Jesse can see the drool drip from its mouth as its claws reach out from its feet.

"*Br*eeech!" Yardley screeches, not knowing whether to land or to retreat, hovering over the shoreline.

"Move back! Move back!" Drumbell yells.

But Yardley isn't quick enough. With velocity, the Kelptar lunges at Yardley midair. The Kelptar grabs Yardley in its claws, and Yardley squeals. Then, as suddenly as the Kelptar rose, Zena is on it. Fire blazes from her snozzle like a finely-tuned flamethrower. Dead on, she hits the dragon's middle. The Kelptar screams. Crumpling, it splashes into the sea, where it bubbles and then disappears. And once again, it is quiet.

Drakendore flies forward toward the island with Jesse and the Thwackers. As Yardley lands on the island, he limps to a halt, and the remaining Fireflies land. Drakendore sets down. Jumping off Drakendore, Barrington runs to Yardley. Even from where Jesse sits, he sees the bloody gashes where the Kelptar's claws have punctured Yardley's skin.

"Shush!" Barrington holds his finger to his lips, warning everyone to stay quiet. More Kelptars may be lurking.

Shaken from the attack, taking shallow breaths for fear that even his breathing will be heard, Jesse listens.

A few minutes pass until Drumbell breaks the silence and whispers to his companions, "Uhm, there don't seem ta be any more Kelptars. Should we move forward with the advance?"

Barrington nods. "Ask Yardley if he's okay to walk."

Jesse moves closer to Yardley and asks the wounded dragon if he can move. Trying, Yardley takes a step forward before collapsing, blood spurting from his wounds.

In a hushed voice, Jesse tells Barrington, "I think Yardley needs to stay put."

"Tell him to stay hidden," Barrington retorts. "Tell him we'll come back for him. Tell him we all fly home together."

Jesse strains to focus on Yardley. The boy groans as he struggles to relay Barrington's message. The ground where he's standing is like quicksand, and he has trouble standing. He's having to keep moving to keep from sinking into the sodden earth as he communicates with the dragon.

Behind him, Jesse hears Drumbell grumble, "The vegetation's too thick 'ere. There's no way we'll be able ta draw the Kelptars out an' lure 'em to us. It's impossible ta even see anything!"

"Uh-hmm," Barrington answers. "The Gor camp is southeast from here. Let's have the Fireflies break into two groups. One group can head along the west shore." He points. "The other group will travel along the east shore." He motions in the opposite direction. "Moving in the direction of the Gor camp, the Fireflies should be able to flush the Kelptars out."

"Aye, it's as good a plan as any," Drumbell says. "I'd have the Fireflies stop halfway up the island, though, an' circle back. We'll need ta regroup b'fore we get too close ta the Gor camp."

Barrington's nodding. "Jesse, can you tell Zena the plan? Zena's already proven herself. If she hadn't been as quick as she was, Yardley would be dead." Barrington pants. "Plus, Malacor identified her as a leader. She should serve as the de facto head for the Fireflies, I presume."

Walking amongst the dragons, slogging through the mud, Jesse does the best he can to tell Zena what he understands the plan is. In restrained squeaks, Zena relays the plan to the other Fireflies.

The Fireflies break apart. Zena, Firebomb, and Barnum move along the east shore. Gloria, Sprinter, and Breeze skirt along the west shore. Meanwhile, Drakendore, Barrington, Yardley, and Jesse stay put, straining to listen for the Fireflies' progress.

"Argh," Jesse moans, fighting his impatience as he listens. *Was that a branch, or was it a dragon? Was it a Firefly, or was it a Kelptar? This must be worse than being in battle!* He wrings his hands, wishing he could do something to help his dragon friends.

"Can't we do anything? Can't we help them?" he asks Barrington and Drumbell, thinking anything would be better than staying idle here like this.

"We must wait," Barrington tells him. "We must wait for the Fireflies to find the Kelptars. We must wait for the attack."

"Blech." Jesse sighs, so anxious, he could spit. He struggles to stand as mud the consistency of mashed potatoes oozes around him, smelling like eggs rotting in the sun. *And the humidity! This heat is unbearable!* Jesse gasps. *It must be 105 degrees. This place is hotter than Alabama in the middle of July.* He shudders, marveling that a princess is here, hidden in this misery.

Waiting, Drakendore, Barrington, and Jesse keep moving, shifting their weight, pulling one foot, then the other, from the soupy marshland to avoid sinking. Unfortunately, Yardley, wounded as he is, can't get his bearings on the shifting ground. The Thwackers and Jesse work to pile sticks under the dragon's webbed feet to help him keep his balance, but it isn't making enough of a difference—Yardley's too big. He's still struggling, sinking into the ground, losing more blood as he does so. Giving up on the sticks, Jesse finds a nearby stump for Yardley to stand on.

"Gud idea!" Drumbell grunts, seeing the boy on the stump, motioning for Barrington and Yardley to come.

Together, they move Yardley. Drumbell pulls; Barrington pushes; and Jesse shoves sticks under the dragon's feet each time he takes a step. Just as they're moving him, though, a Firefly calls out. Squeals erupt rapid fire.

"It's a fight!" Jesse startles, thinking that the screams sound like they're coming from southeast of them. But he can't see anything.

Then, *ZING*—a Kelptar shoots into the air with Firebomb on its tail! Like comets streaking, the Kelptar and Firebomb zoom. The only dragons Jesse can see are the Kelptar and Firebomb soaring toward the horizon. But there's lots of noise from dragons that are still on the island.

Then Gloria rockets into the air, tracking Firebomb. Traveling fast and far, the dragons take a southernly turn. Trees block Jesse's view, and he loses his visual on them as they fly away and into the distance. Meanwhile, fighting to the southeast of the island continues.

"There's so much noise, I-I can't tell what's going on," Jesse stammers. "There's so many dragons fighting and screaming."

"How many Kelptars can there be?" Drumbell asks, nervously. "I thought ya said Drakendore only saw four," he mutters at Barrington.

"Umm, I suppose there could be more than the four Kelptars that Drakendore saw initially." Barrington shrugs, confused as well, watching the sky mindfully. "But Zena already killed one. And another is in the air being chased. With Yardley sidelined and Gloria and Firebomb in the air, hmm . . . There should be four Fireflies that are still left here on the island." Barrington counts on his fingers. "Given that Drakendore only saw four Kelptars on her scouting mission, it's hard to think that there'd be four Kelptars left on the ground to fight the remaining four Fireflies, but it sure sounds like there are. And that's a problem," Barrington admits, sounding every bit as anxious listening to the Fireflies' screams as Jesse and Drumbell.

Yardley, hearing his fellow Fireflies' calls of distress, struggles to rise. The Thwackers and Jesse throw themselves at him. With all their might, they try to restrain the wounded dragon.

"He's injured! He can't protect himself!" Jesse shouts. But it's no use—Yardley's determined to help the Fireflies fight. With a swoosh of his tail, he bats the Thwackers and Jesse up and off of him like a lion brushing away a fly.

Ascending, Yardley flies into the fray. And the commotion ratchets up even louder. There's no mistaking it—Fireflies and Kelptars are at war. They're fighting to the death. And from the sound of it, the Kelptars are winning.

"Welp." Drumbell sighs, wiping off his face that's splattered with mud from the tussle with Yardley. "There goes our chances that the Gors'll still be sleeping." He rolls his eyes. "Nobody could sleep through this."

As Drumbell speaks, Jesse sees two dots on the horizon getting bigger. *It's Gloria and Firebomb returning!* Jesse's heart explodes in relief at this realization. "There's no Kelptar with them. They've won! They're coming back! We have reinforcements!" The boy jumps, seeing them.

And for the first time in his life, Jesse feels the drumbeat of war thump in his chest, calling him forward. He pictures Sckabor's blade shimmering in his hand like it did when he was at Barrington and Millie's tree hut. A surge of energy, ancient and knowing, pulses from within. For a moment—only a moment—it seems to him as though he's connected to a knowledge that's not of his own. For a fleeting moment, a confidence—a readiness for battle, a readiness to fight for what Jesse knows to be true and right and good—surges within him like the tide rising before a storm. Then, like a butterfly fluttering from one flower and onto the next, it is gone.

"Hurrah!" Barrington bellows with a glint in his eye, seeing the Fireflies soaring as well. "The time has come. We must move. There's no putting it off any longer. If we move now, at least we'll catch the Gors still out of sorts."

Jesse agrees. Truth be told, he agrees wholeheartedly with Barrington. Now is the time they must go. But his guts are churning like a washing machine. He feels like he did when he was standing next to Noni's car on the first day of school at Eufaula Middle—scared to go, scared to stay. Only this time, instead of feeling like he might puke, he *does* puke.

He can't help it. He's sleep-deprived, and there's so much fighting going on around him. And the smell . . . *I can't stand the smell*, he thinks, embarrassed. Bending over, he throws up the morning's kettle cakes.

Barrington and Drakendore wait patiently for him to finish. When he's done, Barrington leans down. He pats the boy's back. "Uh, ready, Jesse?" Barrington asks.

Wiping his mouth with the back of his hand, Jesse sputters, "Ready as I'll ever be."

CHAPTER 24
EONIA

Eonia pulls her knees into her chest. She rocks back and forth, curled up in a ball, trembling. Sad and alone, the princess pretends her father is in the hut with her. Princess Eonia imagines her father's towering figure, peering down at her from above. (King Mor towers over most everyone; he's quite tall by most anyone's measure.) In her mind's eye, her father's straggly beard hangs down toward her. She imagines his light eyes, twinkling. As he bends toward her, he reaches for Eonia. Her heart explodes with warmth. She opens her arms to greet him; and as she does, she opens her eyes. He evaporates.

Eonia's father isn't in the hut with her. While she was on the ground, daydreaming, King Angus came in. It's not her father standing over her—King Angus is. Ignoring him, the princess turns away.

Trying to close King Angus out as though he weren't hovering, watching her every move, Princess Eonia closes her eyes and tries to picture her father again. Then hearing the door to the hut slide open, the princess peeks out, hoping the sound of the door she had heard was King Angus leaving.

Rather than King Angus leaving, however, a guard is coming in. And as he enters, squaring himself off with Angus, his king, Eonia senses fear on him. With his face deep red and his eyes bulging, the guard looks horrified. Even Angus, balancing on his heels with his fists clenched, looks flustered.

Is Angus scared? Eonia smirks, suddenly hopeful. She flushes pink with the thought that King Angus should be fearful. Up until now, Eonia hasn't noticed any holes in King Angus' cold exterior since she's been here. He's hardly shown any emotion at all. Eonia's realization that something is getting to him and throwing the Gor king off-kilter is cheery news for the girl. She's fed up being the only one who is terrorized.

"It's dragons on dragons, m'lord. It's other dragons that are attacking da Kelptars. Farlen saw 'em on the southeast end of da island," the guard announces, trembling at his own words.

Eonia had been hearing the dragons' screeches. But the Kelptars always screech. Day and night, the dragons fight. *This time, though, their screams had sounded different than usual,* Eonia reflects, trying to remember exactly what the dragons sounded like. Up until now, Eonia hadn't given much thought to the Kelptars' latest round of fighting. Thinking of it now, though, the princess determines, *Yes, the dragons' screams seemed more frantic than normal. Their rapidity and shrillness made them sound like animals being hunted and wounded,* Eonia concludes.

This time, too, the princess thinks she may have heard the call of another cry amongst the Kelptars. "It wasn't as high pitched as a Kelptar's screech is. It was throatier," Eonia whispers. "It must have been the cry of a different dragon species." *But why are other dragons on the island? Could it be that there are dragons of Light on the island who have come for me?* Eonia's hope blooms.

"How many of the other dragons did Farlen see?" King Angus asks the guard.

"He said he'd seen two, m'lord. Bud, Yer Greatness, id sounds like der's more. And id appears that not only can the other dragons fly; but der're fire-breathing dragons, too, like the Kelptars are."

The Fireflies! The Fireflies! It must be the Fireflies! Eonia alights, burying her face in her hands to hide her glee, thankful King Angus can't read her thoughts unless she wants him to. There's only so many dragons in the Land of Miriam that fly and breathe fire. The Kelptars are the only Dark agents that can do it. *That means it must be dragons of Light who are here on the island fighting,* Eonia cheers inwardly. *And if they are here, they must be here to save me. Why else would Light agents be here on this dreaded island?*

And as Eonia dares to consider something so wonderful, she's catapulted back into the land of the living. She's thrown into a world of hope. She glimpses an endless string of possibilities.

If agents of Light have come for me, perhaps I will live! The princess finds enough hope to dare to dream. *Maybe they finally understand that Lord Letch is evil. Maybe my parents sent them!*

Angus, sensing Eonia's happiness, snarls, "Mind your business, Princess. This doesn't involve you."

"*What* doesn't involve me?" Eonia retorts, trying her best to sound naïve, despite her mounting confidence.

Angus ignores her. Turning his back on her, he turns to face his guard—and at that very moment, the door to the hut slides open yet again. Another

Gor pushes in. Only this time, it's not a guard Eonia's seen before.

It must be a Gor from the village, she thinks, looking over the frightened Gor. It's early afternoon, and the Gors should still be sleeping. *Noise from the dragons must be waking them.* And even as the Gor from the village scurries in, Eonia hears the noise from the dragons pick up outside.

The Gors tense, listening.

"Wad should we do, m'lord? Should we attack 'em?" one of the guards asks nervously.

"Or should we try ta get off the island as quick as we can?" the Gor that's just entered offers, trembling.

Hearing the Fireflies' cries, Eonia breaks into a radiant smile. She doesn't even try to hide her joy any longer. The Fireflies are here for her; she knows this now with near certainty. They've got to be. There's no other reason Fireflies would be on the island taking on the Kelptars. And if agents of Light are here, Eonia's next question is whether they understand the stakes at hand. Are agents of Light aware that the Dark knows that the *Book of Good and Evil* exists? And if they do, do they understand Princess Eonia's involvement? Does the Light know that she's the key to breaking the spell?

If they know, Eonia rationalizes, *there's no way they'll leave the island without me.*

Indeed, it's far too risky to the fate of the kingdom for agents of Light to leave the island without the princess.

I have to break free, Eonia thinks. *King Angus isn't dumb. He'll know that the Fireflies are coming for me. I have to get to them! I have to warn them! I can't let Angus use me as a lure to trap and kill them.*

Longing to run through it, Eonia stares at the hut's door behind King Angus, who's conversing with the Gors. As though drilling a hole through the splintering wood, she focuses on the makeshift enclosure. *All I need is one chance to make a run for it.*

CHAPTER 25

JESSE WALKER

Instead of skirting along the water's edge like the Fireflies, the Thwackers, Jesse, and Drakendore cut through the heart of the island.

"We can't afford to get caught up in the tumult of dragons. A Kelptar could incinerate us in an instant," Barrington announces, "and we'd cause defeat to the whole operation."

Jesse shivers, remembering how fast the attack on Yardley unfolded. The shrillness of Yardley's screams still rings in his ears. He pictures the Kelptar's talons ripping through Yardley's leathery skin, like a knife puncturing a grapefruit. Jesse hadn't even seen the Kelptar coming when it had launched off the island. Yardley had no time to assess how to defend himself.

What will we do if a Kelptar comes upon us now? How will we save ourselves?

Jesse imagines himself caught in a Kelptar's path. Like a marshmallow in a fire, one moment plump and pale and the next moment burned to a crisp, he imagines himself withering in the dragon's flames as fire laps around him. *What's to keep that from happening to me?*

Behind Jesse, Drumbell grunts, "Do ya think we'll be able ta slip into the Gor village without the Gors noticin'?"

Leading the way, Barrington shrugs. "I sure hope so, Drumbell. It's our only ho—"

And as though Jesse's darkest fears have sprung into life, a dragon hiding in the brush jumps out at them!

Barrington ducks and dodges the Kelptar that hurtles through the air. Having missed Barrington, the dragon lands in the bushes where it thrashes, righting itself. Straightening its neck, it points its snozzle at Barrington as the Thwacker tries to run. Jesse can hear the clicking sound from the Kelptar's throat, the sound dragons make when they ignite their fire. The Kelptar hones in on Barrington, preparing to shower the Thwacker in its flames. And as it does, Breeze launches over the bushes and tackles the Kelptar, knocking it down on its side.

For a moment, the dragons wrestle. The Kelptar and Breeze roll in the mud, each one fighting to gain the upper hand and pin the other one down. Wings flap, and talons fly. The dragons topple over each other, somersaulting on the ground. Flames spurt this way and that way, shooting out of the dragons' snouts haphazardly, like lightning bolts that've run astray.

Unable to move, struck with awe and fear, Jesse stares at the beasts. Determination glints in the Firefly's eyes. Hatred is etched into the Kelptar's face. Claws reach out. Backs brace. Mouths open.

"Run!" Barrington screams at Jesse. "Run, boy, run!"

Barrington's voice jolts him. Sliding through the mud, Jesse chases after Barrington, slipping through the marsh, trying to get away. The Thwackers and Jesse don't stop running until the sound of the dragons is far behind them in the distance.

"Gracious, that was close." Drumbell grunts.

"Too close," Barrington pants. And with concern and a hint of agitation, Barrington looks to Jesse. "Next time—if there *is* a next time, Jesse—don't stay to watch the dragons fight. Run!"

For a while longer, the Thwackers and Jesse, together with Drakendore, travel in silence. Slowly, mindful of their surroundings, they pick their way through the quagmire of the Isle of Mires. With each step they take, the earth makes a sucking sound like it wants to swallow them.

"Ich!" Jesse yelps, slipping and falling yet again with a heavy thump.

Despite his best efforts, Jesse's already fallen twice since they started walking. Mud drips from his elbows; it's running down his legs. *It smells like eggs, for sure,* he decides of the mud, gagging. He snorts and sneezes, trying to blow the mud out and away from his nostrils. *And it's not the good kind of eggs either—* the boy spits—*not the fresh, cheesy scrambled eggs like Mama used to make.* Nope. The smell from the Mires is not a good smell. *This mud smells like dry, crusty eggs that've been sitting in the sink for two days.*

Even Barrington, who's closer to the ground and quicker than Jesse is, has slipped and fallen in it once. Only Drumbell and Drakendore remain clean and unscathed. As for Barrington and Jesse, they're covered in the muck. Barely recognizable, covered with seeping sludge, they look nothing like themselves.

We're just shadows of disgustingness, wandering through a depressing marshland. Jesse scrunches his face with disgust.

And that's when an idea hits him. "That's it!" Jesse cries out, looking Barrington up and down. "I can't tell who you are!"

With mud matted to his fur, Barrington knits his brows. "No kidding, Jesse? Who else would I be?" The Thwacker shakes his head.

But Jesse's not kidding, not in the least. "No, *seriously*, Barrington. I can't tell who you are with all that mud on you. Why didn't we think of it when we started?"

Drumbell's wheels spin. "Aha!" His eyes light as the realization sets in.

Together, Drumbell and Jesse drop and roll until they're practically soaked through, sopping in the heavy, wet, stinking mud of the swamplands. Jesse rubs it out of his eyes. He picks it out of his ears. Tasting it on the tip of his tongue, he spits and seals his lips, so more doesn't get in. Beyond the whites of their eyes, nothing's left visible on Jesse and Drumbell beneath the coating of muddy brown earth that's on them.

"Covered as we are, no one should be able to tell *what* we are, let alone *who* we are," Jesse declares. He studies Drumbell and himself, unable to hide a hint of pride from creeping into his voice for having come up with the disguise. "At least, my *hope* is that nobody can tell." He beams, eyes shining.

Finally, Drakendore and Barrington drop and roll as well. Barrington smooshes his face into the wet earth, and Drakendore rolls, coating her fine fur.

With slop running down him, Barrington mumbles happily, "This revolting mess may be our best ally yet. The Gors won't know what hit them!"

"Yee-haw!" Drumbell grunts, grinning.

And seeing Drumbell, his teeth shining out from the muddy darkness, makes Jesse think of Irvin smiling, his teeth glistening against his dark skin.

I'd give anything to have Irvin here, Jesse thinks, longing for his friend. *If Irvin was here, he'd be cracking jokes. He'd be telling me I look like a turd.* Jesse smirks. *This would all be so much more tolerable if Irvin was here.*

Camouflaged, the Light agents continue their advance toward the Gor village. As they walk, the mud begins to harden. Jesse feels it crusting on his skin, drying. It's in his armpits. It's caught beneath his armor, grinding against his skin. And with every step he takes, uncomfortable and worried, Jesse thinks of home. He thinks of taking a shower. Closing his eyes, he can almost feel the water run down his body, washing off the grime of the Isle of

Mires. But when he opens his eyes again, he's still here, crawling through the marshland.

Slow and sluggish, Jesse progresses with the Thwackers and Drakendore toward the Gor village. Then hearing the murmur of voices, they stop.

Barrington motions for Drakendore to wait.

"Continuing with Drakendore by our side is suicide," Barrington whispers. "She's our only means of escape off the island. An alicorn—even one covered in mud—can't pass through a Gor village unnoticed," he says, gesturing toward Drakendore's unmistakable wings.

"If she's detected, she'll be captured, then tortured, then killed." Jesse's breath shortens, hearing Barrington's words. He's come to love Drakendore. The thought of something happening to her is horrific to the boy.

"Drakendore must stay hidden," Barrington says seriously. "We must split from her. We will rejoin her after we find Eonia."

Jesse pats Drakendore goodbye, like one would a good friend. And together, the Thwackers and the boy continue deeper into the swampland. Glancing back, Jesse sees Drakendore alone in the shadows, her wings tucked in against her sides. A stab of fear runs through him, like the blinking light at a train crossing, warning of an oncoming train. *Will I see her again?* he worries. *Will the Gors find her?*

Reaching the base of the Gor village, Jesse and the Thwackers come to a halt. The village is panicking. Gors are in a frenzy, running this way and that. On first glance, the Gors look normal—*like people at home*, Jesse thinks, *just wider and taller.* But when he looks closer, the boy's blood runs cold.

"They're not human," Jesse murmurs, covering his face. Their body parts—eyes, ears, lips, hair—are not as they should be. *They're closer to monsters than they are to people.* A wave of nausea ripples up through him like a tsunami toppling onto a beach. *They look like science experiments gone wrong, as though they've been fed gallons of toxic waste.*

Jesse cowers, waiting for his nausea to pass. Meanwhile, Gors scamper before him like animals. Frantic and searching, they scatter like the kooboo did, fleeing the oubré. Yet despite the telepathy Barrington insists that he has, Jesse can't tell what the Gors are thinking. All he can see is that they are agitated, full of torment and fear.

Jesse starts, suddenly hopeful. "Do you think the Fireflies might've won?" he asks under his breath, daring to speak loud enough so that Barrington and Drumbell can hear. "Is that why the Gors are so frightened?"

Eyes bright, Barrington mutters, "Let's hope so!"

Drumbell grunts. "Glory be, mebbe they did!"

With renewed confidence, Jesse and the Thwackers walk into the Gor village. Jesse steps onto the village's beaten path, and the smell of waste and smoke and sweat hits him. *There's no order. There's no civility.* This village is unlike anywhere else he's ever been.

Jesse and the Thwackers pick their way through the Gor village, clinging to the edge, hiding in the bushes as best they can. Some Gor kids, holding sticks and knives and covered in scabs, run by Jesse without a second glance.

Aah, the misery of this place! I can't stomach it! I can't think. Jesse cringes.

Across the path, two Gors fighting over what looks to be an axe stop and watch them. Jesse stiffens and rests his hand on Sckabor's hilt. Drumbell, noticing the Gor's attention, too, draws his bow. A minute passes. The Gors look at Jesse and the Thwackers, noting Jesse's sword and Drumbell's bow. Jesse and the Thwackers look at the Gors. Then the

Gors dismiss them and start fighting with each other once again, deciding Jesse and the Thwackers aren't worth the hassle of fighting as well.

"Phew!"

The Thwackers and Jesse proceed on through the village. All of the sudden, seemingly rising up from the mayhem, Jesse senses a spirited presence. *Pure. Strong.* A presence not from this place is seeping out from the decay. Jesses feels its energy. He senses its goodness. A crisp, well-meaning voice sounds from the squalor that's before him.

"Who is that?" Jesse asks. Barrington and Drumbell appear unphased. "Don't you hear it?" he asks them. Barrington and Drumbell look at him quizzically. *It must be her!* he realizes with a jolt.

"Princess Eonia!" Jesse grabs Barrington's shoulder. "I think she's near."

Ahead, he makes out what looks to be a shed built into a tree. Seeing it, too, Drumbell motions to it. "It must be the hut that Drakendore saw on her scouting mission," Drumbell says.

"I think that's where the princess is," Jesse whispers back to him.

Barrington, Drumbell, and Jesse situate themselves out of sight and wait quietly, not daring to speak more than is necessary. Crouched in the bushes near the hut, Jesse picks at the mud on his fingers. His head pounds, and his heart thumps.

Will we be spotted? Can we save the princess? Will I survive this?

Finally, the door that's wedged against the hut opens. A ginormous Gor emerges. Over six feet tall and nearly as wide, the Gor is as big as a bear. His face is hideous. Even from here, Jesse sees the crown of weeds on his head. There's no mistaking that it is King Angus, the king of the Gors, of whom Barrington had spoken.

He's worse than he was in my nightmare. Jesse shrinks, feeling as though he's caught in a horror movie, unable to extricate himself. Wanting to scream but unable to breathe, Jesse hears himself gurgle instead.

King Angus talks with the two Gors who are standing guard at the hut's entrance. Then turning back into the hut, the king goes in. One of the guards follows him. Tensing, the remaining guard draws his weapon.

"Great." Barrington frowns. "Not only is Angus awake, but he's also on alert—not exactly the situation we'd been hoping for."

CHAPTER 26

EONIA

The fighting continues for hours. Blood-curdling screams ring out, draping the island in a torrent of uncertainty over whether the Light or Dark will win.

Sweat drips down Eonia. She tingles with anxiety, longing to run out of the hut that she's trapped in. She wants to scream at the top of her lungs, *Here I am! Come and find me and save me. Or if not, let me end it. Please put an end to my misery.*

Unfortunately for the princess, she knows all too well that her fate depends upon the outcome of what's happening outside, beyond the walls of the hut that enclose her.

"Will the Fireflies win? Will I see my parents again? Can I survive this nightmare and return to the life I once lived?" Eonia whispers to herself, wondering if that future is possible. "Or will Darkness be galvanized to unite and prevail against us?"

So much hangs on what's happening in the air a half-mile above where the princess is. And most traumatizing for the girl is that she knows she can do absolutely nothing about it. She closes her eyes and imagines the dragons tussling, ripping into each other at ferocious speeds, somersaulting through the air, claws extended like oubré wrestling.

The screaming outside picks up even more.

The door to the hut that's rarely been opened since Eonia first arrived on the island seems to be a revolving door as Gors push their way in. The Gors are seeking guidance from Angus, their king. But Angus has none to give them.

"Well, m'lord, wad if we light da village on fire ta keep the dragons from comin' in?" a Gor asks King Angus.

"They're fire-breathing dragons, Schnog. They're not going to be scared of a little fire. Plus, where would we go, then? We can't survive the village being on fire either."

"Gud point, Yer Highness. Gud point."

"My vote's ta get off the island immediately," another Gor insists.

"If we leave the island as a group, the Fireflies will see us and follow us," Angus counters. "They'll pick us off in the sea more easily even than they can on land."

"Shud we try ta trick 'em, Yer Greatness? We cud hide in the brush an' then run 'em through wid our spears?"

"We can't play games with Fireflies," Angus spews incredulously, offering no better solutions than those presented. "Fireflies aren't dumb like the Kelptars are. If they figure out that we're hiding from them, they'll light the whole place aflame."

King Angus is being pushed into a corner. Will the Gors fight or run? The guards and village men want to know. Insecure and frustrated, he locks in on Eonia. His voice, sneering, flashes inside of her.

Do you find this intriguing, Princess? he asks. *How intriguing will it be when we kill your precious Fireflies?* He chides her.

"The Fireflies!" Eonia chirps, elated by King Angus' confirmation of her hopes. She guessed correctly; it *is* the Fireflies—the most gifted dragons in all of the Land of Miriam. *If anyone can match the force of the Kelptars, it's the Fireflies.* Eonia smiles. *And King Angus knows it, too.*

Even King Angus, the king of misery, can't hide the fright that's taking hold of him. Like moss growing up a tree, wrapping its spindly threads, fear is beginning to strangle him.

Since the Fireflies are here, the Light must know Lord Letch's scheme, Eonia determines. *He and Angus are in the crosshairs.* She presses the tips of her fingers together.

But one thing Eonia fails to consider as she contemplates the Light's attack on the island and its implications is that even if the Fireflies fail to capture King Angus today, the Gors will come for him in the night. With Angus' plans cratering and his leadership floundering, his weakness is splayed open for all to see. The Gors will prey on him for it. Like animals, they will kill one of their own for power and territory. King Angus knows this. Such is the world of Darkness. It feeds on anything it can, even its own. Such knowledge is influencing the king's response to the Light's attack as he weighs his options.

King Angus throws the door of the hut open and walks out, leaving the Gors to squabble amongst themselves.

Is the fighting over? Eonia considers with a seed of hope in her heart. She listens for the dragons' screams through the din of the Gors. Despite King Angus' departure, Gors remain in the hut with her, enjoying the flimsy protection the hut has to offer.

She hasn't heard the dragons recently. *Did the Fireflies win?* She squints, focusing on the noise beyond the Gors chattering beside her, beyond the drum of the Gor village outside of the hut's walls. It's chaos out there, it sounds, but there's no noise of dragons.

"The Fireflies must have won," Eonia tells herself, hearing the screams and disorder. And the princess lets out a long sigh of relief, reveling in her hope of the Light's victory. Happiness rushes in like spring rain following a summer's drought. She doesn't notice when King Angus opens the door again. She barely feels his hands wrapping around her, gathering her up from the ground. Like a sleeping child, Eonia's gone limp, lost to her blissful thoughts as Angus gathers her up and pushes her out the door in front of him.

Once outside the hut, though, the subversive cruelty of the Gor village accosts her. Never has Eonia been anywhere as disgusting as here. The whole village—men, women, children, air—smells like a wound. Scenes of torture submerge her. Scores of bloodied bodies, whimpering Gors with bloodshot eyes, run around her like madmen. Frightened, the Gors are turning against each other. Desperate to grasp hold of the fleeting power that's left to them, they're pommeling one another.

King Angus plops Eonia down on the ground while he confers with Gors in the village. The Gors are swarming, blocking Angus' path forward with the princess. Smelling flesh and blood and feces, the princess groans. She closes her eyes, summoning all the courage she has left to confront the scene of terror unraveling before her.

Then she hears his voice. *Eonia,* the boyish voice begins, *it's Jesse Walker. I think you're my cousin. I'm here with Barrington and Drumbell. You know them, I'm told. We've come to help you. We've got to get you off this island.*

Standing in the middle of the Gor village beside King Angus, Eonia falls to her knees. Gratitude for God's grace floods her heart.

Oh, the sanctity of a pure soul, unblemished by evil. The wonder of shining life near! Eonia sobs quietly, pressing her face to the earth. She searches the crowd for Jesse, mindful not to draw attention to her efforts for fear of giving him away. Overcome by the love bursting forth, pulsing through her veins, Eonia thanks the Lord above for sending help to save her.

Thank You! Oh, thank You! Thank You, God! Her eyes swell with tears, and then, she sees him.

CHAPTER 27

JESSE WALKER

King Angus returns from the hut carrying a girl. Stopping to rally some Gors who are frightened and fleeing, he drops her to the ground, keeping hold of her wrist. The girl's dress is tattered. She's barefoot. Her face and arms are smeared with dirt, and her hair is tangled with leaves.

Despite all this, there's a strength to her, Jesse sees. *She has an air of majesty,* the boy thinks, seeing his cousin for the first time.

Eonia's strength is written on her brow. It's alive in her movements. The girl holds her head high, as though refusing to give in.

Regardless of the grossness that surrounds her—the Gors, the swamps, the village—Princess Eonia's nobility shines brightly, Jesse reflects as he watches her.

As he had done with the Fireflies, Jesse pictured the words he wanted to send to the princess. He imagined

264

the shape of the letters of each word in his head as he tried to communicate with her telepathically.

Although Jesse's crouching, hiding in the bushes, barely breathing so as not to be seen, Eonia looks straight at him.

She knows I'm here, he realizes excitedly, noting the look of surprise and then excitement that passes on the girl's face like a curtain rising. Eonia's eyes flash, and her lips quiver.

Barrington squeezes Jesse's shoulder. "We have her!" he whispers, seeing the princess' expression as well. "Now, the question is, what to do?"

In a hushed voice, Drumbell says, "If we rush into Angus and his guards now, our outlook's bleak." Drumbell makes a cutting motion like a guillotine lopping off a head. "Gors are everywhere. They'll jump into the fray. We don't stand a chance out in the open against all of 'em together like this," he huffs. We've got ta wait fer—"

King Angus pulls Eonia beside him, and Drumbell stops talking mid-sentence. Angus is dragging the princess away, taking her away from the hut, leading her deeper into the Gor village. He's taking her away from where Barrington, Drumbell, and Jesse are hidden. The Thwackers and Jesse have no choice but to follow King Angus and Eonia or risk losing track of the princess amongst the throng of Gors crowding the village.

Keeping a safe distance, Jesse, Barrington, and Drumbell trail behind the king and the king's guards, keeping Eonia in their line of vision.

"Angus is flushing us out," Barrington whispers to Jesse, careful to keep his voice trained below the din of the Gors humming around them.

The Thwackers and the boy can't stick to the swamp's undergrowth as they had been. Even among the chaos, it's a worry that the three of them stick out like a sore thumb, following King Angus and his guards into the very heart of the Gor village. Barrington motions for the three of them to split up and spread out. Puffing himself up, Jesse grimaces and tries to make himself look as much like a Gor as he can.

What I wouldn't give to be home playing video games! Jesse stares at his feet, desperate not to make eye contact with one of the Gors. The last thing he wants is a Gor thinking that he's trying to engage with him. So, he follows the only advice his grandpa's ever given him (that the boy remembers, at least). Jesse keeps his head down and his nose to the ground as he follows.

That's how Grandpa says he got through the war. Jesse shuffles along. *I'd have to give Grandpa credit. It's pretty good advice, given the mess that I'm in. At least, if there's ever been a time in my life when it's been relevant, there's a solid argument that it's now,* he determines.

Jesse has friends whose grandparents live to tell their life stories, passing on one life's great lessons to the next. "That's not my grandpa," Jesse grumbles beneath his breath. Jesse understands this about him. His grandpa's never been one for conversation. *He's not much for talking in general,* Jesse thinks with a smirk. *He doesn't have to. Noni talks for him.*

It's not that Jesse's grandpa doesn't love him and Maddie. Jesse knows that his grandfather does. *It's just he doesn't say it out loud.* Jesse frowns. *I bet my whole life that Grandpa's only spoken two or three hundred words to me.* Jesse tilts his head, tabulating the sum of conversations he's had with his grandfather over the years. "And twelve of those words have been, 'Keep your head down and keep your nose to the ground, son,'" Jesse mutters, repeating his grandfather's words, nodding to himself. *And you know what? Those words are meaningful now!*

Stealing a glance ahead, Jesse looks up to see where he's fallen relative to Barrington and

Drumbell and King Angus' position; and as he does, the boy catches sight of Angus pulling Princess Eonia off the village's main path.

Thankfully, we can get out from the center of this. Jesse blinks, wondering if this is how his grandpa felt when he'd made it through enemy trenches. *I'm not on friendly ground yet.*

Jesse rubs his head, remembering the Kelptar that had nearly killed Barrington as he and the Thwackers picked their way through the marshland before reaching the Gor village. "Doesn't matter," he mumbles wryly. *I'll take the swamps over what we just went through any day of the week.*

Approaching a narrow trail leading out of the village, Jesse falls in line between Barrington and Drumbell. The Thwackers bookend Jesse protectively as they follow Angus and his guards down the uneven path and into the marshland. Not long after turning down the path, Jesse hears Barrington's muffled call from in front of him.

"Look up!"

And as the trees close in around him, the boy glimpses two Fireflies soaring above, wings spread out wide, victorious.

Like a crack of thunder that's sudden and powerful, Jesse's heart explodes with a pride he's never experienced. It's not a pride in one's self that is so bothersome. Rather, it's an honor for fighting for what's good. The boy blooms with pride for fighting on the side of right, for fighting with the Fireflies. And in an instant, hope and love and strength ignite within him, expanding like a balloon being filled with helium.

"They've won! They've really won!" Jesse beams.

"It appears so." Barrington dips his head in a salute to the warriors flying over. "We have to hurry, though!" Barrington hustles down the path in front of Jesse and Drumbell. "Angus is headed toward the sea. He knows he's under siege, and he's fleeing. We must get to the princess. We can't let him get off the island with her!" Barrington swings his hands, motioning for Jesse and Drumbell to move even faster through the marshland.

Sprinting, with Drumbell on his heels, Jesse races to keep up with Barrington. The Thwackers and Jesse are going as fast as they can, yet the Gors are moving faster.

They're taller, and they've got longer legs, he thinks of the Gors as he runs, trying his best not to slip and fall again. *Plus, they're used to traveling through this cruddy muck,* he reflects begrudgingly.

Meanwhile, the sounds of the Gors with Eonia are getting farther and farther away.

CHAPTER 28
EONIA

Isle of Mires, Land of Miriam

Aunt Lillian's eldest child? Of course! It's brilliant!
Eonia smiles, resisting Angus' powerful pull to the
best of her ability. *Jesse is the perfect answer to counter
King Angus' talents.*

How did I not piece it together before? Eonia asks
herself. *That's how the Fireflies came to the island. It
would've taken forever to clue the Fireflies into what has
been happening. Jesse was able to communicate with
the dragons. The kingdom recruited Aunt Lillian's son
because he inherited Aunt Lillian's gift. He's telepathic!
The Light brought him into the fold to help us. Bless him!*

"But how did they get him here so quickly?" the
princess murmurs, eyes widening. *And how did they
bring him up to speed on all that's been happening? Last
I heard, Jesse didn't know anything about the Land of
Miriam.* "He must be so confused," she whispers.

Finding out about Aunt Lillian's role in the kingdom and discovering his true identity would be a lot to digest.

"Hurry up," King Angus snarls. Stopping abruptly, he turns on his heel and stares at Eonia, trying to decipher her thoughts. Failing, he tugs at Eonia harder.

Eonia winces but tries not to show her pain. The throbbing radiating up her arm from King Angus' death-like grip is the least of the girl's worries. She'd been hearing the noise of the Gors from inside the hut, but even she hadn't been prepared for the mayhem she witnessed. Plodding behind Angus, bloodied Gors had wandered around her aimlessly, lugging weapons behind them. Fights were everywhere.

And now, here we are, rushing down this path. To go where? The princess weighs the situation, alarmed by Angus' sudden determination.

"I can't keep up with you if you hurt me," Eonia yells at the Gor king, doing the best she can to slow him down. She resists scanning the trail behind them in search of Jesse and the others, worrisome of tipping Angus off as to their whereabouts.

Even as dirty and disgusting as they appeared, the Gors will eventually sniff out the Thwackers and Jesse. Eonia struggles not to think about what happens then. She needs to break free from Angus. She knows she needs to get to Jesse. But Angus is dragging her, forcefully pulling her down the path. Eonia's barely able to keep her feet on the ground as it is.

"Pick up your feet, Princess," King Angus growls, angrily.

Angus, too, seems taken aback by what's happening, Eonia observes, dragging her feet even more, despite Angus' constant protestations. *He's unsure how to handle the mess that's breaking out among his men,* she estimates. *He's desperate.*

"What do your men aim to do?" Eonia dares to ask. "They seem upset."

Angus ignores the princess and moves faster.

Eonia had noticed how the Gors had locked in on her and King Angus as Angus had pulled her through the Gor village. *They looked at us like we were prey,* she decides. Yet, uncertain how best to capture and kill their king, the Gors had let Angus pass unscathed through the village with Eonia. Emboldened by the mayhem unfolding and swimming in adrenaline, some of the villagers had approached their king, perhaps to accost him at a moment of weakness. But the guards had pushed them back and away.

"Walk faster, Princess, unless you want to get hit and stop asking questions that aren't your business,"

Angus orders, urging Eonia again to move faster. As he does, Eonia, sensing movement, glances up from the palm fronds and the grasses that surround her. Through the trees and swamp brush, she sees the dragons flying.

"Ooh!" she cries, unable to hide her glee as the Fireflies stretch out their wings, streaking through the air. She sees the dragons' distinctive red and black striping. Without a doubt, these beautiful creatures are not the Kelptars she has seen on the island from time to time since she arrived. *No, sir, not these graceful dragons!* She grins. *These are the Fireflies who have come to save me*! Overwhelmed with a desire to thank them, Eonia wishes with all her might that she could float up to greet them.

His neck straining skyward, Angus sees them, too. Snarling, he shoots Princess Eonia a disgusted look, and he picks up the pace even more so. Desperate to slow down the Gors, Eonia doubles down, dragging her legs.

I need to stall, she thinks, suddenly frantic. *I need to let the Light agents catch up with us.* But knowing all too well what's at stake, Angus plunges through the brush, rushing forward with the princess.

To where? Eonia wonders again. *Where is he taking me?*

Try as she may, Eonia isn't able to slow down Angus much. For sure, she is fierce. But she's half the size of the Gor king and probably only a third of his weight. Frustrated by her resistance, however, Angus finally grabs her up like one would a doll. He slings her over his shoulder like a load of firewood as he thunders down the path. Pressed up against him, Eonia's head bangs against Angus' back. She cranes her neck, straining to glimpse down the path behind her.

Is that rustling in the brush behind us? She holds her breath, hoping with her whole body that it is Jesse and Barrington and Drumbell that she hears.

And at that very moment, as Eonia dangles over Angus' back, straining to determine if Jesse and his cohorts are behind them and how far back they might be, King Angus steps out of the brush, and the path opens to the sea.

"Noooo!" Eonia cries. Now she understands where King Angus is taking her. Now she understands what his plan is! "Coward!" she screams. "You're trying to get off the island. You're leaving your men!" She kicks her heels. "COWARD!"

The princess reels, her anxiety surging. *He's sneaking away! He's leaving the Gors to the fate of the Fireflies. I can't let him take me! If he gets off the island with me, there's no telling what he will do. Besides, Lord Letch is still in the mix. Together, King Angus and Lord Letch can recruit more Dark agents.* Eonia quivers. *I may never get back to the kingdom. I've already spent several days locked away on this island in the middle of the sea. There's no telling where Angus may take me from here. And the Dark's search for the book could go on and on and on. This needs to end,* Eonia thinks desperately.

Reaching the shore, Angus throws Eonia to the sodden ground. "Don't move," the Gor king barks at her. Then he grunts at his guards. "Get a rope off one of the boats."

CHAPTER 29

JESSE WALKER

Isle of Mires, Land of Miriam

Running as fast as they can, they soon come to a break in the trail.

"The Sea of Sunderway." Drumbell huffs. "Those are the Gor boats."

Three long, slender, wooden boats are docked in the water not far off from the shore. "They look like Viking boats," Jesse pants, remembering the video his third-grade teacher had uploaded online.

The video, part of a three-part series that the class was doing for social studies on Vikings that year, discussed Viking boats at length. It showed sketches of a boat's hull—long, thin, and turned-up at the ends. There had even been a picture of a Viking vessel that archeologists had found in a burial mound in Norway and preserved. Jesse was enamored with Vikings at the time, and he had paid close attention to the lesson.

Jesse traces the smooth lines from the hull to the keel of the Gor boats. *They look just like the boat from the burial mound,* he thinks, picturing the image of the archeologists with the Viking boat from Norway. Then, noticing a serpent carved on the front of each of the Gor boats, the boy gags. Serpents stretch out their long, wooden tongues as though hissing. Despite the heat of the Mires, Jesse shivers.

Angus and his guards hoist a sail up the mast of a boat anchored several feet off the shore in the sea. Catching the wind, the sail ripples and unfurls, revealing a black skull stitched into its fabric. The skull looks down at Jesse.

Did that skull just grimace?

Swaying in the breeze, it seems as though the skull's come to life, as though it sees Jesse and the Thwackers huddled up at the edge of the trail looking up at it. Mesmerized, Jesse can't take his eyes off the black holes in the skull's barren head.

"This is our chance!" Barrington blurts, snapping Jesse's attention away from the boat's sail. "Look at Eonia!"

Eonia, who's tied to a tree, is close to where Jesse and the Thwackers stand.

Angus and his guards are distracted, Jesse agrees, noting that the Gors are still very much entangled with the sail.

Without a moment's further hesitation, Drumbell jumps out from the brush from behind Jesse and Barrington. Sprinting, the Thwacker shouts to them, "Now er never," without bothering to look back to see if Jesse and Barrington are following.

Jesse runs after Drumbell.

"ARRRRRRGH!" Angus' blood-curdling scream ricochets through the Mires like an explosion. Seeing the intruders making a beeline for Eonia, Angus cries out like a lion, cold and fierce, awakened to find deer in its den.

"He s-s-sees us!" Jesse stammers, not daring to slow down. His heart beats wildly. His mind fogs. *If he catches us, he'll kill us,* Jesse understands. He doesn't stop moving—*left, right, left, right, left, right—stay close to Drumbell,* he tells himself, and he keeps his legs pumping.

Reaching Eonia, Drumbell pulls the rope taut that the Gors have wrapped around the princess' wrists, binding her to the tree.

"Cut it!" Drumbell orders the boy, hurriedly.

"You're Aunt Lillian's son?" Eonia asks Jesse as the boy fumbles, drawing Sckabor from the sheath.

The boy nods in reply to Eonia's question and prays he doesn't accidentally cut his cousin instead of the rope that binds her. "I haven't had much practice with magical swords," Jesse offers. With shaking hands, he works as quickly as he can. Blessedly, Sckabor slides through the rope like scissors snipping a thread, freeing Eonia, notwithstanding Jesse's clumsiness.

It's like it's on autopilot, Jesse thinks of the sword in his hands, curiously. *I was holding it.* He tilts his head. *But it's like the blade knew what to do before I did anything with it.*

Re-sheathing the sword, Jesse jams Sckabor into its scabbard. He scurries away from the sea back toward the trail, tracking Eonia and Barrington. Down the narrow path, he scrambles after them, headed back into the heart of the swampland, not daring to look behind him. And anyway, he doesn't have to look back to know that Drumbell's behind him. And behind Drumbell, Jesse hears King Angus and his guards coming.

"We have to get to Drakendore!" Barrington shouts back to him, without slowing down.

The guards are gaining. Jesse hears the Gors pounding down the path, getting closer. He hears the grass rustle. He hears the Gors' uneven grunts and breathing.

"I need to stop them! I've gotta do something!" Jesse shrieks.

Slowing, the boy falls behind Princess Eonia and Barrington. *There's no time to explain.* He comes to a full stop. Ahead of him, Barrington slows, urging Jesse to hurry.

"Go!" Drumbell, who's stopped behind Jesse, yells to Barrington. "I'll stay with Jesse. Go and get Eonia out of 'ere!"

Barrington makes a motion like he's going to argue but instead grabs Eonia by the hand, forcing her to move faster. Diving into the brush, Jesse watches Princess Eonia and Barrington disappear down the trail. From where he's hidden, Jesse no longer sees anyone at all. He can't even tell where Drumbell is.

Barely a moment passes, though, before the grass on the trail sways. Seconds later, a guard comes barreling down the narrow path like a freight train. From where Jesse's hidden, he sees the guard's feet run past him without so much as even slowing down. Then, there's a hissing sound. The boy doesn't understand what the hissing is or what it could mean before he sees the guard falling forward, an arrow in his back.

Then the second guard is on them, looking around. Reaching the first guard, the second guard stops. Stooping, the guard leans over for a closer look at the arrow sticking out of the first guard who's on the ground moaning, writhing like a squirrel that's been run over but hasn't yet succumbed to its injury.

Hissssssss—another arrow from Drumbell sails through the air. *Thwack*. The arrow hits the second guard in the forehead. The guard stumbles and falls backward where he comes to rest near the first fallen guard.

King Angus reaches the spot where Jesse is hidden as the second guard falls. Having seen the direction from where Drumbell's arrow had launched, King Angus scans the marsh for the perpetrators. Bent low to the brush, Angus draws his knife. He searches the area, working to determine exactly where the arrow came from.

Jesse pictures Drumbell hiding. He thinks of the Thwacker's accent. He imagines Drumbell's laugh. He remembers the smothering hug Drumbell had given him the morning at Barrington's tree hut when he had first given Jesse the bow and arrows.

He couldn't have known that I've no idea how to use them! Jesse frets of the bow and arrows that Drumbell had made such a point to deliver. *Does he know I haven't a clue how to help him against Angus?*

King Angus stops. The Gor king locks in.

He's found Drumbell! Jesse realizes, seeing Angus raise his knife in the air.

Hisssssss. THWACK.

Another of Drumbell's arrows flies out from the brush straight into King Angus. King Angus sways backward and then catches himself. Jesse watches as Angus rips the arrow out of his own chest and then lunges into the bushes after Drumbell.

He's going to stab him! Jesse stiffens in horror.

Then everything goes dark. Jesse doesn't remember running. He doesn't remember drawing Sckabor. He doesn't remember the feel of the blade sinking in. All Jesse remembers is whimpering and King Angus crumpled at his feet. Jesse sees the pain in King Angus' twisted face flicker. The king's dark eyes turn colder and colder, then darker. It seems a long time to the boy as he stands there frozen, wondering what he's done. Although, in reality, it's only been seconds.

Noise from Drumbell brings Jesse back to his senses. Hidden in the brush, Drumbell's groaning. Rushing, Jesse searches for him and finds the Thwacker wedged beneath some bushes. Using every ounce of strength he's got, Jesse rolls Drumbell's hefty body out from under the branches. He pulls Drumbell back onto the trail and crouches down beside him. Jesse's breath quickens. Blood pools around him, mixing in the mud where he crouches over the Thwacker.

Drumbell is wounded, but alive.

CHAPTER 30
EONIA

Isle of Mires, Land of Miriam

AHHHHH! Eonia wails, blundering through the marshland like a drunkard. Overcome by a sickening sensation of guilt and fear and pain, she's unable to pay any regard to where she's going at all, it seems.

We were sprinting down the path when he stopped. Jesse stopped in his tracks in the middle of the trail. "Angus would've been on him in seconds!" Eonia cries out. Eonia would have never left the boy there, but Barrington grabbed her. He forced her to run and leave him.

"Why didn't I scream?" Eonia gurgles, fraught with disbelief that she let this happen to her own cousin. "I should've screamed, 'I won't leave you,' at the top of my lungs. But I didn't!" she blubbers at Barrington. "I ran, and I left him. I left Jesse and that other Thwacker alone with vicious killers. They've never been up against Gors! They've never seen the likes of King Angus! They don't stand a chance—and I left them there *alone* to face him. How will I live with myself?" she sobs.

"They may be all right, Princess Eonia." Barrington pats the princess' shoulder. "Drumbell's a fighter. He's the best bowman in Miriam. And Jesse's tougher than he might seem."

"But how?" Eonia bellows. "How is it possible that a Magus and a Thwacker could have survived King Angus and his guards? Even if Drumbell *is* good at archery, his tricks wouldn't rival the brutality of the Gors!"

Eonia wants to sink to the ground and weep, allowing her weak body to give in. But Barrington won't let her. He won't let her slow down.

"We have to find Drakendore," Barrington tells the princess over and over. "She should be hidden in the marsh where we left her."

But Barrington and Eonia are having a hard time finding Drakendore.

"Maybe she's dead," Eonia huffs at Barrington, venting a sense of nothingness she feels. Like waves, sadness is roiling her, tossing her about like a ship in a storm. She feels lost and empty. She's left questioning her very existence. Sadness is smothering her vitality like a veil that's been draped over a flame.

"That's how everything ends up here, isn't it?" Eonia fumes. "Dead. How could I have let this happen to him?" she trembles, ashamed. "Jesse, Aunt Lillian's only son. I did this to my own cousin! And after everything he's been through," she squeals, her voice raspy and strained. "Of course, I should've known it was him from the start. I should've known it was him as soon as I heard the Fireflies on the island. He talked to them, didn't he?" she asks Barrington. "Jesse actually did inherit Aunt Lillian's gift. He talked the Fireflies into coming here. That's it, isn't it? I'm alive and free because of *him*—and I *left* him!"

And the thought of her dead aunt and her sense of disloyalty brings Eonia to tears all over again. Unable to restrain her cascading emotions, she sputters like a spigot. "There's nothing I can do for him now," she whimpers.

Still, she can't push the boy from her mind. She can't dismiss him. Drained of all feeling, the princess plods along behind Barrington. And all she sees is an image of Jesse, face-down in the mud. She sees nothing else. She thinks of nothing else. A tiny voice inside of her wants to yell at the image that's haunting her, *Get out! I can't do anything to help you!*

But deep down, deeper in Eonia's conscience than where her frustration lives, deeper than where the tiny voice originates, Eonia doesn't really accept that the voice is right. She doesn't accept that there isn't more she can do.

Trailing behind Barrington, Eonia puts one foot in front of the other like a lifeless rag. Wrestling with herself, she stares into the marsh as her eyes blur. Then through the blur of her tears, Eonia sees movement.

"Is it Drakendore?" she asks, eyes wide with surprise.

Drakendore looks nothing like the alicorn the girl knows. With her white fur covered in mud, Drakendore's nearly unrecognizable to the princess.

But yes, it is her, Eonia realizes. *It is Drakendore.*

Barrington and Eonia hurry over to greet the muddy alicorn. For a moment, Drakendore looks at them as if to ask where Jesse and Drumbell are. Then understanding what must have happened, Drakendore drops her head, her eyes wet.

Seeing Drakendore's sadness, Eonia strains yet again to keep from falling into pieces and collapsing to the ground.

"Climb on," Barrington urges Eonia, holding the girl up by the hand. "We've got to get you out of here."

Eonia shakes, too upset to climb onto Drakendore.

"We can't leave them," she sobs.

Barrington's face softens. His eyes, too, are watery. Gently, he says, "We must, Princess. We've no choice. We need to get you out of the Mires. We need to get you back to the mainland, where it's safe."

"So, that's what this vile place is." Eonia jerks. "The Isle of Mires." And as she hefts herself onto Drakendore's back with Barrington's help, she bawls. "We can't leave them here!"

Barrington swings himself onto Drakendore in front of Eonia. Grabbing her by the hands, Barrington wraps Eonia's limp arms around his middle. Drakendore heads for the shore, searching for a space to become airborne. Galloping, Drakendore reaches the water's edge and launches out and over the sea and into the air, leaving Jesse and Drumbell on the Isle of Mires to fend for themselves.

As the island becomes small beneath her, memories of Lillian awaken within the princess, swimming through her thoughts like minnows darting hither and thither, making her head throb. The thought of her aunt's only son, alone, left to die a terrible death, gnaws at her. Like a bleating animal, she cries over and over, "We can't leave them! We can't leave them alone!"

Barrington yells back to her, "They are not alone, Princess! The Fireflies are still in the area." He squeezes Eonia's hand wrapped around him, comforting her. "None of this is your fault, Princess Eonia," he tells her. "And all is not lost. Jesse is more resourceful than you're giving him credit for. And Drumbell is a fighter. I wouldn't write them off just yet," he insists. "We need to alert the Fireflies that they are still on the island, though." Barrington looks up, directing Eonia's attention toward dragons flying above. "The Fireflies need to know that Jesse and Drumbell are still stuck on the Isle of Mires so that they can look for them."

As they rise, Eonia sees four dragons circling. They soar with wings spread wide—powerful, graceful, and pure. Eonia sucks in her breath. Even in her grief, the princess reflects on the Fireflies' loveliness. They're breathtaking. Seeing them, it is impossible for the girl not to feel a sense of peace pass over her, no matter how fleeting. And for a moment, Eonia can breathe.

Is it possible Barrington's right? she dreams. Hope bursts forth within her for the first time since

Barrington and she split from Jesse and Drumbell on the trail. *Is it possible Jesse is still alive? Maybe he, with Drumbell's help, did escape King Angus and Angus' guards.*

Drakendore flies for the closest dragon. Seeing them, too, the Firefly swoops down toward them.

"It's Barnum," Barrington tells Eonia of the Firefly, recognizing the dragon's size.

Flying close, Barrington frantically gestures to alert Barnum to Drumbell and Jesse's absence. Then, Barrington points the dragon to the area of the island where he and Eonia split off from the Thwacker and Magus. Barrington motions for Barnum to go and look for Jesse and Drumbell. And Barnum, seeming to understand Barrington, screeches and changes his trajectory.

"I think he's calling the other dragons to him," Barrington announces, listening to the dragon as he is departing. "They'll scour the island for Jesse and Drumbell, Princess. Dead or alive, the Fireflies will find our friends. They will bring them home to us." Barrington sags slightly.

As Drakendore flies for the mainland, Eonia peers over her shoulder, watching Barnum behind them. She sees the other Fireflies responding to his calls. She watches them flock around the largest dragon. And when the island is almost out of sight, Eonia thinks she sees the Fireflies—now mere dots on the horizon—disperse, flanking the island in search of her cousin.

CHAPTER 31

JESSE WALKER

In a groggy voice, Drumbell moans, "Leave me, Jesse. Find Drakendore an' leave with Barrington an' Eonia."

"I won't! I won't leave you," the boy cries.

Drumbell's blood is turning the mud into a brownish red. Unfortunately, there's too much blood for Jesse to see where it is coming from, so he's unable to assess Drumbell's wound. Not to mention, the boy's no doctor; he doesn't know how to stop the bleeding.

"You've got to walk," Jesse suggests, choking back his tears, trying to sound confident.

Drumbell understands Jesse doesn't want to leave without him. He allows the boy to help him roll off his back and onto his side. And Drumbell groans even louder. Slowly then, Drumbell comes to his knees. Sinking into the earth beneath him, he gets his feet up and under him. He pushes himself

293

upright, standing as his blood drips from him, splattering the mud around him like drops of rain.

Jesse wraps his arm around Drumbell's back as far around as he can to support the Thwacker as he moves. Together, the two of them start out through the muck, headed in the direction where they had left Drakendore.

"Bah," Drumbell croaks as they go. "That boggart stabbed me in mah shoulder." Then looking the boy up and down, he says, "You, though, Jesse—ya were unbelievable. If ya hadn't come up when ya did, I'd fer sure be dead."

"Err . . . I don't remember any of it," Jesse stammers, glancing down the path in the direction where Angus' body remains strewn across the path and in the bushes, lying in a puddle of red.

"Ya don't?" Drumbell asks, raising his eyebrows. "Ya don't remember comin' up behind 'im?"

Jesse shakes his head no. "I don't remember anything," the boy mumbles beneath his breath. Jesse doesn't want to think about what he's done, or how terrible it may be, or what it could mean about him. He doesn't want to think about King Angus lying on the path not moving or the Gor guards, bodies bent in odd directions, with arrows run through them.

All I want to do is get off this miserable, stinking island. The boy squints, not saying a word.

"Well, one thing's fer sure," Drumbell says. "Once the Gors find King Angus, then the hunt'll truly begin. Gors'll try to track us down. They'll be on that hunt fer the princess. They'll wanna kill any outsiders before doin' anything else they have planned. We need ta get ta Drakendore as fast as we can."

And wincing, gritting through the pain of his injury, Drumbell starts to move a little bit faster. He's still bleeding, but his situation is not as dire as it seemed when the boy had first found him in the bushes. The blood—that Jesse now sees is coming from Drumbell's shoulder—has slowed. Drumbell used some mud to seal it like a bandage, which seems to have helped.

Unfortunately, with Drumbell wounded as he is, they can't go very fast as they skirt around the village in the swamps to avoid the Gor camp. Plodding along, not wanting to talk about Gors or death or what happens next if they can't find Drakendore, Jesse asks, "So, why do you and Barrington have different accents?"

After all, the boy had been wondering about the question since the night of the party. Barrington's accent is distinctive, relative to the other Thwackers that he has met.

"Ah." Drumbell grunts, and his eyes glint. "Barrington wasn't raised in Tanglewood. He was raised in the kingdom, and I was raised in the ramble. That's how Barrington met yer mum and knew her so well. Barrington knew yer mum since she was a babe."

"Really? Barrington knew my mom when she was a baby?" Jesse asks, surprised the Thwacker should know his mom long before he'd ever been born himself.

"Oh yes." Drumbell snorts. "Barrington, at least, knew yer mum since she was born. That's how he an' Millie were so close ta yer mum all those years. Ya know, Jesse, everybody 'ere loved yer mum. She was special. Just like you are."

Jesse remembers Barrington wiping the dirt off his back after he'd fallen from Drakendore. He recalls the sadness in Barrington's eyes when he was talking about Jesse's mom being sick. He remembers the hurt in the Thwacker's face when Jesse didn't recognize who he was in the bedroom the night Barrington had come for him at Jesse's home in Eufaula. *I guess Barrington is like family,* Jesse thinks, remembering his mom's words.

"Why was Barrington living in the kingdom?" Jesse asks Drumbell. "I thought just Magi live there?"

"Oh, the kingdom is a Magi city." Drumbell squints. "But all different Light agents live in the vicinity. It's just that most of us have our own villages where we prefer ta live instead." He shrugs.

"Barrington's kin, though, have always served the crown," Drumbell explains. "His family's been a Thwacker liaison fer as far back as I can remember. That's how he met yer mum an' came ta love her so." Drumbell gestures toward Jesse. "Barrington grew up in the kingdom. He didn't move ta Tanglewood till after he an' Millie got together."

"So, how close was Barrington to my mom?"

"As close as an uncle, I'd say. He loved her. He was heartbroken when he found out that she was sick. When yer mum passed, he and Millie didn't come out of their tree hut fer days."

"Mama didn't tell me about any of her life here until she was sick," Jesse says.

And the question *why not* pesters him. The same questions that have been grating on the boy's conscience since he crawled out of his window and realized that he really was traveling with Barrington to the Land of Miriam, the land his mother was from, are rising within him, taunting him as to why he's been in the dark all these years.

"Why did Mama hide it all from me?" Jesse cries. "Why didn't she share her life in the Land of Miriam with me? She was my own mom, and it feels like life with her was a lie. Didn't she love me enough to want to bring me here? Didn't she trust me?" Jesse trembles, allowing the thoughts he's been wondering all this time to be spoken.

"I didn't know Lillian as well as Barrington did, Jesse. But I'm sure ye've determined by now the Land of Miriam isn't without its dangers." Drumbell grabs Jesse and pulls him toward him. "I'd bet yer mum had her reasons fer not wantin' ta bring ya 'ere inta this." He gestures toward the swamps that surround them. "And judgin' by the mess we're in, they were pretty good ones."

Drumbell and Jesse stop talking. They've reached the place where they'd left Drakendore.

CHAPTER 32

EONIA

En route to the Kingdom, Land of Miriam

For hours, Eonia, Barrington, and Drakendore fly over the Sea of Sunderway. Eonia rests her head against Barrington's back as she gazes into the sea. She hasn't spoken to Barrington since they left the Isle of Mires. She has nothing left to say to him. She can only pray that Jesse somehow survived King Angus and that the Fireflies have found him. Finally, though, her curiosity gets the better of her. She asks Barrington what's become of Lord Letch.

"What do you mean?" Barrington asks, turning to look at her.

Tension shoots through Eonia like a shot of adrenaline. "What do I *mean*?" The princess' eyes flash. "Lord Letch is behind all of this!"

Barrington tilts his head. Like a child taking his first step, he asks her, cautiously, "Princess Eonia, do you think Lord Letch was involved in your kidnapping?"

"You don't know!" Eonia exclaims. *If Barrington doesn't know, then no one knows! No one at all knows that Lord Letch is evil!* Eonia squeals with frustration, "Aaaargh, I don't *think* Lord Letch was involved in kidnapping me, Barrington. I *know* he was!" Eonia rails in anguish. "Lord Letch was the demon who orchestrated it all. Doesn't my father know anything? Doesn't he know that Lord Letch pledged himself to Darkness? Doesn't he understand that it's Lord Letch who had me kidnapped? It's Lord Letch who's been working with King Angus! Lord Letch wants to take over the whole land of Miriam!"

And all this time, Eonia thought that Lord Letch had been found out. Since the Fireflies had first arrived on the Isle of Mires, she thought that Lord Letch had been exposed. She thought he'd be imprisoned by now. But Lord Letch isn't in prison; he's roaming free! He's with her parents in the kingdom!

Still to this day, no one even knows he is responsible for all this! Eonia rocks, hitting Barrington in the back in frustration. "Noooooo!" she cries. Violently, she shakes.

As though waking from a nightmare, still unsure of reality, Eonia hears Barrington say, "We didn't know, Princess Eonia. Are you certain? What do you know that implicates him?"

"Yes, I'm certain!" she howls. She squelches the overwhelming urge to shake Barrington as a means of venting her rage, but instead, she tells him everything.

She tells him how she awoke in the night, hearing Lord Letch's voice outside of her bedroom. She tells him how her captors, disguised as Magi, tore her from her bed and tied her up, binding her arms and her legs. She tells him how they dismissed her pleas and gagged her to stifle her screams. And all the while, Lord Letch stood in the corner of her bedroom, watching. And finally, Eonia tells Barrington what she saw when she and Lord Letch locked eyes that night.

"Lord Letch is dark!" she sobs. "There's no mistaking it. There's no Light left in him. He lives for himself and himself alone. He doesn't care about the destruction he brings. Don't you see? He is *evil*!"

Eonia pictures Lord Letch walking the halls with her father. She imagines him sitting next to her mother. All this time that she's been imprisoned, he's moved freely, biding his time, plotting to kill her parents. Eonia is in agony. Tortured as she is, she would do virtually anything to hide from the ugly reality that Lord Letch is no doubt with her parents now.

Barrington is quiet. He hasn't uttered a simple word since Eonia began rehashing the events from the night she was taken. He has no words of comfort to give, no helpful suggestions to pacify her. What can he offer Eonia now? She's too smart to be calmed by mere platitudes.

Finally, though, having mulled the matter over, Barrington sighs a long sigh and solemnly says, "Princess Eonia, if what you say is actually true, then your parents are, indeed, in grave danger. We must be careful. We must act swiftly when we reach the kingdom.

"If Lord Letch realizes his plan has failed and that you have returned safely to the kingdom, he may become desperate." Barrington pushes up rigidly through his athletic frame. "There's no telling what he might do. We must alert your parents of Lord Letch's culpability without raising red flags for him. And you, Princess"—he catches her eye—"must remain out of sight until Lord Letch is handled."

Eonia aches with frustration and fear. She roars at Barrington, "I thought the Light knew! When I heard the cries from the Fireflies, I thought, 'The Light is here to save me! Lord Letch has been thrown from the kingdom. My parents are safe!' But I was wrong," she screeches, tugging at her hair. "I've been so wrong!

"While I've been suffering under King Angus' hand, Lord Letch has been gallivanting through the kingdom. He's been rubbing elbows with my father. He's been catering to my mother." Flushing red at the thought, Eonia tingles from the tips of her toes to the tip of her nose. "All of the time that I've been here, useless, slave to Angus and his grubby guards, Lord Letch has been free, plotting my parents' murders, planning the Land of Miriam's downfall."

CHAPTER 33

JESSE WALKER

"This is the right place, isn't it?"

"Aye," Drumbell coughs, gripping his injured shoulder, allowing his wounded arm to hang limply.

This is where they'd left Drakendore; Jesse's sure of it. But she's gone. They're all gone. Drakendore is gone; Barrington is gone; Eonia's gone. Drumbell and Jesse are alone on this miserable island. And the Gors are hunting them down.

Drumbell scans the marshland all around them. "Eonia an' Barrington mus' be on their way ta the kingdom."

Jesse sinks to the ground in despair. *I did this. I doomed us. I left us here to die among these awful creatures.* The boy shakes. *What did I think would happen?* He winces, remorseful and surprised by his previous hopes. *I stopped running, so Barrington and Eonia could leave!*

"Isn't there a way out? Isn't there another way for us to get off the island?" Jesse sputters, hoping against hope that Drumbell knows some other way to get back to the mainland without Drakendore's aid.

Drumbell sits down slowly next to the boy, maneuvering his injured body gingerly. The Thwacker studies the ground, dejectedly.

"What about the Gor boats?" Jesse asks, trying to come up with a solution to save themselves, no matter how farfetched it may be.

"Er, I don't know how ta sail, Jesse."

Jesse shakes his head. "Me neither." The boy's panic grows.

He thinks of his dad at home in Eufaula walking around the family's house, discovering that he's missing. He imagines his father as the days pass, realizing that Jesse's never coming home. He pictures his dad alone in his bedroom, staring at his things like parents do in movies when their kids run away or are killed.

"We have to think of something!" Jesse chokes, tasting a chalky taste in his mouth that he's come to correlate with fear. "We must get out of here! I can't die here, Drumbell!"

"Slow down there, Jesse. I'm not a fan of dying 'ere either," Drumbell assures him. "When Barrington an' Eonia reach the mainland, they'll send help fer us. Problem is"—the Thwacker glances sideways—"that the Gors might find us bef—"

A screech sounds! Cracking the silence, it explodes like a siren. Drumbell's eyes widen, and like bells, the screech sounds again.

"It's *them*! The Fireflies are here!" Jesse yelps, jumping up from the ground.

Without a doubt, it's the unmistakable cry of the Firefly warriors.

"I've been given a second chance to live!" the boy squeals, jumping up and down with glee. And in an instant, too, Jesse's pulling Drumbell up beside him, trying to get the Thwacker up and off the ground.

Drumbell stands and groans. "We've gotta get ta the shore," he instructs Jesse. "It'll be easier fer the Fireflies ta see us from the shoreline without all of this brush around us."

Moving as quickly as Drumbell's injury allows, Jesse and Drumbell rush for the western shore of the island. They travel away from the eastern shore, away from where the Gor boats are docked. It's best, they decide, to stay away from the area of the island where the Gor boats were docked, in case other Gors are trying to flee as Angus and his guards had aimed to do.

With all of his might, Jesse drags Drumbell toward the western shore, begging the injured Thwacker to move faster. But Drumbell's so much bigger than he is, and Jesse has trouble in the mud as it is. Struggling, slipping, and falling every few feet, Jesse flashes back to the day his dad had taught him how to ride a bike. Jesse imagines his dad is running next to him now, helping him like he did then, when he had guided the steering wheel and instructed him to look out ahead.

We've got to get to the shore, the boy tells himself doggedly. *We have to get there. We have to find a Firefly to take us away from here.*

Jesse thinks of Maddie, too. He thinks about how much his sister loves her baby dolls and dresses. He thinks of Maddie laughing, jiggling on the ground, her cheeks turning as red as the tomatoes in his grandpa's garden. *Will Maddie be the girl who's lost her mom and her brother all before she turns six?* Jesse frets.

And then he thinks of his mom. Jesse imagines her with him, urging him on, encouraging him to run faster.

There's a picture of Lillian at home in Jesse's living room. In it, she's dressed in white; her mouth is set as though ready to laugh, and her skin is pink. She looks healthy. The picture was taken from before she was sick. When he thinks of his mom, that's the image the boy likes to think of. It's the image of her that he thinks of now. Jesse doesn't know if he remembers his mom from the day the picture was taken; he can never be quite sure. But regardless, although she's kept so much from him, there's some things about his mom the boy knows for a fact.

I know she wants me out of here, he thinks. *I know she doesn't want me to die here. She wants me home with Dad and Maddie . . .* So, he pushes himself harder.

Reaching the shore, dragging Drumbell, he gasps for air. Over the treeline, he sees a Firefly.

"It's Gloria!" Jesse calls out to Drumbell, who's beside him. Gloria is cutting across the southeast end of the island. She's searching. She's looking for something.

Leaving Drumbell, Jesse runs up and down the shoreline, crisscrossing the marshland, trying to get Gloria's attention. "Hey! Look at me! Look at me, Gloria!" The boy is shouting, running back and forth along the water's edge.

Still, the Firefly doesn't see Jesse on the ground. Darting frantically hither and thither, yelling, Jesse tries to catch the dragon's eye. Jesse is so focused on the Firefly, he doesn't notice the shadowy figures in the marsh, congregating.

"Get 'em! Kill 'em! Chop off their heads!" The Gors erupt, chanting in a battle cry. Charging toward Jesse and Drumbell on the shoreline, Gors sprint out from the marshland like a crashing wave, littering the beach, swinging their weaponry.

Even still, the dragon seems not to see him.

The boy plops down in the mud. Closing his eyes, he concentrates with all of his energy, focusing on Gloria flying above him two hundred feet in the air. In his mind, Jesse pictures Gloria with her wings spread out wide above the trees. He sends her his plea. *Gloria, I'm here. Come down. Save us.*

When he opens his eyes again, Gloria is swooping toward him.

"She sees me! She's heard me! She's coming for us!" Jesse booms to Drumbell, who's hobbling up the shoreline toward him, away from the charging Gors.

SWOOSH. Gloria lands. The dragon plants herself between Jesse and Drumbell and the oncoming Gors. The Gors—who moments ago were rushing for Jesse—turn on their heels. Gloria blows a stream of fire out her snozzle, sending a torrent of flames lapping at their ankles. Yipping and yapping, they run as fast as they can back up and into the marshland, trying to get away from the dragon. The brush ignites beneath them as they jump over it, fleeing.

Jesse helps Drumbell onto Gloria. "Oomph, you're so heavy!" he grunts, bracing his slender body up and under the Thwacker's big behind and pushing with all his might.

Thankfully, even though Drumbell's injured, he's still strong. Drumbell pulls himself up onto Gloria as the boy pushes him. Once Drumbell is securely on top of Gloria, Jesse scrambles up and onto the dragon behind Drumbell. Together, they hold on tight as she launches into the air. They speed away from the island and rise into the muggy sky.

Gloria shrieks over and over, sending her cries to the other Fireflies. *I've found him! I've found Jesse! I've found Drumbell. Retreat. Retreat. I've found them. Let's get out of here.*

And Jesse realizes now, *Gloria was looking for us! She was scouring the Isle of Mires for me.* Smiling, with tears in his eyes, he watches the Fireflies fall into formation behind them.

But then, there's only four Fireflies besides Gloria. Firebomb, Sprinter, Barnum, and Breeze are here. He asks Gloria.

Gloria drops her neck and releases a pained squeal. *They're dead,* she replies quietly.

Oh. Jesse sags.

They travel the remainder of the flight in silence.

CHAPTER 34
EONIA

Fear eats at Eonia. Screaming, it's drawing her in. All she sees is red.

"Ahhhhh!" Eonia seethes, flushing with a heat the likes of which she's never known. Her wrath is making her feel as though she's being consumed by flames. Oh, how she wants revenge. The thought of Lord Letch's screams, shrill and suffused with agony, excites her.

She wants to run into the kingdom. She wants to storm the capitol's steps. She wants to scream, "He's a murderous traitor! Lord Letch is a murderous traitor!" She wants to throw open the capitol's doors, grab hold of him, and hear his breath quicken. She wants to see the fear in him before she kills him.

But no. *No!* Instead of rushing to her parents' side, she must sit here, camouflaged among the trees, waiting for night to come. Once night falls, Eonia and

Barrington can continue the rest of the way to the kingdom on Drakendore. Only then, under the veil of darkness, can they approach the capitol building.

Barrington remains motionless, watching Eonia pace back and forth.

"Eonia, I know you're upset," he pleads, "but do you think you could maybe calm down?"

Eonia stops pacing and glares.

"Calm down?" She snickers. "You want me to calm down? I'll calm down once justice is brought down upon Lord Letch's head." Eonia makes a chopping motion. "He's probably with my parents now, Barrington!"

Nearing the kingdom, the sun was still high. Barrington had insisted that the three of them find a clearing in which to land. Here then, in the shadows of the forest, Eonia, Drakendore, and Barrington must hide.

"If we fly before it is dark, everyone will see us soaring on Drakendore," Barrington insists. "I understand your concern for your parents, Eonia; and I am concerned also. But they'd be amongst others now. Lord Letch would not commit any harm to them currently. Unless he knows he's been found out, that is." Barrington widens his eyes at her. "And that is exactly why we must remain here until we can avoid detection."

Eonia looks at Barrington as though she is seeing past him, and she remains silent. *He's right,* she knows, although she will not admit it.

The entire Magi city that surrounds the kingdom would watch Drakendore fly in with Barrington and the princess if they were to fly in now. Word of Princess Eonia's arrival would travel through the city's streets and up the steps to the kingdom, where the capitol is situated, faster than a wildfire. It would make its way up the steps and through the halls of the capitol building quicker than you can count to three.

Barrington is right; they cannot allow themselves to be seen. They need to be careful. Yes, they must be patient. Unfortunately, waiting is doing a number on the poor princess. Somewhere between the Isle of Mires and the woods on the outskirts of the kingdom, Eonia's patience withered and left her. Any patience she once had (which wasn't very much to start with, one might add) is gone. She's none left to give.

"Why did my father trust him in the first place? I don't see why he had to make Lord Letch an advisor. I don't see why he had to practically throw the keys to the kingdom at him." Eonia squints.

Barrington looks away. "I think, Princess, that King Mor initially saw some of himself in Lord Letch. Lord Letch's ambition, the crux of his very downfall it seems, drew your father to him. And your father wanted to give the Magus a chance. Not to mention, it's not as though King Mor has not had reservations about bringing Lord Letch into the fold. Your father has not been oblivious to Lord Letch's flaws." Barrington ventures a glance at the princess.

"King Mor gave Lord Letch the benefit of the doubt simply too much, or so it turns out." Barrington frowns. "All of us strive, though, Princess, to appreciate others' God-given talents as much as our own, but it is a difficult perspective to cultivate. King Mor understood Lord Letch's weakness in this area and tried to work with him to overcome it. King Mor was hoping, I believe, that love and trust would pull Lord Letch out of his ambition, away from his jealous nature."

"Ideally, Princess, you or I can appreciate the gifts and creations of one another to the same extent as if we created them ourselves, but even I occasionally struggle with this. I know I should relish a masterpiece created by another—a concerto, a painting, a magnificent speech or an architectural feat—for what it is—a beautiful creation made by one of God's creatures employing the skills God has blessed him with. It is God's will that makes it so. But it can be challenging to set aside one's own aspirations to appreciate others' accomplishments. King Mor extended grace to Lord Letch to allow him to grow and mature, to feel comfortable in his own skin, presuming Lord Letch would mellow and learn to be happy for others rather than trying to one-up everyone. Unfortunately"—Barrington shakes— "your father misjudged Lord Letch's proclivity. Lord Letch's jealousy won out."

CHAPTER 35

JESSE WALKER

Turrets spiral heavenward, piercing the blue sky like the crests of snow-capped mountains on a clear day.

"The kingdom," Drumbell announces, slumping in front of Jesse, relieved.

As they fly over what appears to be a town, people materialize from their homes below, faces turned upward.

"We mus' be quite the spectacle up 'ere, "Drumbell grumbles. "Five great Fireflies closin' in on the kingdom with a Thwacker and a Magus ridin' 'em."

Jesse studies the people beneath them as Gloria lowers. "Um, who are they?"

"They're Magi like you are, Jesse."

A tingly sensation runs up the boy's spine. "Those are Magi!" he repeats, anxious to meet others like him.

And indeed, the people below do look just like Jesse. He sees no difference at all between the Magi in the town below and the people he knows from home. They look exactly the same as anyone else the boy's ever known.

Traversing the kingdom's gates, Gloria lowers with Jesse and Drumbell while Zena, Barnum, Sprinter, and Breeze remain hovering in the air.

Ahhhhh, Jesse moans, sliding off the dragon's back, thighs aching from the long ride. He grabs hold of Drumbell's hand to help the Thwacker down. Slowly, Drumbell slides off and then tumbles. Jesse tries to catch the falling Thwacker, but they both end up falling instead; and somehow the boy ends up on top of Drumbell.

"Thanks fer the help." Drumbell grabs his shoulder, grimacing.

"Sorry," Jesse pants, rolling off his friend.

"Don't bother apologizin'." Drumbell smiles wryly. "It wouldn't be any fun if I didn't give ya some grief every now and again. In all honesty, I'm jus' happy ta be 'ere, alive." Drumbell snorts as he struggles to stand.

Jesse helps Drumbell up. Then the boy rushes to Gloria, who's readying to leave with the other Fireflies. Jesse wraps himself around the dragon's neck and feels her cool skin against his. *Thank you for saving me. I'll never forget you,* he tells her, surprised how natural he finds telepathy to be. Like mastering another language, it's no longer a strain for him to communicate.

Gloria nudges Jesse's shoulder with her snout. *We will meet again,* she promises. And the dragon ascends to rejoin the waiting Fireflies. Together, the dragons fly from the kingdom, headed home, back to their lair in the Rickenbacker Mountains.

"Gloria told me she'd see me again," Jesse says to Drumbell, confused, as the Fireflies cross the sky, leaving. "What do you think she means?" he asks Drumbell, thinking it a very odd thing for Gloria to have said as her parting words.

"Not a clue." Drumbell shrugs. "Some dragons have foresight. Maybe she knows somethin' we don't."

"Strange that a dragon should have foresight," Jesse answers softly. *But then, isn't it strange to be thinking of dragons at all?* He ponders the situation he's found himself in. So much has changed since he left Eufaula. The world is not as it seemed. There are things he'd never known and never seen. *And I have a place in it. I am worth something. I have meaning.*

Jesse looks out at the kingdom that sprawls before him, marveling at its beauty, feeling as though his heart has grown two sizes since he left home in the night with Barrington. He gazes up from where he stands in the grass at two spiraling staircases. The staircases twist and twirl, rising up from the ground. Then coming together, joining as one, they lead to a large, white building at the top of a sloping hill. On top of the building, domes and turrets extend, soaring up toward the sky above them. The building itself reminds Jesse of an image he had once seen of La Sacré Coeur, a cathedral in France, that his mother had shown him. Only, the building before him now is bigger and ten times more impressive.

"That's the capitol," Drumbell says, gazing up at the building as well. "We'll need ta climb up the stairs ta find the king an' queen. No doubt, they'll be wantin' ta see ya promptly," Drumbell says, still staring up at the building. Then Drumbell shakes his head. "Err, Jesse. I'm not sure, though. That's a lot of stairs ta get up." He raises his eyebrows. "I don't know if I can make it up all those steps. I can hardly walk as it is." He snorts.

"What do ya think? Wud ya consider goin' without me jus' this once?" Drumbell implores, rubbing his shoulder, and looking very much like Jesse's dog when it's begging to be let in.

The thought of climbing up all those steps to an intimidating (and undoubtedly guarded) castle to ask for the king and the queen, by himself, looking like this, doesn't seem to be a good idea at all to Jesse, really. *I'm covered in mud and blood and who-only-knows-what-else,* he thinks of himself, ashamed. As Noni would say, he's not exactly looking presentable at the moment.

"Do I have a choice?" Jesse asks Drumbell.

"Bah. I jus' don't think I can make it, Jesse." Drumbell eyes the boy, feeling a heaping load of guilt. "You'll be fine without me, though," Drumbell says, assuring himself as much as Jesse. "Yer aunt an' uncle'll be thrilled ta see ya. And Princess Eonia an' Barrington shud've arrived by now. They shud be up there already." He points at the capitol. "They'll be expectin' ya.

"I'd luv ta go up ther with ya, Jesse; really, I would." Drumbell wrings his hands in consternation. "But I'm spent. And I'm still bleedin'." He gestures to his shoulder. "I did get stabbed in ma shoulder with a sword not long ago, ya know."

"Okay. Okay." Jesse shrugs, giving in, despite his hesitation.

"One favor while yer up there," Drumbell wheezes. "Have somebody sent down fer me, a'right? I need some bandages, an' I'll need a ride back ta Tanglewood."

"Well, all right." Jesse gulps, not feeling the least bit confident in his ability to accomplish Drumbell's requests.

Stair by stair, the boy starts to climb, wondering how many other Magi climb all of these stairs on a regular basis. *Isn't there a shortcut?* he wonders. Then reaching the three hundredth stair, he turns. "Wow!" he gasps.

The Magi city spreads out before him in the distance. Even in storybooks, he's never come to know of a city as beautiful as this. Trees canopy the alleys. Grassy lulls with colorful homes flank the rolling hills. Brooks crisscross the terrain, carving the city into swaths connected by majestic bridges. It is lovely. Then turning back to the capitol, Jesse continues to climb.

Nearing the building, he sees a red door that is nestled beneath three arches, peeking out from the shadows. It's a huge door, at least five times taller than he is.

It must be the main entrance, Jesse thinks. He takes the steps faster, his heart thudding in his ears. *This is where Mama's from. Magi who loved her live here. I have family in there!* He jumps stair to stair, reveling in possibilities. *Will they look like her? Are they really expecting me?*

The dual staircases wind upwards infinitely, as if suspended in air. Then coming together, they form a wide pathway to the front door. As the boy nears the entrance, he prepares to knock; but before he can, the door flings open. A woman shoots out. Dressed in a velvety gown, she balances a sparkling crown on her head.

"Ummm, Queen Marakee?" Jesse's voice wobbles.

The woman bends toward him, studying him intently. And before another word is said, the woman is hugging him. "Call me Aunt Marakee," the woman coos. Her hands press the boy's forehead, smudging away the dirt so she can kiss his widow's peak. "Jesse, we've been so worried for you," she wails, her ribs trembling against him.

"But where is Eonia?" she asks, releasing him.

"Uh. What do you mean?" the boy croaks, confused. "Eonia should be here."

CHAPTER 36
EONIA

Eonia presses her face to the ground. Smelling the earthy smell of dirt, she groans a primeval, *Errrrg!*

"This is unbearable!" she shouts at Barrington.

All that time languishing in that hut with those decrepit Gors seems like nothing to the princess now compared to the torment she's in. Biding her time in the woods, waiting until the sun is gone, is driving her mad. She feels her will crack and splinter. "Lord Letch lurks the streets of the kingdom free. His heart, riddled with sin, remains hidden. Unhindered, he strides the capitol's halls. He is there. He is with my parents!" Eonia's body jerks haphazardly.

And there, hidden in the woods outside the kingdom, teetering on the edge of sanity, an image of Eonia's mother, Queen Marakee, floats before her.

Lord Letch is by her mother's side. Her mother reclines in the capitol's dining room at ease. Queen Marakee, sipping wine, smiles. She's engaged, talking to someone. The queen's warmth and goodness shine brightly. Then there, nestled in beside Eonia's mother, is Lord Tenebris Letch. His elbow brushes her mother's elbow. His eyes rest on her mother's face. Studying her, Lord Letch clenches his fists, considering how best to dispose of her mother's remains.

As the image of her mother floats before her, anger ripples through Eonia like an earthquake. Seething, Eonia turns to Barrington. "What if Jesse did live?" she asks him. "What if the Fireflies found him? Jesse could be in the kingdom *right now.*" She raises an eyebrow. "Lord Letch may know that I'm alive *right now.* What then, Barrington? What would be the point to all this waiting and hiding in the woods, then?" she huffs at him.

Barrington clears his throat. "I have been considering that possibility, too, Princess." He nods.

"I would think, though, that it would take a while for the Fireflies to find Jesse and Drumbell on the Isle of Mires among all of those Gors." Barrington tilts his head. "Unless, hmmm . . . unless, of course, clever as he is, Jesse managed to catch the Fireflies' attention and call them to him."

Barrington looks up into the trees and squints at the sinking sun.

"Unfortunately, Princess, we both know that's not likely," he says morosely. "You spent time with King Angus. You, of anyone, understand King Angus' nature," he mumbles. "I am afraid, ugh, that you and I both know that it is more likely Jesse and Drumbell fell to King Angus than it is that they've beaten us into the kingdom. It's not likely that they liv . . . "

Barrington's voice trails off. Eonia can't stand to hear him finish his sentence, and he can't stand to finish it. Shrouded in a morbid silence, the three of them—Eonia, Barrington, and Drakendore—wait for darkness to come so that they may continue their advance on the kingdom.

CHAPTER 37

JESSE WALKER

Kingdom, Land of Miriam

Queen Marakee stutters, "E-eonia isn't here, Jesse. We thought she was with you."

A pit in Jesse's stomach starts churning. *What could've happened to them?* he frets. *Eonia and Barrington left long before Drumbell and I did—Gloria told me so. Did they stop somewhere? Was one of them injured? Was there a Kelptar alive that could've followed them as they flew from the Isle of Mires to the kingdom?*

"She was with me," Jesse tells his aunt, noticing the distress in her face as well. "But Princess Eonia should've beaten me here with Barrington. They left the Isle of Mires on Drakendore long before I did."

His aunt opens wide the capitol's red door and motions for Jesse to enter. Her face is white. Her lips tremble. "Let's discuss this inside," she says.

Inside, evening light floods in through stained-glass windows, lighting the capitol's entrance. Above the boy is an enormous arched ceiling. On it, Jesse notes, a battle is painted. In the center of the painting, there is a beast portrayed in a lush forest that's surrounded by trees that are ripe with fruit. The beast, who has three heads, bows. Horns twist and twirl from each of his heads, spiraling toward the ground.

Beyond the beast, there's a fire that is painted. Figures that look to be angels and demons with mouths open as though in a scream reach for the beast through the flames. The beast's outstretched arms reach back toward the tormented beings. The beast seems to be pleading with them—angels and demons alike—to cross over the fire that besieges them and to come to him.

Struck by the beauty and power of the painting, Jesse points to the beast on the ceiling. "What's that meant to be?"

"Life," his aunt answers. "He takes different forms."

Countless questions well up within the boy, gazing up at the painting, unable to tear his eyes from it—questions of life and death, heart and soul, and goodness versus evil. The strangeness of the beast's image strikes a chord with him, and he wants to know more. But before he can ask his aunt what she means or what the image—"Life," as his aunt calls it—signifies, she is leading him hurriedly down a hallway.

They come to a room. Outside of it, through the room's windows, Jesse sees men gathered inside, sitting around a large table. Queen Marakee knocks on the door. The door opens.

"Mor, I need you," his aunt pants.

Sensing the urgency in the queen's voice, the entire room looks at Jesse and his aunt. And a very large man's eyes come to rest on Jesse. Wrestling himself up from his chair, the man grabs his cane.

"Jesse, I'd like for you to meet your uncle, King Mor, the king of Miriam," Jesse's aunt announces. "These are Mor's advisors." The queen motions to the other men.

Jesse's uncle hobbles over to him. He snatches the boy into him. "Ahh, I'm so glad to see you, Jesse!" his uncle belts, squeezing him tightly.

Twisted against the king like a pretzel, the boy peeks out at the boardroom. His uncle's advisors watch him curiously. *They seem friendly. They're all smiling, at least.* Jesse breathes a sigh of relief—all except for one of them, that is. One of them—his eyes like slits, his mouth in a line—doesn't look happy at all, Jesse notices.

Uncle Mor lets go of Jesse. Turning back to the boardroom, the king booms, "Excuse me, Gentle Magi. I believe you've all heard of my nephew, Jesse Walker—Lillian's son.

"I need to meet with Jesse privately." King Mor motions toward the exit. "Rest assured, though, I will brief you on the state of Miriam when I return."

The Magi smile and nod. Spinning Jesse on his heels, Uncle Mor steers the boy out of the boardroom and down a hall, away from the king's men.

"This way," his uncle tells him. "We can talk in the den."

Opening a side door to a private compartment, the king leads Jesse into the room. As soon as the door shuts behind them, Queen Marakee starts ringing her hands again.

"Mor, Jesse doesn't know where Eonia is. He thought she was here."

King Mor does a doubletake at the queen's words, and Jesse squirms. The pit in the boy's stomach aches with dull pain.

"Jesse, why would you think Eonia to be here?" his uncle asks kindly.

The pit in Jesse's stomach expands.

"Umm, well, ya see, Princess Eonia and Barrington left the Isle of Mires before me," Jesse explains. "They . . . uh . . . left on Drakendore before the Fireflies even found Drumbell and me there." He shakes his head. "They should've arrived here already. Umm . . . th-th-they should've gotten to the kingdom a long time before I did," he stammers.

And remembering he's forgotten to tell anyone about Drumbell, Jesse slaps his forehead. "Drumbell! I've forgotten Drumbell! I told him I'd send help for him!" Jesse jumps from the sofa.

"He's hurt," Jesse tells his aunt and uncle. "After Eonia left, Drumbell got hurt. You need to send someone to help him! Please!" he shouts, imploringly. "He couldn't climb up the stairs. He's at the base of the kingdom!" Jesse points in the direction of the winding staircase.

"Not to worry, Jesse. We'll send help for your friend," his uncle answers serenely, patting the boy on the back. Then furrowing his brows, King Mor sighs. "If Eonia is with Drakendore and Barrington as you say, I am sure she is fine. There must be an explanation for their delay," the king offers. "Perhaps Eonia was hungry, and they stopped for some food.

Or maybe after being cooped up for so long, Eonia wanted to stretch."

Jesse sees his uncle's lips are moving, but his words seem muffled as they come out of his mouth. Jesse is having a hard time understanding what the king is saying to him.

There's no doubt Eonia and Barrington should've been here by now, the boy worries, watching his uncle's lips. *Something happened to them. They wouldn't have "stopped to stretch." And if Eonia's not here with Barrington and Drakendore, then where are they?* he considers, his anxiety mounting. *Did they have trouble over the Sea of Sunderway? Was Drakendore unable to finish the flight with them?* He carefully weighs the possibilities.

"Once we know the facts," his uncle is saying, "then we will be in a better position to secure Eonia's safety."

Jesse takes a deep breath. He tries to focus on his aunt and uncle. He tells them everything he can. He tells them about Drakendore's scouting mission and about his journey with Barrington and Drumbell to Rickenbacker River Gorge. He tells them about Malacor, and the swamps, and the Gors. Careful not to say too much about King Angus so as not to upset his aunt further, he describes how they had found Princess Eonia in the hut on the Isle of Mires. He tells them how he, together with Barrington and Drumbell, tracked King Angus and his guards through the swamps to rescue their daughter.

"How did Eonia look?" his aunt asks, her eyes wet.

"Umm . . . "

The boy's got an idea of what his aunt's getting at. She wants to know if Eonia looked worn down. How was her health? Did Darkness break her daughter down? He understands enough to understand where she's coming from. She wants to know if there's a possibility, no matter how small it is, that things can go back to how they were before all of this happened. And Jesse recalls, too, wondering the same question after his mom had left him. *I wondered if life could ever be the same again,* he thinks, recognizing the pain in his aunt's eyes and remembering his own.

Sucking in his breath, Jesse imagines the Isle of Mires when he had first sensed Eonia's presence. He recalls Eonia's purity, rising up and out of the wickedness of the Gor village like church bells ringing on a crisp morning.

Looking his aunt in the eye, he tells her, "Princess Eonia seems strong. But you know your daughter better than I do." He shrugs. "It seems at least, uh, like Eonia's out of the Dark's grasp. Almost like she's impenetrable or something."

Relief floods his aunt's face. Her hands shake.

King Mor says, "I see. Thank you for that, Jesse. And how did Eonia escape with Barrington and Drakendore?" Then his uncle asks more softly, "How did you get split off from them on the Isle of Mires? Why were you and your companion—what was his name?"—King Mor looks at the ceiling trying to remember—"Drumbell, I believe you called him? Why were the two of you left behind, as you say?"

Jesse explains how he ran to Eonia with Drumbell and Barrington. He tells his aunt and uncle how he used Sckabor to untie the princess. He tells them how the four of them—Barrington, Drumbell, Eonia, and Jesse—raced for their lives, scurrying into the marshland, fleeing from the Gors.

"And then I stopped . . . "

His aunt and uncle raise their eyebrows.

"King Angus and his guards were on us. I, uh . . . I had to do something," he tells them, his breath quickening. "Eonia and Barrington ran, while Drumbell stayed with me . . . We hid in the marsh until the first guard came."

King Mor and Queen Marakee's eyes are as wide as saucers.

"Drumbell hit the guards with his arrows, and they, umm . . . they fell," Jesse pants. "King Angus was close behind us, though. He saw the second guard go down. He saw where the arrow came from. King Angus looked around. He saw where Drumbell was hiding. King Angus lunged for Drumbell!" Jesse cries out. "Drumbell shot him in the shoulder, but King Angus pulled the arrow out and . . . uh . . . he went for him . . . Then, everything went black," the boy chokes. "I don't remember . . . umm . . . I must've stopped King Angus. I-I stabbed him . . . at least, Drumbell said that I did," the boy sobs, his heart bursting. "I didn't mean to kill him!" The boy wails in abject shame.

Queen Marakee rushes to him. Gathering Jesse in her arms, she cradles him. "Jesse, my dear, dear Jesse. You didn't have a choice." The queen smooths his hair as she comforts him. "You saved Eonia. You saved Barrington. It was self-defense, my sweet nephew. If you hadn't done what you did, they would all be dead." She rocks him, reminding him of his own mother. "If you hadn't done what you did, dear boy, *you* wouldn't be here!"

Jesse pictures King Angus on the ground, covered in blood. "It all happened so fast," he mutters. And even now, telling his story to his aunt and uncle, it doesn't feel like he lived it. It feels as though he's telling someone else's tale.

King Mor leans in. He presses his fingertips together. Gently, his uncle asks him, "What makes you certain that Eonia and Barrington managed to get off of the island, Jesse?"

"I *know* they did!" Jesse jerks, his voice cracking. "After King Angus found us, Drumbell and I walked a long while not knowing what to do. We tried to find everyone, but they . . . umm . . . they were gone." He closes his eyes, trying to block out the horror he had felt. "Then, we heard the cries of the Fireflies. We ran to the shore to call them. That's how we're here now," he tells the king and queen. "A Firefly found us and flew us to the kingdom. The Firefly—Gloria is her name"—he chews his lip—"told me that Barrington and Eonia had found the other Fireflies. She told me that they had left on Drakendore. She told me that they were all safe." He scrunches his face. "Don't you see?" he yelps. "Princess Eonia and Barrington should've been here already, long before I made it."

King Mor grabs his cane, standing. "I need to brief Parliament on all that's happened," he says, resolutely. "Night is falling. We need to dispatch a search crew for Eonia immediately. And I'll send help to your friend, Drumbell. You say he's at the bottom of the staircase to the capitol? The main steps to the kingdom?"

Jesse nods, and King Mor grabs the boy's shoulder. The king's voice shakes with emotion. "All of Miriam is indebted to you, son," he declares. "You're Lillian's eldest child. We've always known you were special," he says. "But never could I have expected you to be as strong as all this."

King Mor opens the door to the private room and walks out.

CHAPTER 38

EONIA

Kingdom, Land of Miriam

Finally, nightfall is upon the kingdom. The sun is low behind the trees, and the dusty hue of sunset hangs in the air, lighting the Land of Miriam. Finally, the time has come that the waiting trio—Eonia, Barrington, and Drakendore—may leave.

Motioning to the sky, Eonia scrunches her nose. "It's time, Barrington. It can't be completely dark before we get out of here. Drakendore still needs some light to fly," she directs. "We need to go." She clenches her hands into fists so tight that her nails nearly puncture her skin.

Barrington nods his head but instead of getting up, he says, "Just a little while longer, Princess."

Eonia moans and sits, dropping her head between her knees. "Fine," she groans.

Barrington nods but says nothing more.

"Mother, my mother," Eonia mutters to herself over and over, rising from the ground and pacing back and forth once again, like a caged animal.

The entire time they have been here, hiding in the trees outside of the kingdom, this has been the plight of the trio. Barrington has been patient and calm, while Eonia paces angrily. She cannot sit still. Barrington is the "voice of reason," as he tells her. And there's no doubt that Eonia is the "voice of emotion," as Barrington also tells her.

Eonia doesn't care. *What is reason? What is emotion?* She stopped caring about any of it when she and Barrington left Jesse standing there. She stopped caring about *reason* when she learned that Lord Letch is still in the kingdom.

Sanity, though, is a temperamental thing. Eonia, tortured as she is, has spent the time waiting in the woods oscillating between thoughts of her parents to thoughts of killing Lord Letch. One moment, she's ripping out Lord Letch's heart; and then in the next moment, she's imagining her parents dead. In her sorrow, she switches back from a feeling of hopelessness to once again feeling emboldened to take on Lord Letch herself.

In a word, she is confused. Poor Eonia is miserable. She's wallowing in her pain, indulging herself in her anguish. And there's no doubt the uncertainty over her parents' fate is making things worse for her. Helplessly useless, stuck here in the woods, she's cycling through scenarios, living in a fantasy. Many fall prey to it at some point or another. While still harnessing the energy and vigor so indicative of the young, it is not uncommon for one to also be hindered by a psyche that is still quite fragile. Indeed, many, perhaps even the majority of individuals, spend more time living in the land of what could happen than they care to admit.

And it's no help at all for the poor girl's imagination that in just a few short days she has witnessed enough misery to last her a lifetime. Up until the moment she was taken from her bedroom the night she was kidnapped, Eonia had lived a charmed life, sheltered from sinister thoughts and souls. She was innocent; and she is innocent no more. It happens to everyone at some point, doesn't it—the fall from innocence? It doesn't make Eonia any less noble than she was before. She didn't fall from grace; her blinders are just no more. Indeed, one might argue it makes her more noble. Rare is the flower that can bloom in adversity. And Eonia's a fighter through and through.

"Come on!" Eonia kicks Barrington to get up.

Barrington looks at Eonia. "All right, Princess. Let's go."

CHAPTER 39

JESSE WALKER

Alone in the meeting room, Queen Marakee observes Jesse.

She's got the same expression Maddie had when she found that dog on Lake Road that had been hit, Jesse notes of his aunt's expression.

"You're a mess, Jesse," Queen Marakee finally declares, rubbing Jesse's arm, flaking off a dollop of hardened, cracked mud. Having long since dried since he had rolled in it in the Mires, the mud bounces off the boy like a rock off a mountain. "I know you were in the swamps," his aunt says to him, "but how did you get so unbelievably dirty?"

Thinking of Drumbell and Barrington on the Isle of Mires with the sludge dripping from their elbows, Jesse nearly smiles. "Er, we rolled in the mud to camouflage ourselves," he says, still not believing his plan worked. "We walked through the whole Gor village without being noticed," he tells her, unable to hold back his delight at having come up with such a useful plan. "I, umm . . . I don't think we would've survived without it. The Gors would've known we weren't one of them." He looks at his feet.

Crinkling her nose, Queen Marakee coos, "That was certainly ingenious, I'll grant. But mightn't it be time to wash it off?" She pats his knee, creating another small avalanche off his body. "You're in the kingdom now, Jesse," her voice rings. "You're safe. You don't need mud on you anymore. Besides, I want to see your handsome face.

"I'll show you to a room so you can have some time to bathe," she says, rising. "We'll be having supper soon. And I don't want the dirt falling off you and onto your plate," she quips, the corners of her mouth turning upward. "How does that sound? Are you ready to wash off all that grime?"

Aunt Marakee pulls Jesse up and off the sofa from where he was sitting. Everywhere that he's touched, clumps of dirt remain—on the sofa, by the door, on the floor.

"I'm so sorry." Jesse coughs, bending down to wipe a clump of dirt off the sofa from where he was sitting. "I didn't mean to make such a mess."

But more dirt keeps dropping from him, even as he tries wiping the sofa clean, making it dirtier than it was before he started trying to clean it.

"Never you mind," Aunt Marakee says sweetly. And taking hold of the boy's elbow, she leads him out through the doorway.

Jesse notices his aunt's steadiness. Her steps firm, she leads him with a graceful speed down a long hall and through the capitol. It occurs to Jesse that the queen is not as fragile as she first seemed when she had greeted him at the capitol's front door. *There is a grit to her,* he observes, thinking, too, of Eonia and how formidable she had seemed when he first came upon her on the Isle of Mires. *Like mother, like daughter,* he surmises, following his aunt down a hall that dead ends into a table and chairs.

On top of the table, there is a leaflet. Queen Marakee places her palm in the center of the bound parchment, and a door that Jesse hadn't noticed before slides open.

Queen Marakee guides Jesse through the door into a narrow corridor. "Before she went to the other world," his aunt tells him, "your mother lived here. She always loved the light in the West Wing." She smiles and lightly brushes Jesse's arm. "Even when she came to visit us, she preferred to stay here, rather than in the remodeled rooms."

Walking through the corridor, Jesse stays close to his aunt. Torches on the walls cast a flickering glow along the otherwise dark hallway as he follows. The walls seem to be closing in on him, like the jaws of an animal clamping down, trapping him in its belly.

There's no way Mama would've "loved the light" here. Jesse furrows his brows. *This place looks like a dungeon, like a medieval castle where cloaked men with dark hoods lead prisoners to be tortured.*

Counting the doors—*one, two, three, four*— Jesse and his aunt come to an orange door with an engraving of a tree. Queen Marakee places her hand on a panel to the right of the door's handle. Jesse hears the deadbolt slide open.

"Your mother was particularly fond of this room, if I remember correctly." The queen says warmly, as the door creaks open by itself.

In contrast to the dark hall, the room in front of Jesse glistens. Orange light from the late afternoon sun streams in through a wall of windows. The afternoon sun dances off chandeliers that are hung from the ceiling. Stunned, breathless at the sight of it, Jesse remains at the entrance, gaping.

"Let me show you where everything is," Aunt Marakee chirps, looking past Jesse's bewilderment. "Soap and towels are in the bathroom. Fresh sheets are on the bed." She looks Jesse up and down. "I'll have clean clothes brought in for you while you rest."

Turning to leave, she asks him, "Are you sure you're all right, Jesse? Do you have everything you need?"

Jesse nods, grateful for the opportunity to be left alone for a while to think on things.

"Get some rest then. I'll come back for you when supper is ready." His aunt clucks. And she leaves, shutting the door behind her.

Alone in the room, Jesse turns, mesmerized by the vibrant warmth of light streaming in from the windows. And there in the center of the room against a wall is the most inviting bed the boy has ever seen. Like puffy clouds, fluffed pillows sit at the head of the bed, beckoning to him. A thick duvet covers the cushy mattress end to end.

How wonderful it would be to take a nap, he thinks, alone in the empty room. He's exhausted. Since he left Eufaula with Barrington, he's hardly had time to breathe. *But first things first,* the boy thinks, wiping another blob of dried mud off his leg. *I can't crawl into clean sheets like this. I'm dirtier than a pig in a pigpen.* He chortles, borrowing one of Noni's preferred phrases.

Jesse wrestles out of his armor. Dropping it to the floor, he watches the dirt scatter. With his feet, he sweeps the dried mud into a pile, trying his best to keep it contained. Then he heads for the bathroom.

There's no shower in the bathroom, but there's a tub made of stone unlike any he's ever seen. The tub is dark and shiny; and most surprisingly, there's already water in the tub's basin. It's nearly filled to the brim. Thinking it unlikely that the tub should already be filled with warm water for him, Jesse tests the water. Dipping in the tips of his fingers, he expects the water to be cold—or, at the very best, room temperature. *But no, it's hot!* He laughs inwardly and shakes droplets off his finger.

Jesse climbs in. Allowing the water to close in over his head, he thinks of his mother. *She's been here.* Jesse is strangely comforted by this reality. *She grew up in this strange land. She's been in this room.* And he thinks of his home. *What would Dad think of all this?* He can't imagine his dad's reaction to all of this. *I met Mama's brother today . . . I met my aunt. There's a whole world here I never knew about. Why did Mama keep so much from us?*

Like a refrain from a repetitive song, the same questions that have been bothering Jesse since he left home are confronting the boy yet again. But the questions don't sting as much as they have before. He remembers his mother's words from the letter: "Understand how much I love you . . . I shouldn't have shielded you as I have, but I wanted you to have a childhood, a true childhood where you could discover things on your own time and in your own way."

Safe and warm, he is at peace. *I'm so comfortable,* he thinks. *Bed.* The word sounds wonderful in his head. He closes his eyes. A blurry haziness begins to take hold of him.

"Urgh!" he gurgles, bolting upright in the water, having nearly nodded off. Quickly, he finishes washing. He steps out of the tub. Drying himself, he rubs his legs with a towel and flinches. "Ow!" He yelps at the tiny cuts on his shins, crisscrossing his skin like folds in paper mâché. "It's from those blasted bushes in the swampland," he grumbles. He remembers his legs burning as he ran. He remembers the palm fronds scraping against him.

And on top of his lacerations, the boy realizes he doesn't have any clothes to change into. "I'm not putting that crusty armor back on." He bristles, spying his armor on the floor. *Worry about it later,* he tells himself, dragging himself to the bed, too tired to bother with anything further. He pulls the covers back, slides under the sheets, and nestles in.

CHAPTER 40

EONIA

A few thin clouds, like cotton balls pulled by their ends, form whiffs across the sky, reflecting the last embers of the sun's golden glow as Eonia, Barrington, and Drakendore fly in. It's not too late really—only a little after the dinner hour. There's still activity in the Magi city. Eonia sees movement along the cobbled streets, and lights in the houses below flicker on. The darkening sky hides the trio as they approach—at least, that's their hope.

Someone might see a shadow passing by. A boy playing ball outside with a friend before he washes for bed might see the alicorn's shape with two riders on it, soaring. But he shouldn't be able to see *who* are riding on top of Drakendore.

Getting closer, Eonia feels the loosening of the knot that's been in her stomach since the night she was taken. *Is there any comfort for Jesse, though?* Eonia sags, wondering where the boy is. Unlikely as it may be that her cousin escaped from the Isle of Mires alive, he doesn't seem dead to her. Indeed, while she was grounded in the trees waiting for night to fall, her certainty grew. She feels him. *Jesse is alive in the Land of Miriam somewhere.* Eonia would nearly stake her life on it.

Assuming that Jesse is alive, she wonders, *is he still stuck on the Isle of Mires fending for his life with Drumbell? Or is he in the kingdom?* She purses her lips in concern, unable to stop the cascade of worry overwhelming her. *Did the Fireflies find him and save him? Is he already in the capitol?* She considers this hopeful option, wishing it to be true. *And if he's already in the capitol, then surely Lord Letch knows that I escaped King Angus and am free. If Lord Letch knows I am alive, then he must know I am coming for him. Regardless of whether we're seen flying now or not, Lord Letch knows he must do something. And he knows he best do it quickly. Yes, I am coming.* She takes a breath in.

After all of her time on the Isle of Mires with King Angus and the Gors and the Kelptars, Eonia can't help but feel a sense of peace settling in on her as she approaches the kingdom. Seeing the capitol spiraling up toward the heavens, she's nearly home, back to the only place she'd ever known before she was kidnapped and taken to the Isle of Mires a few days ago. She's nearly back to the very home that, just this morning, the princess wasn't certain she would ever see. She finds herself so close to it now that she smiles—while the capitol's inhabitants remain on the ground, living life as they normally would.

Dishes are being washed, floors mopped, tables wiped, beds untucked, nightlights lit, teeth brushed, shutters closed. A child asks for another cup of water. A mother kisses a forehead. All appears placidly calm to Eonia from where she sits. The familiarity of the scene cools her skin like a summer's breeze.

It's not Eonia who's stressed anymore—it's the rest of the ruling class of Magi who now feel the burden. *Where is Eonia? Where is Barrington,* they wonder. And, oh, how the tables have turned—it is not Eonia, but rather, Lord Letch who now feels the weight of the world on his shoulders. It is Lord Letch whose heart races as his blood pumps with adrenaline.

Lord Letch knows all too well what is happening and is worried beyond belief. Lord Letch, lounging beside Eonia's bed the night she was taken, did not suspect the princess would *ever* return to the kingdom. "And now s-s-she's due back any minute." He curses beneath his breath.

When Lord Letch had ordered the Gors to abscond to the Isle of Mires with the princess, he had not thought through a contingency plan should the princess return to the capitol. Eonia obviously knows he is evil. *Does Lillian's son know, too?* the dark lord wonders. *Would Eonia have had the opportunity to alert the boy to my involvement?* His eyes nearly roll out of his head at the thought of the mess he is in. The lord strains to keep his face placid; and as he does, his right lip droops, and the vein on his forehead bulges.

"Unlikely," he mutters to himself, relaxing slightly. *If Eonia had told Lillian's son of my involvement, he would have told the king and the queen already; and I would not be sitting here right now,* he determines.

In as nonchalant a manner as he can manage, Lord Letch crosses his arms across his lap and glances sideways, peering out from where he sits to the hallway where the king confers with his armed guards. "Indeed, where is-s-s Eonia?" Lord Letch snarls, repeating the phrase that is echoing up and down the capitol's corridors. *And how much time do I have before they find her?* he wonders, assessing how quickly he must take action toward the crown.

By what means must I kill the king and the queen and recapture Eonia?

Lord Letch scans the hallway for the boy. *And where did they take the boy?*

Having finished giving orders, the king departs. Lord Letch stands and follows.

CHAPTER 41

JESSE WALKER

Kingdom, Land of Miriam

Knock. Knock. Knock.

Jesse jumps with a start. "Didn't I just fall asleep?" he groans.

Knock. Knock. Knock.

"Uh . . . hello?" Jesse calls out to the empty room, answering the knocking.

"Jesse, it's Lord Whissiper," a voice from the other side of the door says. "Queen Marakee sent me." Jesse jumps from the bed. "She, uh . . . she requested that I take you to dinner. I'm excited to meet you, Jesse. I knew your mother well." Jesse dives for the towel on the ground to cover himself. "Were you sleeping? Can I come in?"

"Er, just a minute," Jesse shouts. On a dresser by the door, he notices a fresh change of clothes. Frantic, he lunges for them. And wondering how they got there—in his room while he was asleep—he fumbles, dressing. The pants and the shirt, woven in an elaborate gold and blue pattern, feel like silk.

This is different. Jesse wouldn't be caught dead wearing these clothes at home, but somehow, they feel right in Miriam. "I look like an avatar," he mumbles to himself half-joking. Dressed, Jesse flings open the door. He finds himself face to face with a rosy-cheeked Magi, beaming at him like it's Christmas morning.

What did he say his name was? Jesse tries to remember, blinking away the grogginess of sleep. Then smirking, he recalls, *It was Lord Whissiper. Everyone here seems to be a lord or a king.*

"Hi, I was ju—" Jesse starts to say to the rosy-cheeked little man. But mid-sentence, Lord Whissiper grabs the boy and pulls him in toward him. Before Jesse knows it, he's pressed up against Lord Whissiper's squashy belly, recoiling yet again in frustration over what little regard there is for personal space in the Land of Miriam. And it reminds Jesse—locked in Whissiper's arms as he is, squashed up against Whissiper's ample stomach—of Drumbell the first time Jesse had met him in Tanglewood.

Lord Whissiper lets Jesse go and wheezes, "It's good to meet you, Jesse. King Mor, Queen Marakee, and much of Parliament await you for dinner. We should make our way to the Great Hall as soon as you are ready."

"Is Eonia here yet?" Jesse asks, flustered and red from Lord Whissiper's sudden intrusion. "Also, did my uncle find Drumbell, the Thwacker who brought me here? I'd asked King Mor to send help for him."

"Unfortunately, no, on both counts." The lord sniffles. "I'm not familiar with your Thwacker friend, Jesse, and I understand he hasn't been found yet. But I can tell you that I heard the king checking on the status of the search for him moments before I came up here to get you.

"As for Eonia, a crew is now out searching for her as well. After the king met with you, he briefed his advisors, including me, on all that has happened and the princess' status. It shouldn't be long before we find her." Whissiper's belly jiggles as he rocks back and forth. "Until then, there is nothing we can do but wait, I'm afraid. May we go? Are you ready?" Whissiper asks, pointing Jesse out the door.

Jesse follows Lord Whissiper down the same corridor he had traveled down earlier with Queen Marakee. The torches lighting the hallway cast moving shadows as he and Lord Whissiper walk. At the end of the corridor, Lord Whissiper presses a button. Once again, the door slides open, revealing the main halls of the capitol. The door closes behind Jesse.

From out of the corner of his eye, the boy sees a flash of fur.

Lord Whissiper frowns. "Oh, don't mind him," Whissiper assures Jesse of the animal skulking toward them. The animal—tall and lanky and looking rather like a cross between a red panda and a cat—is wrapping around Jesse's legs, emitting a deep, intermittent grumble that Jesse can only guess is akin to a purr.

Whissiper picks up the kavat and gently tosses him out of the boy's way. "How was your nap?" Whissiper asks him.

"It was good." Jesse shrugs in reply to Whissiper. "Umm, what is it?" Jesse asks Whissiper of the animal that's already back at his feet once again, smoothing its fur against his legs, emitting the haphazard grumble that reminds Jesse of a lawnmower choking.

"A kavat," Whissiper says with disdain. "It's Thomas. He's a pet—although, he's become more of a pest these days, if you ask me." And before Thomas the kavat can react, distracted as he is trying to get the boy's attention, Whissiper swings his bulbous leg and boots the kavat across the kavat's behind. The animal screeches and skulks away, catching Jesse's eye as he goes.

That bulbous, out-of-shape ninny kicked *me. I never liked him, I tell you! He makes that smacking sound when he eats. He slurps when he drinks his tea. He's always smiling about nothing, shaking his portly body. He is so monstrously annoying.* Jesse hears the kavat's thoughts as he leaves.

"Thomas lives here in the capitol," Whissiper explains with a wave of his swollen pink hand. "When he's not out causing trouble in the fields."

"Ah," Jesse mumbles, embarrassed at having heard the kavat's disparaging remarks about Whissiper. Jesse's eyes dart toward the ball of fur departing— but only for a moment before he refocuses his attention on Whissiper.

Then they're moving fast down the stairs away from Thomas the kavat and toward the hum of voices below.

"Lord Whissiper, when Queen Marakee led me to the room before you came to get me," the boy tells Whissiper as they near the bottom of the staircase, "there was a tub full of hot water. And then, just now, there were these clothes left out for me," he says, pulling at the clothes Queen Marakee sent. "Do you know how they got there? Who put them in the room?"

"I presume Queen Marakee had a worker draw a bath and deliver the clothes for you," Lord Whissiper answers. "They fit you quite well." He chortles.

"Yes." Jesse nods. And on Whissiper's wobbly heels, Jesse walks into a truly magnificent room. "Wow!" The boy marvels at the opulence of the room that's before him.

"The Great Hall, as the name suggests," Lord Whissiper bellows, swinging his zaftig arm, "is the largest and grandest room in the capitol. Murals from the Land of Miriam's most famous artists— long since dead—blanket the walls." Whissiper turns up his nose. "Chandeliers, each weighing five hundred pounds, illuminate the room. It is a great hall, indeed." He winks mischievously.

As Jesse enters the Great Hall, everyone, including Queen Marakee and King Mor at the front of the room, stop talking. Jesse feels the eyes upon him. His neck is hot, and his cheeks are burning. Suddenly, a thunderous applause erupts. Jesse fights the overwhelming impulse to run. *Why are they clapping?* Everyone is looking at him, applauding, and he wishes for nothing more than to sink through the floor. *I haven't done anything!*

King Mor cuts through the crowd. Grabbing Jesse's arm, he holds it up in the air and proclaims, "To my nephew, Jesse Walker. Three cheers for Lillian's son!"

The room explodes, cheering. "Hip hip hooray! Hip hip hooray! Hip hip hooray!"

King Mor guides Jesse through the sea of Magi. Swarming him, they smother the boy with their well-wishes. The king leads Jesse to a table at the front of the room where Queen Marakee is conversing with King Mor's advisor from earlier, the one who had scowled at Jesse in the boardroom. As Jesse nears them, the queen and the lord smile at him.

"Jesse, allow me to introduce you to Lord Letch," the queen says.

The boy sits down between his aunt and uncle, nearly missing the chair as he sits. "B-b-but where is Eonia?" Jesse stammers, not understanding why the Magi are having a lavish banquet while Eonia is still missing.

"We will find her, Jesse," King Mor assures him. "This banquet always takes place on the twentieth evening of the month. I couldn't call it off if I wanted to. And on this particular occasion, we have the honor of celebrating you."

Regardless of his words, Jesse sees his uncle's worry. *His eyes are even redder than before, when we'd met in the room with Aunt Marakee. And his mouth is twitching,* Jesse notes of the king.

The band begins to play as the servants stream in, carrying trays of food.

A waiter places a plate down in front of Jesse. The boy's hunger explodes. Vegetables, sweet from the Land of Miriam's brilliant sun, are velvety on his tongue. Meat that Jesse is told is kooboo is rich and tender. Porridge that tastes like grits dissolves as he eats it.

Throughout the dinner, Magi stop by Jesse's table. They tell him stories and ask him about his dad and Maddie. Even Lord Letch, seated next to Queen Marakee, seems to be friendly. *I was wrong about him,* Jesse decides, watching Lord Letch at the banquet. *He doesn't seem to dislike me. He seems nice enough.*

Lord Whissiper, dunderheaded and plied with food and drink, asks Jesse a million questions about his home, most of which the boy can't answer. "What is school like? How do people fly in your world without alicorns? What do young people do for fun?" Whissiper inquires incessantly like a frustrating child.

Eventually, though, Queen Marakee interrupts Lord Whissiper. "You've been through enough today, Jesse," the queen tells him. "You need time to rest. Are you ready for bed?" she asks, standing.

Jesse doesn't want to leave the gathering. He loves being in the Great Hall with the Magi (some of whom are his relatives, being kin to the throne as he is). But he's exhausted. And he's tired of being at the center of attention. "Is it rude if I . . . if I leave the party?" Jesse searches his aunt's face for an answer, then glances around the room. He's torn between wanting to stay—*needing* to stay, even—and exhaustion creeping in.

"Oh yes, more than acceptable! I will walk you to your room myself," Queen Marakee chirps, taking Jesse's hand. But, as if summoned, Lord Whissiper jumps up.

"No need, Queen Marakee! I'd be honored to show Jesse back to his room," Whissiper blubbers.

"Very well. But go easy on my nephew with your questions, Lord Whissiper," Queen Marakee insists. "He is tired."

Jesse says goodnight to the other Magi at his table. They stand to say goodbye to him with handshakes and smiles.

Then, *BAM!*

There it is again! Jesse startles, recoiling. Lord Letch's eyes flash, narrowing in on Jesse.

In an instant, it's gone. Lord Letch's eyes soften. The lord moves toward Jesse, extending his hand. But the rage that Jesse glimpsed in his uncle's advisor has already made its impression on him. Stumbling backward, Jesse tries to get away. But Lord Letch catches his arm. The lord's hand is hot on Jesse's skin. Like steam rising from bathwater, anger seems to be seeping from Lord Letch like slime from a slug.

Aunt Marakee pulls the boy toward her. "Jesse, you're so worn down that you're nearly falling over," she says softly. "If you're going to take him, Lord Whissiper, you'd better take him now. Jesse has put in too long of a day."

Shaken, Jesse follows Lord Whissiper out of the Great Hall. Glancing back, Jesse sees Lord Letch stand. Smiling, Lord Letch takes the queen's hand.

"Excuse me, is there a washroom nearby?" Jesse asks Whissiper as they exit.

"Of course. Did you have too much to eat?" Whissiper asks, noting the boy's pallor. "It takes a little time to let a meal like that digest." Whissiper grins and rubs his portly belly. He leads Jesse to a washroom off the corridor outside the Great Hall and stands guard, waiting for Jesse to return.

Inside the washroom, Jesse scrubs his trembling hands. Candlelight flickers off crystal, making the walls appear alive with movement. "I look like a ghost," Jesse mumbles to himself, catching sight of his reflection. "Aunt Marakee was right. I need sleep."

Jesse dries his hands on his pantlegs and rejoins Whissiper in the hallway. He follows Whissiper through the capitol and up the stairs to the capitol's West Wing. As they approach the top of the stairs, Thomas, the same creature who had accosted Whissiper and Jesse before, emerges from the shadows.

It's that animal again, Jesse notes. *The cat . . . or kavat . . . or whatever Lord Whissiper called it. Was it waiting there for us?*

Thomas plants himself at the top of the stairs, blocking Jesse and Whissiper's path. The boy looks up at him, surprised. Thomas locks eyes on his. And in an instant, Jesse knows everything.

Eonia's kidnapping flashes before him. Jesse sees two figures pulling Eonia from her bed. Thrashing, the princess is kicking, wrestling to get away. Then she's screaming, "Help! Help me!" And her captors are tying her up. Eonia's begging, "I can ask my father to forgive you. You don't have to do this! Don't do this!" Now they're gagging her.

And in the corner of the room, there is a figure sitting, snickering.

"It's Lord Letch!" Jesse yelps. He's recognized the king's advisor, the very same lord he was sitting next to at the banquet mere moments before. Jesse careens, understanding.

"Go away, Thomas." Lord Whissiper swings his arm, shooing the kavat. Holding his ground, Thomas keeps his eyes trained on Jesse. He wants to be doubly sure the boy understands what he is telling him.

Lord Whissiper reaches down and picks up the kavat. Thomas scratches and hisses and rips at his flesh. *Down.* Whissiper throws Thomas out of the way, rubbing his bleeding arm where Thomas clawed him.

"I don't know what's gotten into him," Lord Whissiper mutters as he shakes his fat fists. "Ever since the night Princess Eonia was taken, that kavat's been out of sorts, crying, whining outside of the king and the queen's chambers all hours of the night."

With heavy legs, Jesse plods up the final two steps. Reaching the landing, he tries to catch his breath and recover from what Thomas has just shown him. He's trying to make sense of it. "How's he here in the capitol?" Jesse asks Whissiper of Thomas, panting.

"Thomas is Eonia's pet kavat," Lord Whissiper huffs. "The king and the queen won't let us kick him out of the kingdom for good, although several of us have tried from time to time. He makes me nervous always showing up in the shadows. It feels as though he's drilling holes into your brain with those yellow eyes of his." Whissiper squints. "Now that you mention it, I think he might've been your mother's pet at one time, Jesse. Or perhaps I am mistaken." Whissiper rubs his head, trying to recall the affiliation from so many years ago.

Jesse stops. *Thomas is Eonia's pet!* The boy reels, confused again by the mention of his mother. *The kavat must've been in the room the night Eonia was taken. He saw the whole kidnapping! He replayed his memory.* The boy is starting to understand.

Reemerging, avoiding Whissiper's grasp, the kavat circles Jesse's legs, rubbing up against him.

He's been trying to tell everyone what happened. But he can't! He can't speak! Somehow, though, he knew I would be able to understand him.

Thomas licks Jesse's torn skin.

He figured out that he can communicate with me. I'm the only one who knows what's happened! I'm the only one who knows that Lord Letch is evil!

The boy grabs Lord Whissiper's arm. "It's Lord Letch!" Jesse says hurriedly.

Lord Whissiper scrunches his fat face. "What's Lord Letch?"

"It's him! It's him! Lord Letch had Eonia kidnapped! Lord Letch is to blame!" the boy blurts frantically, shaking like a leaf.

"Slow down, Jesse. What're you talking about?"

"The cat—whatever you call it—told me! He's Eonia's pet. *He saw the kidnapping!*"

And for the first time tonight, Lord Whissiper isn't smiling. His face is gray and ashen. "We have to get to the king and the queen," Whissiper whispers.

CHAPTER 42

EONIA

In twilight's glow, Drakendore lowers down with Eonia and Barrington a fair distance away from the staircase that leads to the capitol's main entrance.

"Stay here out of sight until we know it's safe to come up," Barrington tells Eonia, helping her dismount. "We can't risk Lord Letch catching sight of you."

Eonia starts to protest, "I want to hel—" But hearing a rustling in the bushes, she stops and raises her fists.

Leaves sway. "Oh, it's the two of ya!" a familiar voice says. And in the dim light, out pops Drumbell from the bushes.

"*Drumbell?* Drumbell! You're alive! You're here!" Barrington exclaims joyfully. He catapults off Drakendore and runs to Drumbell, bowling the Thwacker over.

369

"Yes, it is I—the one an' only Drumbell." Drumbell winces, having twisted his wounded shoulder in the tussle. "Jesse's already in the capitol. He said he'd send somebody down for me, but I've started ta think the lil' boggart forgot."

"Are you all right?" Barrington asks, studying Drumbell's bloody shoulder. He prods the wound with his finger, inspecting it.

"Aye!" Drumbell yelps. "Yes, I'm a'right. But that doesn't mean I need ta have ya going around an' pokin' at me."

"You must have that tended to." Barrington scowls.

"No kiddin'? Thanks fer the insight." Drumbell rolls his eyes, shaking his head at the obviousness of his friend's suggestion.

"Listen," Barrington says, brushing away Drumbell's sarcasm, "Princess Eonia is going to stay here while I brief the king and the queen on the status of things. Can you stay with her? Can you ensure that she stays out of trouble? It's important she remains unseen. As soon as I can, I will send someone down for the both of you."

"More waitin'," Drumbell grumbles.

"That's how I feel," the princess chimes in.

"A'right, very well. But be quick about it, Barrington. It's gettin' dark," Drumbell interjects, looking the princess up and down and noting her impatience.

And with that, Barrington climbs onto Drakendore and trots off.

Drumbell insists that Eonia hide with him in some trees to remain out of sight for the time being. As they wait, Drumbell recounts how he and Jesse escaped from the Isle of Mires. In turn, Eonia explains to Drumbell how Lord Letch had her kidnapped. Eventually, though, Eonia and Drumbell fall into silence, each retreating into his and her own thoughts until Eonia can't contain herself any longer.

"I'm not waiting anymore."

"What?" Drumbell cries out. "I'm not in the business of tellin' princesses what ta do. But, Princess Eonia, ya heard Barrington. He said you're ta stay 'ere, hidden in the brush ta remain unseen."

Eonia shakes her head. "I was imprisoned for days on the Isle of Mires unable to do anything. I hid in the woods outside of the kingdom for hours with Barrington. And now, at the base of the capitol's steps, here I am waiting again. You'll have to forgive me, Drumbell, but I'm not waiting any longer. Don't worry, I will send someone for you." With that, she runs off.

Drumbell mutters to himself, slumping to a seat, "Everybody keeps tellin' me they'll send somebody fer me." He sighs, glancing at his shoulder. "Argh!" He huffs. "I guess I've gotta go after her then." He picks up his war-torn body and staggers off after the princess in the direction of the capitol's stairs.

By the time Drumbell reaches the base of the main stairs leading into the kingdom and begins to climb them, Eonia's already halfway up. Two by two, she leaps the steps toward the capitol's main entrance like an oubré scaling a mountain. (One of Eonia's more admirable traits is that she is remarkably athletic.) Reaching the capitol, Eonia avoids the main door and cuts to the side of the building. She scans her hand on a panel, and a door opens to a rarely used corridor.

Which way? Eonia considers, knowing she must find her parents but also knowing she must avoid being seen. *I'll go to their private chamber,* she decides, thinking eventually they'll turn up there, given the time of day it is. She races down the hall. Reaching a spiraling staircase, she climbs.

Coming to the third floor (the majesties' level), she cracks the door open and peeks out from inside the stairwell. *No one's here. Where's all the guards?* Normally, guards are stationed at each of the interior doors. *This is unusual,* Eonia reflects, thankful there's no guards to block her passage.

Cautiously, Eonia tiptoes down the hall toward her parents' bedroom. But halfway down the hallway, it occurs to her how awful she appears. If her mother sees her in this state, dirty and disheveled in ripped eveningwear—the same eveningwear she wore the night she was taken—Queen Marakee will be distraught. Eonia's room is right there. *I'll just sneak in, change clothes, and wash my face,* she decides. *There's no point to making my parents see me like this.*

Eonia crosses the hallway to her bedroom and scans her palm on the room's panel. Her door unlocks, and she scampers inside, so as not to be seen. Eonia's bedroom door clicks behind her.

But there inside her bedroom and before her is Eonia's worst nightmare. It's as though Eonia's most gruesome fears have been given breath and sprung into existence. Eonia's father, the king, lies at Eonia's feet, barely breathing. Her mother is tied to a chair.

Gagged and rigid, her mother's eyes widen with fear as she looks at Eonia.

Poor, dear, kind Eonia begins to dry heave.

"Welcomsey to the party, Princess," Lord Letch hisses. "How nice of you to dropensy in. I must admit, you have superb timing. I was just asking your momsy where the book is."

CHAPTER 43
JESSE WALKER

Kingdom, Land of Miriam

In a full out sprint, Jesse and Whissiper run for the Great Hall. Each stride Whissiper takes, his flab undulates like a waddling walrus. Jesse bursts into the Great Hall behind Lord Whissiper, weaving his way through the Magi who are still at the banquet, mulling about and chitchatting. Jesse spins, looking for his aunt and uncle.

"Where are they?" Jesse calls out to Lord Whissiper, who's doing his best to push his way through the crowd as well. Red-faced, Whissiper inquires amongst the other Magi as to the king and queen's whereabouts.

"They left with Lord Letch," Whissiper calls back to Jesse after receiving an answer from a group of Magi that have gathered around him in confusion.

Jesse hears Lord Whissiper tell the Magi to look for the king and the queen. "Lord Letch is evil!" Whissiper pants out of breath. "He's pledged himself to Darkness. We need to find them!" He presses his palms against his cheeks. "We have to save the king and queen! The kingdom's at risk! Alert the guards!"

Then turning, Whissiper grabs hold of Jesse and drags him along. Together, they run out of the Great Hall.

"We should check the East Wing first," Whissiper wheezes, directing the boy toward an area of the capitol he has not yet been. "The king and queen's chambers are in the East Wing. Lord Letch is more familiar with the East Wing than the other areas of the capitol." He waves his arm, pointing excitedly. "I'd nearly stake my life that he'd take them there before he'd take them anywhere else."

Jesse and Whissiper make their way through the capitol, their footsteps echoing as they go. They climb one flight of stairs, then another, then another. Running down one hallway to the next, Lord Whissiper yells, "Find Lord Letch!" to each guard they pass.

Reaching the third level, Lord Whissiper scans his hand and opens a door into a well-lit hallway, covered with tapestries from floor to ceiling. He swings the door open, nearly hitting someone hairy and small.

"Barrington!" Jesse yelps, recognizing the Thwacker before him. Barrington's eyes twinkle. "What are you doing here?" the boy asks. "How did you find us?"

"Where's the king and queen?" Barrington asks, not answering.

"Lord Letch has them!"

Straining, the boy hears cries in the distance. "It's the cat!" Jesse sputters, recognizing Thomas' screech. A kavat's cries are shrill, indeed. Hearing it once is hard to forget.

Jesse runs down the hall and turns right, heading straight for the noise. He turns another corner, then another. Ahead, he sees the kavat at the door, clawing, trying to get into Eonia's bedroom.

"It's the princess' chamber," Barrington calls to Jesse from behind.

"Move out of the way. I have access to get in there," Whissiper huffs, breathless, struggling to keep up.

Thomas the kavat holds his ground, clawing at Eonia's door. Screeching at the top of its lungs, the kavat drags its dagger-like nails, splintering the door's wood like scissors, marring it with haphazard scrapes.

Barrington and Jesse move so Whissiper can pass them. Lord Whissiper scuttles up to the door, bumping Thomas out of the way with his fat foot. Whissiper scans his hand.

Unfortunately, Whissiper doesn't even make it through the doorway.

"Oh no!" Barrington cries.

Whissiper stumbles backward, a knife sticking out of his chest. Whissiper's eyes roll to the side.

"It's Lord Letch!" Whissiper gasps as he falls to the ground.

Barrington and Jesse throw themselves into Eonia's room, past the fallen lord.

"Mother! No! I can't do this!" Eonia is screaming.

Then, there's the sound of glass breaking and a *thud* as Barrington's body hits the wood floor.

Jesse, unarmed, is the only one left standing. The boy's face is nearly as white as a sheet. His lips tremble. The blood is drawn from his youthful face as he reflects upon the scene.

The king's on the floor, bleeding. The queen's gagged in a chair. Eonia is bound. Barrington's on the ground, not moving.

Jesse meets Lord Letch's gaze.

"Well, I'll be," the evil lord snickers. "If it isn't a family reunion for your ickensy family. How well this has workensy'd out for me, cherished Letchy," he slithers, petting his own cheek with his bony fingers. "I can kill all of you together. Except for you, of course, dearsy," Lord Letch declares, patting Eonia, who's tied, sitting in a chair next to Queen Marakee.

Lord Letch takes a step closer to Jesse. "I'm going to enjoy killing you, Jesse. I never liked your mealy-mouthed momsy. She was so pompous, always skipping around, singing about how great life is."

Lord Letch casually swings a knife toward Jesse. Raising it, he prepares to strike down the boy.

Sensing his imminent demise, Jesse's mind wanders from the horror before him. In place of Lord Letch's face, he sees his mom's face. He sees Lillian smiling, the same smile from the photo at home in the boy's living room, the one of Lillian in the white dress. He sees his little sister Maddie's elephant painting from the day before he had left. He sees Noni and Grandpa sitting in their Adirondack chairs, gazing out at the lake. He sees Irvin holding a fishing rod. He sees his dad bending down to wish him good night.

Lord Letch lowers his sword, bringing it down on the boy.

CHAPTER 44
EONIA

Kingdom, Land of Miriam

"Don't hurt him!" Eonia screams, fighting the battle both seen and unseen.

So much pain, so much fear, so much anger she feels. It's the perfect storm. The visible battle doesn't scratch the surface of the turmoil that's been haggling the poor princess since she walked into her bedroom. Lord Letch has offered Eonia the same offer that King Angus had extended. He's offered to spare Princess Eonia's parents if she tells him where the book is.

Queen Marakee had caught Eonia's eye when she had walked into the bedroom. Eonia had sensed her mother's determination. The princess had sworn to herself then and there not to divulge the book's location, no matter what the situation. She knows her parents would rather die than betray the Land of Miriam. But it hasn't been easy for the princess to remain wed to her conviction.

Her life, like Jesse's, has been flashing before her. Only, instead of seconds to brew over her existence, she has had minutes. Each second, within each minute, feels like an eternity to the girl since she entered. She has been bouncing back and forth between life-and-death scenarios, fighting to breathe, contemplating her parents' murders and what life will be like without them.

One moment, she imagines her mother cradling her, soothing her like she did when she was nine, when Eonia had lost the ring that she'd been given.

"Oh, Eonia. It's my fault," Eonia hears her mother say, replaying her mother's words from the time her mother had discovered Eonia had lost the precious heirloom. *"I shouldn't have given it to you yet. I should've known."* Eonia is comforted again by the memory. *"Don't cry, sweetheart. I'll help you look for it. You're so much more precious to me than a ring is."*

Even replayed, her mother's voice is gentle and reassuring.

Cycling through the past, Eonia imagines her father hugging her, laughing after another of his practical jokes. Then, her mother kissing her forehead. Next, her father clasping the amulet around her neck on her fourteenth birthday, holding her in tight to his chest.

And all the while, as Eonia remembers her life, and it passes before her like the swandocks flying, a voice inside of her, calm and melodious, taunts, *You can save them, Eonia. Don't let this happen. Help your mother and father. Help Jesse. Help Barrington. Tell us where the* Book of Good and Evil *is, and Lord Letch will let them live!*

"I'll tell you where it is!" Eonia cries as the knife nearly grazes Jesse's scalp.

Lord Letch pauses.

"I'm *sorry,*" Eonia blubbers, praying for forgiveness for her weakness. "I cannot bear the pain! I'm not Divine! I'm just a girl!"

And there Jesse is—alone, unarmed, and left with nothing to defend himself with but spirit and brains. Eonia cannot bear to witness her cousin's murder. She can't bear to watch her parents being killed.

Thomas the kavat steps forward. Closing its eyes, the kavat screeches as loud a scream as an animal has ever made. Cries roll off the kavat's tongue, erupting rapid fire. Screeching, the kavat squints at Jesse.

Spreading out its claws, Thomas launches for Lord Letch like a cork from a bottle. The kavat takes hold of the evil lord, digging in its claws. The lord's skin pops beneath the tips of the claws, and the kavat continues to screech over and over and over. Lord Letch's fists rain down on the animal, trying to get it off of him. Then there's yelling. Lord Letch is slipping backward, falling toward the floor as the kavat clings to him, digging the tips of its claws ever deeper into Lord Letch's threadlike skin.

The impact of the lord hitting the floor beneath Thomas reverberates up through the animal like an earthquake, and the kavat's screeches cease. Together, the kavat and Lord Letch thump to the floor—Thomas on top, Lord Letch beneath.

CHAPTER 45

JESSE WALKER

Kingdom, Land of Miriam

"Ya a'right, Jesse?" a familiar voice asks.

With his heart thumping and his palms pressed into his forehead, Jesse takes a minute before confirming, "Yes, I'm here. I'm okay."

Lord Letch is lying on the floor, gripping his head, an arrow sticking out of his temple. The lord's sword, having fallen next to him, still clangs and vibrates. Barrington lays motionless on the ground covered in sparkling crystal, having been hit over the head by Lord Letch with a vase. The king, also motionless but breathing, lays on the floor. The queen and Princess Eonia are tied and bound.

Scanning the room with interest, Jesse surveys his surroundings. The kavat slowly crawls off Lord Letch's chest as the lord rolls from side to side in pain.

"Quite a mess ye've got 'ere," the voice comes again.

"Drumbell?" Jesse gasps, startled out of his stupor and turning to the Thwacker at the entrance of Eonia's bedroom. "How'd you get here?"

Guards rush the room (thanks to the kavat's shrieks and Drumbell's yells, presumably). The guards push Drumbell out of the doorway and run to the king and the queen.

"Well, Jesse, since everybody left me waitin' fer help that never came," Drumbell answers over the frantic bustle, "I couldn't very well bide my time at the base of the capitol forever." Drumbell smiles wryly. "So, I came lookin' fer ya and the princess. And from the scene 'ere, it's a good thing I came when I did."

Drumbell motions to Thomas, sitting on the floor minding his own business, licking his paws. "What's with the kavat? If I hadn't heard his screechin' down the hall, I would've never have found ya."

Jesse looks at Thomas, the corner of his lips curling upward. "He's Princess Eonia's pet. He showed me what happened the night she was taken. He's how I figured out Lord Letch was evil. I guess there is something to be said for telepathy." Jesse's eyes widen. "Did you see him jump on Lord Letch?"

"Yeah." Drumbell nods. "When I arrived, that kavat was attached to Lord Letch, goin' after him like a Thwacker on kettle cakes, bitin' em, scratchin' at his jugular. I had to aim m' arrow high just ta avoid hittin' him. Otherwise, I would've aimed fer the lord's heart. I don't like head shots much, but I didn't wanna risk hittin' the kavat," Drumbell says contritely. "Some kavats are said ta be magical."

Magi dignitaries flow into the room, adding to the mayhem. Word of what transpired has trickled down to the Great Hall, where the banquet was still winding down. In grief, Magi from the banquet wring their hands and whisper, "Lord Letch, an agent of Darkness? How can this be? He has injured the king!"

Unbound and free, Eonia and Queen Marakee kneel at the king's side. King Mor's eyes open. He moans, and a physician barks orders at medics to lift him. Meanwhile, Jesse and Drumbell stay close to Barrington, who is still unconscious and bleeding.

From across the room, Eonia watches. She crosses to Jesse.

Eonia's eyes are like Mama's eyes, Jesse thinks of the princess as she approaches. *They're the same shade of gray, stormy like the sea.*

Eonia's eyes lock on Jesse with determination.

In spirit, Eonia is anything but fragile. She's not unlike Mama on that front either, the boy thinks.

The tension in Eonia's face subsides a little. She touches Jesse's shoulder. "You rescued me. You saved my parents. Jesse, you saved Miriam. I am so honored to finally meet you."

EPILOGUE

Something soft and gentle brushes against Jesse's arm, rousing him from a deep sleep. He scans his body without moving. His mouth is as dry as tumbleweed, and his tongue feels thick. He's dying of thirst, and his body aches all over from the abuse and overuse he has absorbed these past few days.

I should get some water, Jesse thinks, rolling over, wanting nothing more than to go back to sleep.

Then, panting sounds in his ears, and a thump hits his arm, harder this time. *Whoa!* He shudders, bolting upright. *Am I in the Mires? Is it dragons? Is it Angus?* He shakes, pulling himself out of a blurry sleep.

Fur is in his face. A glob of slobber wets his cheek. A bumpy tongue runs across his skin the length of his face, chin to ear.

"Jerry!" Jesse exclaims, recognizing his dog. Dumfounded, he pans the room. *My room? I'm home!* He darts his eyes wall to wall, taking it all in.

Everything is exactly how he remembers it from the night he left with Barrington. A crumpled t-shirt and shorts are balled up next to his bed. *I'd dropped them on the floor before showering,* he remembers. *The Catcher in the Rye* earmarked at page ninety-five is on his nightstand, crammed between a water glass and his bobble head of Stephen Curry.

Nothing has been touched, the boy observes, an uneasiness welling up within him. The windowpane is closed and latched. *How did I get in?* he thinks, trying to remember the details. *What if I never left?* The thought chills him.

The aroma of pancakes fills the air. *Dad must be cooking.* Jesse sniffs the air, taking in the smell. His family has a tradition—if you would call it that. They have pancakes on Saturdays. Lillian started the tradition long before Jesse and Maddie were born, and Jesse's dad has kept the tradition going. Since Jesse's father became health-conscious, the pancakes taste less like food and more like cardboard. Regardless, it's what they do. His family has pancakes on Saturdays.

Was I gone only a night then? Jesse combs through his memories, remembering Barrington told him time was different in the Land of Miriam than it is at home.

Pushing Jerry off his covers, Jesse swings his legs over the side of his bed and slumps. "Drumbell, Drakendore, Barrington, the dragons, all of the Thwackers in Tanglewood, Princess Eonia, my aunt and uncle," Jesse whispers. "Was it all a dream?"

Pressure hits him like a sledgehammer to the temple. With a sinking feeling, he cries out "It can't have been a dream!" A tidal wave of sadness envelops him. *In Miriam, I was cherished. I was special. Here, I'm just an ordinary kid without a mom.* He trembles, tears filling his eyes.

Yes, the Land of Miriam was a magical place—a place of dreams. But it's more than that to me. It's more than being wanted or needed, he thinks dizzily. "I have family there!" he shouts. Saltwater wets his cheeks. Tears pelt his sheets.

A knock on the door jolts him from his sorrow. His dad's voice sounds. "Jesse, are you okay in there? I let Jerry in to wake you up; she was pawing at your door. Breakfast is ready."

Dad! Oh, how Jesse longs to see his dad! He jumps to open the door for his father; and as he does, he glances at his legs and stops dead in his tracks.

Scratches cover his shins. Bloody scrapes blanket his arms and his legs, stopping where his armor covered him and protected his skin. Jesse raises an eyebrow. *The scratches are from the Mires.* He remembers the burning of his legs scraping against the bushes as he ran through the marsh. He remembers the scratches from when he'd taken the bath at the capitol.

"It wasn't a dream," Jesse whispers. The image of the three-headed beast on the capitol's ceiling, emblazoned in his memory, flashes. "Life," his aunt had called the beast. Jesse remembers passing under the painting as he ran through the capitol. He remembers the kavat's screams.

I shut and locked my window myself before I crawled into bed this morning, Jesse recalls concretely.

Jesse went to sleep in peace, knowing Princess Eonia was safe, knowing that the Land of Miriam had been saved. He had slept a peaceful sleep, knowing that he had helped the Light triumph. The Land of Miriam wasn't a dream.

"Thank You, God!" Jesse whimpers softly. "Thank You for my life! Thank You for the sunshine and for the birds and for the trees. Thank You for the air that I breathe. Never again will I take these things for granted."

And there's more, Jesse realizes, shaking. *I think I understand Mama now. Barrington was right—Mama wasn't trying to deceive me. She wasn't trying to hide anything. She was afraid. She didn't tell us about the Land of Miriam because she knew I'd want to go.*

Jesse paces the room, sweating, tears pooling in his eyes.

She didn't tell me because she wanted to protect me. She didn't want anything to happen to me. And from what I've just lived, Miriam is dangerous. I almost died.

"Jesse? Can you come out of there?" Jesse's dad calls from the other side of the door.

"Yes! Of course!" Jesse scrambles to get a long-sleeved shirt and pants out of his dresser, wanting to hide the scratches so as not to distress his father. "I'll be out in a minute."

"Well, what do you think about fishing today? I was hoping Noni could take Maddie shopping so we could go together."

Jesse zips his jeans. "Sure, Dad. That sounds great."

He hears his dad's footsteps leave and come back again.

"If you want to invite Irvin along, that'd be fine," his dad offers. "We can pick him up on the way. It's the strangest thing, though, Jesse." His dad pauses. "Someone left a map for you. It was at the door this morning. I don't know what it's for. It looks like a map of some mountains. Maybe in Montana or Wyoming? I don't know." His dad sighs, his voice cracking with uncertainty. "It's a map of somewhere out West with a star on it and an image of a book. Were you expecting it?"

Jesse's eyes widen. His heart begins to race.

"There's a note with it, too, but it's cryptic." His dad's voice drops. "It makes no sense unless it's a game you're playing. Some kind of a treasure hunt you're doing with friends?"

Jesse wrestles his shirt over his head and bursts from his room like lightning. At the doorstep, his dad cradles the map in his hands.

Looking him up and down, his dad fixes his gaze on Jesse's long shirt and pants. "Jesse, it's nearly May, and we're in Alabama." His dad narrows his eyes. "It's nine a.m., and it's already ninety degrees. What's, uh . . . what's with the clothes?"

Jesse throws himself into his dad like he used to do when he was a kid. "I just didn't want to wear shorts and a t-shirt again today," Jesse fibs. "I missed you," he tells his dad, hugging him.

With a confused look, Jesse's father yields the map to him. Jesse pulls it in close and studies it. A small piece of silver paper that had been attached to the map drops and flutters to the floor.

"That was with it." His dad shrugs.

Jesse picks up the piece of paper and squints at it, trying to read the small print. In block letters, the note reads:

Dearest Jesse,

Keep an eye on this for us. We may need to use it sooner than we had hoped.

P.S. Your mother had her reasons for keeping the Land of Miriam out of your and your family's lives. But those reasons are past us now, I believe. Do you think you could tell your father and Madeline about us please? I had to hide in the bushes dropping this off for you this morning. It would be better if I could knock on the door next time.

See you soon. All goodness

—B.

"Do you want to tell me what that's about?" his dad asks, squinting at the letter over Jesse's shoulder. "And why was someone hiding in our bushes?"

Jesse looks at the map again, focusing on a golden star embossed into an image of a book, marking a location that's nestled deep within the mountains depicted.

"Er, there's a few things I should tell you about," Jesse says, not knowing where to begin.

THE END

ABOUT THE AUTHOR

M.K. Sweeney was born at NATO headquarters in Mons, Belgium, and subsequently moved with her family to Montgomery, Alabama, where she grew up. She received her undergraduate degree from the University of Virginia's McIntire School of Commerce and then moved to Manhattan to work with a pension fund prior to attending law school. She lives with her husband and their three children in Atlanta, Georgia, where she serves as senior counsel for a global chemical company and writes fiction into the wee hours of the morning.

For more information about
M.K. Sweeney
&
The Magi of Miriam
please visit:

www.magiofmiriam.com
www.facebook.com/magiofmiriam
www.instagram.com/magi_of_miriam

Ambassador International's mission is to magnify the Lord Jesus Christ and promote His Gospel through the written word.

We believe through the publication of Christian literature, Jesus Christ and His Word will be exalted, believers will be strengthened in their walk with Him, and the lost will be directed to Jesus Christ as the only way of salvation.

For more information about AMBASSADOR INTERNATIONAL please visit:

www.ambassador-international.com
@AmbassadorIntl
www.facebook.com/AmbassadorIntl

Thank you for reading this book!

You make it possible for us to fulfill our mission, and we are grateful for your partnership.

To help further our mission, please consider leaving us a review on your social media, favorite retailer's website, Goodreads or Bookbub, or our website, and be sure to check out some of our other books!

When Luke Alexander's father is "missing, presumed dead," Luke and his friends decide to start a search of their own. Little do they know that their search will take them on the wildest adventures of their lives and make the stories of Solomon's temple and other biblical events seem more real than they ever thought possible. Will their adventures lead them to Luke's father, or will they only wind up with more questions than answers?

The Maker created Monday Egg for a very important reason. Monday just doesn't understand it yet. Being an egg with arms and legs has its advantages. Monday can run like the wind and climb trees easily, but he is an egg. What happens when he cracks? *The Cracking of Monday Egg* is the story of a cranky crow, a sick little girl, a kind squirrel, and Monday's struggle to deal with his own crackability.

In the trees of Treemoonia, the people are content, work hard, and help each other. Tommy is just another Treemoonian child, enjoying a siesta day with his friends, until he stumbles across a stepping vine leading beneath Treemoonia. He soon finds himself going deep down into a dark world, where creatures are not what they appear. Will Tommy be able to find his way back home?